Also by STEVEN M. THOMAS

CRIMINALPARADISE

CRIMINALKARMA

CRIMINAL KARMA

a novel

STEVEN M. THOMAS

Ballantine Books
New York

Published in the United States by Ballantine Books,
an imprint of The Random House Publishing Group,
a division of Random House, Inc., New York.

BALLANTINE and colophon are registered trademarks of Random House, Inc.

LIBRARY OF CONGRESS CATALOGING-IN-PUBLICATION DATA

Thomas, Steven M.
Criminal karma: a novel / Steven M. Thomas.
p. cm.
ISBN 978-0-345-49783-3
eBook ISBN 978-0-345-51517-9
1. Criminals—Fiction. 2. California, Southern—Fiction.   I. Title.
PS3620.H6428C74 2008   813'.6—dc22   2009020354

Printed in the United States of America on acid-free paper

www.ballantinebooks.com

9 8 7 6 5 4 3 2 1

FIRST EDITION

Book design by Casey Hampton

For my wise, wonderful, beautiful wife,
Mary Patricia Thomas

The rabbi of Lublin said: "I love the wicked man who knows he is wicked more than the righteous man who knows he is righteous. But concerning the wicked who consider themselves righteous, it is said: 'They do not turn even on the threshold of Hell.'"

—from *Tales of the Hasidim: Early Masters*, Martin Buber

CRIMINALKARMA

CHAPTER ONE

She was three cars ahead of us on Highway 60, headed east toward Palm Springs in a white Town Car driven by a guy who looked like trouble. We were in my new Seville STS, Reggie behind the wheel, slouched down in the leather seat, steering with one thick finger. I was almost but not quite sure she had the jewels with her, packed in one of the red Samsonite suitcases I'd seen her escort load into the Lincoln's cavernous trunk. People think gangsters drive Lincolns to show off their money, and they do, but they also like them because there's room for multiple bodies in the trunk. Not that the lady was a gangster. That was us. Kind of.

We'd tailed her from the canal-side house in Venice, through downtown and East L.A. Ahead of us to the right, the Puente Hills bulked up in the golden light you get on winter afternoons after the Santa Ana winds have whisked the smog out to sea. With black-and-white dairy cattle grazing on the green slopes, the hills reminded me of an oil painting I'd seen while casing a Santa Barbara museum a couple of weeks before—a plein air vision of SoCal's vanishing rural past worth $30,000, more than the rolling expanse of portrayed acreage was worth when the painter committed it to canvas in the 1920s.

"What's the plan?" Reggie said.

I'd explained everything to him the night before. Either he hadn't paid attention or he was just annoying me now because he was bored.

"We'll play it by ear," I said, annoying him back.

He turned his shaggy head and gave me a look, half exasperated, half disgusted, that I remembered from years before in St. Louis when he had been the tough mentor showing me, a teenage novice, the ins and outs of our suburban underworld.

Traffic was thinning as we left the city behind, the red needle of the Seville's speedometer edging up to 80 mph as Reggie kept close but not too close to the Lincoln. I didn't know much about the lady other than what I'd read in the society pages of a slick coastal magazine where I first saw the pink diamond necklace reproduced on glossy paper, but I appreciated her judgment in leaving for the desert early in the afternoon.

On Friday evenings, the Los Angeles basin is like an ants' nest that has been stirred with a stick. Whether you are heading north along the coast to Santa Barbara, south to San Diego, or inland to the mountain resorts or desert, every outlet is clogged with cars, fumes, and frustration as swarms of the basin's ten million inhabitants rush for the exits of paradise.

One of the things about conventional people that annoys me the most is their tendency to do everything at the allotted time. If it is noon, they go to lunch—at exactly the worst moment, when restaurants are most crowded and the wait for tables and food is the longest. If it is Friday and by some unaccountable oversight they have one credit card left that's not maxed out, then it is time for them to go away for the weekend; they cheerfully edge onto gridlocked highways after work, stubbornly oblivious to the stupidity of their timing. If we had left Venice at 5 p.m. instead of 2 p.m., we would have been part of a hundred-mile-long traffic jam, arriving in Palm Springs with red faces and sparking nerves after a miserable four-hour commute.

Instead, it was clear sailing as we crossed the 57, the 15, and the 215, and entered the Badlands that lurk like a fairy-tale barrier between Los Angeles and the handy Shangri-La of the Coachella Valley. I gave the lady credit for a sense of tradition, too. Instead of hurtling east on I-10, the soulless highway the monads take, she was following the route old Hollywood rolled along when stars first discovered the charms of Palm Springs in the 1920s and '30s. Dressed in flannel and furs, they left L.A.'s gray rainy season behind in favor of warm winter sunshine in what was then a sparsely populated wilderness with old Indians trudging down dusty roads between scattered resorts that welcomed the rich and famous with small swimming pools and large drinks. Today the pools are huge, the drinks small, and the valley full of people who will never ever be famous, but an aura of celebrity lingers, locked in by savvy developers and city fathers who named the main thoroughfares after Hollywood royalty. When you pull up to the intersection of Bob Hope Drive and Frank Sinatra Avenue, it's hard not to feel a little starstruck, if you go in for that kind of thing.

The Badlands take you by surprise. One minute you are speeding along a straight, level road; the next you are in the middle of a civil engineer's nightmare, narrow highway curving and banking crazily through rugged hills. If you're used to the route you can go through at 70 mph, but if it's new to you, the Six Flags centrifugal forces on the steep curves scare most drivers down to about fifty. The tough guy steering the Lincoln must not have been in high society very long. He slowed abruptly as we entered the treeless hills, Galway green after the December rains. Reggie, a talented wheelman, gave a contemptuous snort as he trod on the brakes, keeping pace with the Lincoln.

In the guy's defense, the Town Car isn't nearly as agile as the Seville. With only 210 horses and weighing almost 5,000 pounds, it's underpowered and tends to wallow in normal highway curves. It must have felt like a roller coaster with elastic bolts as it careened through the Badlands. Of course, the hills put some strain on the Cadillac, too—about as much as a politician feels pocketing a brick of hundreds for a favor that will slip his mind as soon as the cash has been converted to scotch and companionship. The Caddie held the road like it was on a rail, 300-horsepower Northstar engine quiet as a wooden top spinning on a wooden table.

I still missed the DeVille that I had lost on our last job down in Newport Beach—the consequences of which we were hiding out from in Venice—but I was starting to love this car, too. Midnight blue, with $2,000 worth of chrome wheels and an artist's touch in its sleek lines, it was a beautiful piece of machinery to look at. More important, it accelerated like a rocket and handled at 120 mph. I liked knowing I had a getaway car that gave me a realistic chance of actually getting away, and that if the cop caravan and TV crews caught up with me, I would at least be branded into the public's memory behind the wheel of *the* classic American success car.

The boulevards of Southern California are jammed nowadays with German and Japanese luxury cars that cost twice as much as Cadillacs and hold their value better, but the American car retains an aura of happiness and well-being that mere economics can't dispel. Whether you are pulling up in front of a club on Saturday night or church on Sunday morning, you have to like yourself a little bit if you are driving a Caddie.

When we dropped down out of the Badlands onto the flat road below Banning, the lady's driver tried to reinflate his ego by pushing the Town Car past ninety. As the Seville's needle edged up toward a hundred, Reggie glanced over at me, bushy eyebrows raised.

"Drop back a little bit but stay with them," I said. "If there's CHP, they'll tag the Lincoln and we can slow down."

"If you say so."

I had no interest in being stopped by the highway patrol, but I didn't know what hotel the lady was staying at so we had to stick close.

The Lincoln flashed past the 111 turnoff, which meant they weren't going to Palm Springs proper but to one of the resort cities farther down the valley. Fifteen minutes later, their big right-turn signal blinked once at John Wayne Boulevard and we followed the Town Car up the swoop of the exit ramp. Half an hour later, we were turning into the elegant entrance drive of the Oasis Palms Resort in Indian Wells, passing between two fountains that mocked the desert with sparkling geysers.

CHAPTER TWO

The front of the hotel was U-shaped, with wings thrusting forward on either side of a loop at the end of the curving entry drive. There was a massive, modernistic porte cochere at the base of the U, a semicircular shed roof sheathed in copper that slanted down from the bulk of the cream-colored building. Beneath it, guests with gold cards committed themselves to the tender mercies of tip-hungry bellboys and valets who hauled their luggage off on gleaming carts and whisked their limos away to precious parking spots. The Bob Hope Chrysler Classic, the biggest golf event of the winter season, was being held that weekend at the Indian Wells Country Club across the street, and the place was crawling with the kind of people who shell out to spend hours sweating along fairways in expensive sports clothes for the doubtful privilege of watching people in even more expensive sports clothes hit little white balls into widely spaced holes. The country club was part of the desert's celebrity past, built by Desi Arnaz in the

1950s, patronized by Ike, Dick, and Arnold. The famous photo of Nixon moving his ball during a Pro-Am tournament was taken on the ninth hole, half a mile from where we sat idling in the Seville. The only reason I knew the Seville was idling was because Reggie hadn't turned the key. There was no discernible noise or vibration from the eight-cylinder engine, its three hundred horses waiting like an army in ambush, silent and powerful.

Carlos Rodriguez, one of the top pros, was getting the royal treatment as he climbed from his silver Mercedes sedan several cars ahead of us, bellhops competing with one another to carry his clubs into the lobby. The Lincoln was right behind Rodriguez's 420 SEL, but no one was paying any attention to it. We were two cars back from the Lincoln.

After a couple of minutes, while Rodriguez was still signing autographs for admiring members of the alligator-insignia set, the driver of the Lincoln got out with a lethal look on his face. He was a white guy in his late twenties or early thirties dressed in gray loafers, tight gray slacks, and a soft supple black leather jacket that looked like it had put a thousand-dollar ding in the lady's total asset account. He was lumpy and awkward, with the deformed muscle bulges of a guy who has slammed a lot of iron on a lot of cell blocks, but he looked like a fast mover all the same. As he stalked over to the valet desk, springy on small feet, the lady opened the passenger door and emerged gracefully from the Town Car.

She was striking in a red satin outfit that could have been pajamas or street clothes. She had the tomboy figure—with subtle curves in the right places—that middle-aged rich ladies get from endless rounds of golf and sets of tennis and laps in country club pools. She had the bored, benevolent air of the West Side wealthy, too, but even at a distance I could see bewilderment behind the façade. She'd know her way around a luxury hotel like a pedophile around a playground, so it must have been her life, not the immediate environment, that had her confused.

Reggie straightened up in his seat as she got out.

"What do you think?" I asked him.

"I wouldn't kick her out of bed."

"I mean about the setup."

"Run it down again."

"It hasn't changed since last night. We let her check in, get the room number, and go in when they leave for dinner."

"How do we get in the room?"

"I got something in mind."

"What if she wears the rocks?"

"The gala is tomorrow night. That's what she brought the necklace for. She isn't going to wear a quarter million in diamonds to a steakhouse." The magazine had noted in breathless terms that Mrs. Evelyn Evermore of San Francisco and Bel Air would be honorary cohost of the annual "Diamonds in the Desert" fund-raiser for the Eisenhower Medical Center, "one of the most sparkling events of the winter social season."

I saw the article by chance. A kid everyone called Ozone Pacific who lived in an abandoned building next door to the flophouse where Reggie and I were staying in Venice had showed me the magazine while I was having coffee on the boardwalk a couple of weeks earlier. He was panhandling his way up toward the pier and I gave him a dollar, same as every morning.

"Aw, thanks, Rob," he said, and gave me the big, bright smile that was his best feature. "Hey, look what I got!"

He pulled the magazine, something called *Riviera*, out of an ancient Batman backpack he carried and opened it to Evermore's picture. The full-page photograph showed her at a ritzy Christmas party in Santa Monica, wearing a scarlet gown and the pink diamond necklace.

"Isn't she beautiful?" Ozone said softly, gazing at the picture.

There was something sad about the guy, beyond being unemployed and homeless. He had to be in his late teens or maybe even his early twenties, but he was still as fascinated as an infant by shiny things and pretty pictures. He had a little pouch of plastic gold coins he played with underneath a palm tree on the beach where he hung out when he wasn't begging, and a brightly colored photograph of a woman he would never meet filled him with religious awe.

"Sure, she's beautiful," I had said to Ozone, even though my attention was locked on the glittering stones fastened around the woman's slender neck.

I wondered what he would do if he were with us now, seeing her in the flesh in front of the Oasis Palms, looking down pensively at her red-sandaled feet.

While I watched her, thinking that, yes, she really was beautiful, she looked up from her thoughts toward a bellboy in a braided maroon uniform who was hurrying toward the Lincoln, pushing a brass-trimmed luggage cart. He was about the same age as Ozone, and he bobbed his head as he passed her.

"Sorry to keep you waiting, ma'am," he said, glancing back over his shoulder at the biceps behind him.

"Everyone was so surprised to see Mr. Rodriguez," he said to the driver as he began loading the Samsonites onto the cart. "We didn't know he was staying at our hotel." It was a fine point whether he was fawning or cringing, but I could sense his fear from thirty feet away. As he leaned over and stretched to get the last piece of luggage from the back of the trunk, the driver glanced around and then kneed him viciously in the ass, knocking him into the Lincoln's capacious body receptacle.

"What the hell?" the bellboy squeaked, red-faced and trembling, after he scrambled back out.

"I'll give you sumpen be surprised at you make Miz Evermore wait again," the driver said in an expressionless voice. He had a long narrow head, and he barely moved his lips when he spoke. The ones who showed no emotion always worried me.

Rodriguez was graciously signing a last autograph. He looked about thirty-five, in great shape and with a good attitude.

"Who's he, a movie star or something?" Reggie asked.

"He's a professional golfer. Favored to win the tournament."

"Big deal."

"Top prize is seven hundred and fifty thousand dollars."

Reggie turned his head and looked at me with his eyes stretched wide open, eyebrows near his hairline. It was the look he used to express surprise. "Why don't we roll him after the game?"

"Good thought," I said, "but I'm sure they pay by check or wire transfer."

By the time a valet got around to us, the lady had disappeared through the double doors that opened into the lobby. The Oasis is a four-star, four-diamond resort, and each door was a massive slab of plate glass, five feet wide by fifteen feet high, trimmed in brass. The tough guy had driven off in the Lincoln without tipping anyone.

"Nice car," the valet said as he opened my door. "Is it an Eldorado?"

"Seville," I said. "Eldorados are coupes."

"Oh, right! I should know that." He had the blond crew cut and permanent tan of a surfer working through the winter so that he could spend next summer sliding down green waves in the surf between La Jolla and Malibu. "Can I get your name, sir?"

"Peter Blake," I said, using an alias that I had decided on a few days before.

Some criminals use the same alias over and over, which helps the cops if they get interested while investigating a crime or series of crimes. Once they figure out that Andy Anatello is just another version of Anthony Antonio, the element of disguise is lost, while a false sense of security remains. I never used a fake name more than once. There was a driver's license, a nonfunctional Visa card, and a couple of miscellaneous ID cards with the Blake name in my wallet. The license and cards had cost me six hundred dollars in the back room of a souvenir shop on the Venice boardwalk, but they would be snippets of plastic in a public trash container when this job was over. Which I expected would be soon. With any luck, we would be back in Venice with the jewels in time to catch Leno's monologue.

My real name is Robert Rivers. Most people call me Rob, a pleasant irony. I tried going straight once—got clean and sober, worked as a carpenter, got married, had a kid—a beautiful little girl we named Sheila. But it wasn't me. I drifted back.

Being a criminal was my karma, and I wasn't complaining. The hours were flexible, the money was good, and freebooting was way more interesting than swinging a hammer or sitting on a numb ass in front of a computer screen eight hours a day.

There were some moral issues, for sure, but I'd dealt with most of them. What I did hurt people sometimes, but so did the actions of most other professions, one way or the other. Bankers with their loan-shark interest rates and foreclosures, lawyers with their sharp practices and subpoenas. The worlds of business and government were packed like a college student's Volkswagen with crooked connivers who, unlike me, topped their sundae of sins with the pickled cherry of hypocrisy. I knew I was a bad guy, and tried to be as nice about it as I could. They thought they were good, which gave them license to be ruthless as hell.

There was danger, too, of course. The claustrophobic specter of prison, where I had spent a couple of memorable years in my early twenties, was a lurking nightmare. I'd been shot at three times, hit once, and I'd killed one person. To be fair, he deserved it.

Did I ever wake up at 3 a.m. horrified at the texture and trajectory of my existence? Sure. But I don't think that kind of dark-night-of-the-soul despair is unique to stickup guys. Everyone in contemporary society carries a layer of anxiety under their bullshit and bluster. With some it's fear of getting fired and losing the house in which they've invested their identity. Others are afraid that Barbie will find a fatter wallet or a bigger schlong to suck, or that Ken will take off with an intern who wears a thong over skin as smooth as satin. Old ladies are afraid that a less-deserving size sixteen will be tapped to sing the solo in the church choir, or that the neighbor's daughter will get married first.

"Are you checking in, Mr. Blake?" the valet asked. Built like a compact welterweight who lacked reach but made up for it with inside punching power, he had the outlaw aura common to dedicated surfers, with hard eyes and a marijuana leaf tattooed on his right forearm.

"No, we're here for dinner," I said.

"Call us on a house phone a few minutes before you are ready to leave and we'll have your Seville waiting."

"Thanks." I traded him a ten-dollar bill for a claim check. "Take good care of it."

"You can count on it, sir," he said, giving me a little salute. "And thank you, sir."

It's so easy to make people happy. If I had given him a dollar, it would have been emotionally neutral, a routine transaction. Two dollars would have given his heart a little lift. A ten-dollar bill, which was nothing to me in pursuit of a quarter million, made him happy. It was just a piece of paper, but it put a spring in his step and made him feel a little bit better about himself, his job, and the human race. If a conflict of any kind broke out between me and another guest, he would be on my side.

"Little prick better be careful or he'll run out of 'sirs,' " Reggie said as the kid wheeled the Caddie crisply out of the line of parked cars, squealing the tires just enough to show he knew where the edge of the power was.

CHAPTER THREE

A **dignified old** doorman grasped the brass handle with a white-gloved hand and swung one of the glass slabs open with a whoosh, air-conditioned atmosphere pouring out into the desert afternoon.

"Welcome to the Oasis, gentlemen," he said in a B-movie baritone.

When I was a kid, most of our family vacations consisted of driving five hundred miles through the summer swelter of Illinois, Indiana, and Ohio to stay with my grandmother for a week or two in her big boxy frame house by the railroad tracks. On the rare occasion when we went someplace besides a relative's house, we stayed in the kind of roadside motel where you park in front of your room and the amenities consist of a phone and a shower stall. Even after several years of patronizing them as a crook and customer, doing my part for the GDP by putting stolen money back into circulation, luxury hotels still gave me soul satisfaction, made me feel like I'd accomplished something that my father never did.

Reggie gave a whistle as we entered the marble-floored lobby. Ahead of us, two wide stone staircases curved down around a fountain to a lounge half as big as a football field with scattered groupings of couches and armchairs upholstered in expensive fabrics. Above us, an atrium rose eight stories, ringed at each floor by a continuous balcony, polished maple with vines hanging over. Beyond a three-story glass wall at the far end of the lounge, the turquoise Jell-O of a swimming pool jiggled in the slanting light.

"Pretty fucking fancy," he said.

Standing at the railing, looking down at chattering groups of vacationers laughing and drinking wine and cocktails in the lounge, I felt a pulse of ecstasy pass through me. The thrill meter had been turned up to three as we followed the Lincoln out Highway 60, powered by thoughts of diamonds, deception, and theft. When we arrived at the sparkling resort, it edged up to five. Now it jumped all the way to ten, banging against the peg, as the whole happiness of the crime descended on me like a blessing, sharpening my eyesight and hearing, bringing adrenal clarity to my mind.

This was what I lived for.

It was a busy Friday afternoon at the peak of the season in one of the nicest hotels in the Coachella Valley. There was wealth all around me—in the expensive shops that lined the upper lobby, in the pockets and on the wrists and fingers of the guests, in the registers behind the front desk, and in the hotel safe—and I had the guts and know-how to take whatever I wanted.

Dressed in Italian walking shoes, brown gabardine slacks, and a finely woven silk shirt—tan with ivory buttons—I blended into the environment so perfectly that I was functionally invisible, which was, of course, my goal. None of the people walking through the lobby, smiling and nodding, could tell by looking at me that I was different from them. Not one of them would have guessed at the gear I had in the black leather bag slung over my right shoulder.

Reggie was getting scruffy again, his inner biker emerging in the hiatus between the barbershop visits he had such strong resistance to. But his clothes were up to par—new khakis and a dark-blue aloha shirt the fortune-teller on the promenade had given him the previous week—so he blended in, too, sort of.

He wasn't an ideal partner for this kind of job—no luxury-resort manners, and too apt to freelance something on the side that might interfere with the main plan. But he had criminal virtues, too. Besides being a skilled driver, he was a good mechanic, a decent alarm guy, and a tricky, explosive street fighter. They didn't come any tougher when there was blood in the water.

He'd shown up at the right time in my personal Kabuki play, too, motoring out from St. Louis on a broken-down trike eight months before, just when Switch, my former partner, decided to get out of the high life, swayed by a beautiful young Mexican woman who was about to give birth to their first child.

And Reggie was fun to be around when he wasn't fucking up. Coming up on fifty, with a droopy bearded bloodhound face and sizable gut, he still exerted the same old mysterious pull he always had on the opposite sex. For as long as I'd known him, women had been drawn to his gruff, monosyllabic charm like lookie-loos to a car wreck. The fortune-teller was sub-par, chubby and in her forties, but she was constantly buying him gifts and cooking him meals and doing his laundry. In between banging surfer girls he picked up on the Venice boardwalk, he afforded her a casual fuck every week or so to keep her cheerful, putting about as much into it as a big-leaguer playing catch with a kid at a charity event.

After craning his head to look up into the atrium and swiveling it to take in the expanse of the upper lobby, Reggie shrugged. "What's it cost to crash in a dump like this?" he asked. Part of his code was never letting anything impress him—unless he was flattering you to get something he wanted—and now he was trying to retract the admiring whistle and the tone of his earlier comment.

"High season, rooms start around three hundred and go up to five grand."

"Five grand! People must be fucking crazy. You could buy a cherry scooter for that."

"I know," I said and smiled. "They've got more money than they know what to do with."

The lady was standing in line at the front desk, off to our right. I didn't see the ex-con.

"Get a cup of coffee and sit where you can see the entrance and front desk," I told Reggie. "Keep an eye out for the driver. I'll go see what room she's checking into."

"Coffee?"

The lobby bar was next to the coffee shop. "All right," I said. "Have a beer. But keep your eyes open. I don't want that muscle-bound prick sneaking up behind me. And take this." I handed him the black leather shoulder bag, which was the size of a large briefcase and heavy as a concrete block.

At the front desk, I joined the line next to the one the lady was standing in. Up close, she was spectacular, with flawless, lightly tanned skin, delicate features, and thick, silken blond hair that was cut straight all the way around. She had lovely hands, with perfectly manicured nails the same red as her outfit and lipstick. It crossed my mind that it would be nice to have those soft, strong sportswoman's hands gripping the shaft of something other than a golf club. The thought surprised me because I'm not usually attracted to older women, and I believed her to be somewhere between forty-five and fifty, five to ten years older than me. Her red lips were parted, showing the tip of her pink tongue. While I watched her without appearing to watch her, she turned and looked around the lobby with a anxious air.

The glittering space was filling up as the Friday-evening rush came on, well-heeled people from Los Angeles, San Diego, and points around the globe jostling for position in the check-in lines. The bobbing faces ranged from doughy-white to dark brown, flaccid to eagle-sharp. Twenty conversations in several languages competed for decibel space around us. As the lady reached the desk, I edged in as close as I could without being conspicuous.

"We have you in a Catalina Suite, Mrs. Evermore," the pretty young Latina desk clerk was saying, focusing on her computer screen. "Room 589, overlooking the pool with a view of the Santa Rosa Mountains. How many keys will you need?"

"Two," the lady said unhappily, glancing around the lobby again.

The clerk ran two key cards through the coding machine and inserted them in a paper folder. "You go left when you come out of the elevator on the fifth floor, left again and then follow the hallway to your suite. A bellman will be right up with your luggage."

"Can't someone bring it now?" the lady said.

"We're very busy," the clerk said. "It will be just a few minutes."

"Please," the lady said. "I'd much rather have the luggage go up with me."

Her words caught my heart like the toe of a punter's shoe, sending it soaring into the blue sky above the stadium. She didn't want that Samsonite out of her sight.

"Let me see what I can do," the Latina said, and walked away to the end of the counter, where there was a traffic jam of laden luggage carts and harried bellboys. She spoke to a plump black man with a goatee, who nodded and pointed to the red suitcases. As the clerk came back, the goatee maneuvered the cart into the clear.

"John will take you to your room, Mrs. Evermore."

"Thank you so much. What is your name, dear?"

"Loretta, ma'am."

"Thank you, Loretta."

"My pleasure, ma'am."

You don't get that kind of service at Motel 6.

As the lady and the black bellman moved toward the elevators on the far side of the lobby, a hulking matron in a green tweed outfit more suitable for wintertime Chicago than Indian Wells charged past them in the opposite direction, bearing down on the front desk as if it were a buffet. Barging through the resentful crowd, she leaned her bosom across the counter to address the clerk next to the one who had waited on Evermore.

"Where are my bags?" she screeched in a falsetto that was comical coming from her pro lineman's body. She was six feet tall, probably 275 pounds, with a big fry cook's head and what looked like size-twelve feet squeezed into size-ten brown leather traveling shoes. "We've been waiting half an hour and we can't even change our clothes to go out to dinner. What kind of hotel is this? My husband isn't paying four hundred dollars a night to be treated like this. We've been on a plane for six hours and we're starving to death!"

"I'm sorry, ma'am," said the clerk, flustered by the onslaught. "Where are you—what room are you in?"

"I'm in room 569, and I want my luggage now!"

While all eyes were fixed on the drama of the bitchy snowbird and the beleaguered desk clerk, I reached over the counter and took a blank key card from the stack beside the coding machine and murmured my way through the crowd to sit on a tan leather couch against the wall.

After about ten minutes, the Latina who had waited on Evermore disappeared through a doorway behind the front desk. I made my way back to the counter.

"Excuse me," I said to a woman arguing with two children at the front of one of the lines, then spoke to the clerk, holding out the stolen card: "There's something wrong with this card. My wife forgot her medication in our room and when we tried to get back in the door wouldn't open."

The clerk glanced from the woman to me and back.

"Go ahead and help him," the woman panted, trying to wrestle into submission a freckle-faced demon who was squealing and kicking a suitcase.

"What room are you in?" the clerk asked me.

"Room 589, Evermore," I said.

She looked at her computer screen, nodded, pressed a couple of keys, and ran the blank card through the machine. "Here you go, Mr. Evermore. Sometimes if you put them next to a credit card in your wallet, it messes them up. It should work now."

CHAPTER FOUR

I found Reggie sitting in a green plaid easy chair in the bar, finishing his second Budweiser. The bag was on the floor beside him.

"No sign of the punk," he said after I sat down in the plaid chair next to him. "How'd it go?"

I held up the key card. "We're in."

A cocktail waitress stopped at my elbow. "Can I get you gentlemen anything?"

"Perrier with lime," I said.

"Another Bud, sweetheart." It was the kind of remark cocktail waitresses usually roll their eyes at, but the woman, who looked like she was in her mid-thirties and had a name tag pinned to her breast that identified her as Tawny, giggled and gave Reggie a lingering sidelong look as she bent over to pick up his empty bottles, grasping the necks with dainty hands. She was built like Bette Midler and looked like she'd know a good time if she saw one.

"I bet she gives a mean one," Reggie said, watching her walk away, swishing her hips. "What now?"

"We might as well wait here. We can't hang around in the hallway by her room, and she has to come out this way when she goes to dinner."

"What if she orders in?"

"She didn't bring three suitcases full of clothes to eat in her room."

I was beginning to think that the guy in the black leather jacket whom I'd taken for the lady's escort was just a chauffeur who had dropped her off and gone back to town. I liked thinking that. But then he came into the lobby through the front entrance, talking on a cell phone, and crossed to the elevators.

His weightlifter's strut reminded me of high school athletes I'd known back when Reggie and I first met, loud-mouthed wrestlers and football players who sometimes made the mistake in freshman and sophomore year of shoving me in the hallway because I had long hair and smoked dope and didn't come to games. They weren't the brightest bunch of jock-straps that ever played grab-ass in the showers, but after I sent the second one home with shattered facial bones they grasped the concept that it might be smarter to pick on a less volatile hippie.

Reggie doctored my hand after the second fight, pouring 100-proof vodka on my gashed knuckles to keep them from getting infected. He was moving ten pounds of Mexican pot and an ounce of soul-satisfying brown heroin each month back then. He had a sky-blue Thunderbird convertible and 650 BSA chopper with a candy-red teardrop tank. Looking back, he was small-time, but he loomed big in the neighborhood. It was the peak of his criminal success prior to joining me in California, and a big chunk of his confidence still rested on that image of himself.

They kicked me out of school for a month after that fight. Since I didn't have anything else to do I started riding with him, learning the Mexican dope business, banging the little biker chicks who were left over.

Reggie was on his fourth beer when the lady and the black jacket stepped out of the elevator. She had changed into a slinky midnight-blue silk dress and had a matching cashmere shawl draped over her bare shoulders. The two were so mismatched that it was jarring, an angel holding hands with an ape. She was a diamond carefully crafted by society to be one of its crown jewels while he was more like a pebble of windshield glass left on the bloody pavement after a fatal collision. I couldn't figure out what they were doing together, if he was a gigolo or if something else was going on. As they crossed the lobby to the entrance, he held her arm more like she was his prisoner than his lover.

"Pay the check," I said to Reggie. "I'll be right back."

I walked over toward the entrance where I could see out the big glass doors. The lady was already in the Lincoln, sitting stiffly in the front seat, looking straight ahead. The valet was handing the keys to the escort, extending his arm full length and keeping his distance, like someone touching a snake with a stick. There was no tip.

When I turned back toward the bar, I saw Tawny standing beside Reggie's chair with her right hand on a thrust hip. As I walked over, she burst out laughing and struck him on the shoulder with the leather check holder in a "Go on with you, now" sort of way.

"Your friend's pretty funny," she said to me as I climbed up the two shallow steps into the bar.

"Don't encourage him," I said.

"Shall I charge this to your room?" she said, holding the leather folder poised between us.

"Sure, sweetheart, why not," Reggie said, reaching out to take the check. He scrawled a name and room number, added 25 percent, and handed the folder back to Tawny.

"Why thank you, Mr. Delmonte," she said, her eyes lighting up when she saw the tip. "You're on the fourth floor, huh?"

"Yeah," Reggie growled, "I'll be home later if you want to come up."

Tawny's jolly face got serious. She looked plainer and older without the smile. "You mean it?" she said.

Reggie winked and nodded. Cryptic. Her smile came back but it was sad. "You're just kidding," she said.

Reggie gave the slightest of shrugs, shoulders going up a quarter inch and then back down, as if to say, "I made the offer."

"Oh, you!" Tawny said and walked away with a little extra swish, glancing back once over her shoulder.

"Did you make that name up?" I asked.

"No! Thad be too risky. Old codger was leaving as I came in. I snuck a peek at the check on his table and got his name and room number. He went out the front with his old lady and got in a limo while you were ripping off the key card."

Over at the register, the waitress was looking closely at the check.

"What if Tawny notices your name is the same as the old guy's?" I said, looking around to see if there was anyone between us and the nearest exit, thinking that I was going to leave Reggie at a rest stop in the desert if he fucked up this score.

"Shift changed right after he left. She just came on." Smug.

"Yeah, well, here she comes again," I said. Tawny was walking across the floral rug toward us, check in hand, funny look on her face. Halfway to our table, another customer tugged on her sleeve, asking a question. She spoke with the man briefly, then continued on toward us.

"I'm sorry to bother you, Mr. Delmonte," she said to Reggie, her manner hovering between apology and coquetry, "but I can't tell if that is a seven or a nine on your room number."

"Nine," Reggie said.

"That's what I thought, but I wasn't sure," she said. "Sorry to bother you."

"No bother, babe," Reggie said, gruff but genial.

He looked at me as she walked back to the counter. "See? No sweat."

"Maybe not," I said, "but it was still a stupid chance to take for a twenty-five-dollar bar bill when there's a couple hundred grand on the table."

I couldn't blame him too much. Both of us were as full of larceny as a slot machine is of quarters.

We rode up to the fifth floor in an elevator lined with mahogany and padded brocade. The elevator floor was covered with a carpet that had the word FRIDAY woven into the wool pile. They changed the carpet each day for the benefit of travelers who had lost their place in the continuum of time.

Coming out of the elevator alcove, we stepped onto a carpeted walkway that went continuously around all four sides of the atrium, numbered doors on one side, railing on the other. At the corners, hallways led to the wings of the gigantic hotel. Standing at the railing, looking down five stories, we had a clear view of the entrance and front desk. The lobby and lounge were crowded with miniature people, and the murmur and clatter of their self-absorbed oblivion rose up to us like faithless prayers to an empty heaven.

Tawny was clearing a table in the bar, looking girlish in the distance. Glancing up the way people do when they sense someone watching them, she saw us and waved, stretching her arm up high and waggling her hand. Reggie gave her a little salute.

I left him at the railing to watch the entrance and started down the wide hallway that led to 589, heavy black bag hanging from my shoulder. Anyone who has ever read the numbers on a lottery ticket over and over, feeling the realization that they have actually won spreading like an orgasm through their bones and belly, knows how I felt approaching the room of Evelyn Evermore in Indian Wells on the last Friday in January 1996. The adrenaline pump had kicked on like an air-conditioner compressor, flooding the spongy tissue of my brain with epinephrine, bringing a fresh surge of exhilaration. I had felt alien and out of place in normal society for as long as I could remember, but I was at home in the world of crime, happy as a soldier at the end of a war he never expected to survive as he crosses the bridge back into the town he came from.

The hallway was illuminated by crystal chandeliers that sparkled above my head. The rose-colored carpet was springy beneath my feet. I passed one dark-skinned housekeeper who snubbed her cart against the wall and stood with downcast eyes as I passed, and one room-service tray piled with dirty dishes and wadded cloth napkins outside the door of a suite.

I walked past 589, which was near the end of the long hallway. At the very end, there was a fire exit. The door opened into a bare steel and concrete stairwell that I could descend in a hurry if I had to. To my right as I faced the fire door, a narrow hallway extended for twenty feet, then jogged out of sight. I didn't explore it.

Back at the door to the lady's suite, I slid the key card into the slot. The green light blinked on, the lock beeped and, with a quick glance up and down the hallway, I stepped into a future far different than the one I imagined.

CHAPTERFIVE

The living room was furnished richly in desert brown and tan with umber and gold accents. Directly in front of me as I entered, a sliding glass door opened onto a large balcony. Through the door, framed by heavy gold drapes, I could see the orange disk of the sun half hidden by the Santa Rosa Mountains, which rose abruptly several miles to the west. Early in the morning when they are bathed in eastern light, the mountains glow red. But they turn black in the afternoon.

The bedroom, where everything of value would be, was through a doorway to my right. The bathroom was beyond the bedroom, corner of a sunken marble bathtub visible through a second doorway.

I entered the bedroom silently. Since the suite was empty, it wouldn't have mattered if I coughed and scuffed my feet, but the habit of stealth was engrained in muscle memory. The king-size bed was crisp and unwrinkled, but I opened the louvered closet doors as softly as if a police captain was snoring beneath the yellow duvet. A small room safe fastened to the closet floor made a flutter in my chest.

Like most precautions approved by security-conscious citizens and their enablers, hotel room safes are actually a boon to serious criminals. The main hotel safe at the Oasis was, I knew without having seen it, a hard-core, high-tech device that would be difficult to access. But travelers in luxury hotels no longer put their valuables in big safes protected by cameras and security guards. Instead, they take advantage of an "amenity" they get for paying exorbitant rates and put their money and jewelry and drugs and weapons in convenient room safes, cracker boxes made of soft metal with no alarms.

I laid the black bag on the bed. It held a .32-caliber Beretta Tomcat; a very expensive, very powerful, nearly silent cordless drill; and a set of ra- zory titanium bits that would cut through the little play safe like a sur- geon's scalpel slicing through a girdle of fat. There was also a flexible, lighted scope that I could insert through a drill hole to see the contents of the "safe," and a hardened steel prying tool which, when the sections were screwed together into a five-foot bar and the hooked tip inserted up to its back spur in that same handy hole, would give me enough leverage to break the lock and pop the door open.

I was all set to crack the safe and steal the lady's jewels, polishing my image of myself as a crafty and competent criminal in the process, but I didn't get the chance. The safe was unlocked. And empty. Either Ever- more was careless with her diamonds or she hadn't brought them.

The three red hard-shell suitcases were empty, too. There was nothing bulky in the pockets of any of the clothes hanging in the closet. The top dresser drawer contained the outfit the lady had worn in the car, neatly folded, a nightgown, pantyhose, and half a dozen pairs of panties, silky and colorful. The middle drawer was cashmere sweaters and folded wool pants. There were no men's clothes.

The bottom drawer held two phone books, a Gideon Bible with a card- board cover, and what looked like a child's jewelry box, flimsy wood with seashells glued to it, secured by a ten-cent latch. I felt the unmistakable weight of something valuable as I lifted it from the drawer and set it on top of the dresser.

Pasted to the underside of the lid was a photograph of a girl about the right age for a seashell jewelry box. She was smiling and waving at the camera, wearing what might have been a Confirmation dress. Pasted next to it was another picture of the same girl, older, sadder, with angry eyes, standing against the railing of a corral, with a barn and pasture in the background. She was wearing a blue jean jacket and her blond hair had been dyed black. A woman who could have been Evelyn Evermore some years back was looking at the camera with a strained smile, her arm placed awkwardly around the girl's shoulders.

In the box was a collection of mementos: an ID card with a third and final picture of the girl, identifying her as Christina Evermore, an eighth-grader at Sea Winds Middle School; a silver thimble; a small magnifying glass; and a pink plastic unicorn with a bedraggled mane. The sense of loss that clung to the trinkets and fading snapshots made me think of my own lost daughter, the little girl who wasn't so little anymore, growing up somewhere in the wide world without me.

But there was also a blue velvet case in the box, three inches wide by eight inches long by an inch and a half deep. It injected a silver shimmer into my dark heart, washing over the sadness like cool surf over disheveled sand after the last swimmer has left the beach at the end of a summer day. In the white satin interior lay the necklace: twenty-six carats of fancy pink diamonds. A set of earrings lay beside the necklace. Each earring was an unadorned one-carat rose-colored diamond in a simple platinum setting.

Diamonds are one of society's most spectacular illusions. The clear, sparkling gems people think of when they hear the word aren't actually all that rare. They are abundant all over the planet, from Africa to India to Siberia to South America. A cabal of South African businessmen and Israeli merchants that has persisted for generations maintains inflated prices by strictly controlling the flow of stones into the market. People routinely pay as much as ten thousand dollars for very fine one-carat clear diamonds, but if you try to sell a stone like that back to a jeweler, you will be lucky to get ten cents on the dollar.

Pink diamonds, on the other hand, are genuinely rare and valuable. Which meant I would be able to fence the necklace for a decent percentage of its quarter-million-dollar appraised worth, netting at least a hundred thousand dollars. Likely more.

Roy Rogers had just started playing "Happy Trails" in my mind when I heard someone move behind me. Whirling, I saw that it was the weightlifter. He was standing in the bedroom doorway holding a big black automatic that looked like it had come from a fascist country. It was an ugly, large-bore weapon that would make an ugly hole. The hall door was open behind him. Rifling the dresser drawers, I hadn't heard him enter. I wondered how he had gotten by Reggie.

"Who the fuck are you?" I said.

"I'm Jimmy Z, the last one you think of, the first one to show," he said. "Who are you?" His leather jacket was stretched tight over his bulging chest and upper arms. It looked like the seams would split if he flexed his biceps. His long narrow ex-con's face was as expressionless as his voice. I had a premonition that one of us was going to kill the other at some point.

"Hotel security," I said. "We had a report of a break-in. What are you doing in Mrs. Evermore's suite?"

"Um her bodyguard," he said. "Show a badge."

"I'm not showing you shit," I said. "I'm going to put Mrs. Evermore's necklace in the hotel vault for safekeeping. Then you're going to answer some questions." I snapped the jewelry case closed and reached for the black bag on the bed. The Tomcat was a much nicer pistol than his industrial piece. It was an elegant James Bond sort of weapon, stainless steel with an ivory grip. At 4.9 inches long and 15 ounces, it was light and easy to conceal, yet had the stopping power of a .38. There were seven 60-grain hollow-points in the magazine and one in the tilt-up chamber. It never jammed.

But I had to get my hands on it.

"Stop," he said, raising his pistol an inch or two so that it was pointing at my solar plexus. The hammer was cocked. "You ain't hotel security. And that ain't Evermore's necklace no more. It belongs to Baba Raba now."

"You better put that pistol away, Jimmy, or you're going to end up back in the clink."

He took a step toward me. "Drop the case on the bed and put your hands behind your head, or you're gonna end up in a funeral parlor," he said, voice flat and uninflected. All the emotion had been beaten out of him by a sadistic older brother or drunken mother, and by the blackjacks of cops in police departments from San Diego to San Francisco. He had probably killed his first small animals in grade school, moving on to larger prey as he matured.

I was running out of options. "Who's Baba Raba?" I said, still holding on to the blue velvet box full of long, leisurely rides up the coast and meals in fine restaurants and trips to Cabo and Hawaii.

"Last chance," he said. The knuckles on his right hand, swollen from hitting the heavy bag, looked like one-inch ball bearings. They were white with tension. Numb heart full of Novocain, he would kill without remorse. He might be able to get away with it, too. He had caught me burglarizing the room. I had a gun that he could put in my hand if he found it in time. His gun was probably unlicensed, but that would be a minor charge. He looked like he could do ninety days standing on his ear. I dropped the jewelry case on the edge of the bed and it bounced off onto the floor.

"Now the hands," he said.

Everyone likes to be tough. I like to be tough. But sometimes when a sociopath is pointing a hand cannon at you, you feel a little scared, or sad. Sometimes you remember walking along a path by a river with someone you loved who you will never see again. A narrow dirt path overhung with alder trees and bordered by all the flowers of a midwestern spring. Sometimes you remember the hopes you had for your life when you were young. But then you get over that and start calculating your odds of ducking under the gun with a fast tackle.

The odds weren't good.

I put my hands behind my head, scrambling mentally, looking for an out. There wasn't going to be anything pleasant in store for me if I let him take me prisoner, arrested at the least, shot and dumped in the desert at the worst.

"Turn around and get down on your knees," he said.

CHAPTER SIX

Before I could turn my vulnerable back to the large bore of the .45, there was a knock at the half-open hall door and Reggie burst into the room carrying the tray I'd seen in the hallway. He had covered the dirty dishes with a white cloth napkin and tucked another napkin in the front of his pants so that it hung down like an apron.

"Room service," he shouted.

The weightlifter half-turned, looking over his shoulder at Reggie, then glancing quickly back at me. He turned the gun away from me, holding it flat in front of his body so that Reggie couldn't see it. "Put it down and get out," he said.

"Where you want it?" Reggie said, panting a little bit. His face was red with excitement or exertion and I saw some lipstick on his right ear. At first glance, with the improvised apron, he looked a little like a waiter. At second glance, not so much.

The weightlifter was noticing that. As he turned for a better look, I dove toward him, tucking, doing a tight somersault on the thick carpet, and coming up to tackle him from a crouch with a lot of momentum. He clubbed me on top of the head with the .45 as he went down, loosening my grip on his waist. Stomping at me, he kicked free, still holding on to the gun. Dazed, I heard a loud crash as he scrambled to his feet, dishes shattering and metal dish covers clanging, then saw Reggie looming up behind him, metal serving tray raised high. The weightlifter spun toward the noise a split second too late, and Reggie brought the tray down on his head with a bong.

His muscular legs wobbled but held. As Reggie raised the tray for another blow, the weightlifter backfisted him with the .45, striking his forehead with the heavy barrel. Reggie dropped to his knees and the weightlifter reared back his right foot for a kick. I was up on one knee and grabbed his foot as it came back. Lifting and charging toward him as I got to my feet, I flipped him onto his head. His gun went flying and landed under the table near the hall door, which Reggie had left standing wide open. As the weightlifter scrambled after his piece, I dove on top of him, flattening him against the floor and knocking the wind out of him. Before he could recover, I got him in a stranglehold, my right forearm across his windpipe, right hand gripping my left bicep, left hand locked on the back of his head.

He was strong. He got up on his hands and knees and nearly bucked me off. He hit back over his shoulder with one hand and then the other, putting knots on my head, and crashed around, bashing my body against furniture and walls. But I kept his air cut off and after a minute or so I could feel him getting weaker. Finally, he stopped struggling. I kept the choke hold tight, grinding his trachea, not taking any chance in case he was playing possum.

"Less get outta here," I heard Reggie say in a weak voice. The weightlifter was sprawled flat on the living room floor with his head near the hall door. I was lying full length on top of him. Looking over my shoulder, I saw Reggie leaning against the wall by the bedroom door. He was holding one of the cloth napkins to his forehead. It was red. Blood dripped from the end of his nose. "Too much noise," he said.

I released the choke hold and sat up on the weightlifter's back, which twitched and heaved as he started to breathe again with his face in the carpet. He smelled like the jocks I fought in high school: too much sweet cologne not quite covering up the stink of old sweat. Thinking about the beautiful, bewildered lady he had somehow gotten his hooks into and remembering the fear he made me feel, I grabbed his hair with my left hand, turned his head so that his face was exposed and slammed my right fist into his nose as hard as I could in a tight roundhouse. There was a crunching sound as bone and cartilage gave way and blood sprayed on my hand and forearm.

"What's the meaning of this?"

Looking up, I saw the snowbird from downstairs filling the doorway. She was wearing a white terrycloth robe with the Oasis's emerald-and-scarlet hummingbird logo perched on her tremendous bosom. Her hair was wrapped up in a white towel turban. A little man with a perfectly bald head and big ears was hopping around behind her, stretching out his scrawny neck and peeking around her bulk from one side and then the other, trying to see into the room.

"My husband didn't pay top dollar to listen to this kind of ruckus! He won't stand for it, do you hear me? What do you think you're doing, anyway? What was all that crashing and banging?"

Thrusting his head in between his wife's plump shoulder and the doorjamb, the bald man made a mean face. "Yeah, what gives?" He was wearing a hotel robe, too. It was way too big for him.

"I'm the head of hotel security," I said, suppressing a nauseating surge of vertigo as I stood up, grabbing the couch to steady myself. "We caught this punk robbing a guest room. I apologize for the disturbance. Everything is under control now. Why don't you go on back to your room and let us take care of this?"

"Don't order me around!" the lady said. "My husband isn't paying four hundred dollars a night for this malarkey!" Her suspicious little eyes were darting around in her head, cataloguing the disorder in the room. "Who's he?" She nodded sharply in Reggie's direction.

"He's my associate, ma'am. I am very sorry you were disturbed. There won't be any more trouble. But you are going to have to go back to your room and let us take care of this."

The man's bald head and big ears poked into the room on the other side of his wife. "Don't order her around!" he said.

"I'm ordering both of you to get the hell out of here, right now!" I shouted, walking toward them, crowding them out of the doorway. "Go back to your room before I arrest you for interfering with a crime scene!"

The man's shiny head disappeared, and the lady drew herself up with a look of outrage on her frying pan of a face.

"How dare you talk to my husband like that!" she yelled. "Come on, Dickey! We'll see what the manager thinks about this. I've never been so insulted in all my born days. I'll have that man's job or know the reason why." Her commentary trailed off as she sailed back down the hall to the open door of 569, a battleship with a dinghy in its wake. Her robe was stretched tight across her ass and shoulders. It stopped just below her knees and elbows, leaving massive calves and beefy-red forearms exposed. The husband looked like Dopey from the Seven Dwarfs in his robe, sleeves covering his hands to his fingertips, hem dragging the floor. Just before he went into their room and slammed the door, the little man looked back at me and made his mean face one more time, pulling his lips back and baring his teeth like a lap dog snarling at a German shepherd through a rolled-up car window.

"We *got* to get out of here," Reggie said.

"No shit," I said, passing him on my way into the bedroom. "How did he get by you?"

"He didn't come past me, man."

The jewelry case was lying twisted and broken by the bed. Someone had stepped or rolled on it during the fight. I saw one of the earrings near it and snatched it up. The necklace was nowhere in sight.

I looked under the bed and on the closet floor, then started searching through the broken dishes and debris.

"What the hell yuh doing?" Reggie said.

"I'm looking for the goddamn necklace," I said. "Help me find it!"

The jewels were crystallized bliss, emotionally potent as pure rock cocaine. I was desperate to find them. But there were voices in the hall.

"I'm not sure, sir," I heard a woman's voice say. Then Tawny came into the room. She was wide-eyed but calm, keeping it together. Her blouse was buttoned crookedly, each button one hole off.

"I don't know who you guys are or what you're doing," she said, her voice low and intense, "but you better haul ass. The security guys are coming up the elevator!"

"Fuck!" I said, and grabbed the black bag from the bed. Pulling out the Beretta, I stuck it in my belt beneath my shirttail, where I could get to it fast. Reggie was following Tawny out the door, wobbling a little as he walked. Crossing the living room, I spotted the other earring and snagged it without breaking my stride, slipping it into my right pants pocket with its mate. Jimmy Z was still out cold. I resisted the urge to kick him in the head on my way out of the room.

There were several people standing in front of their doors along the hallway that led back to the atrium. Rodriguez, the golf pro, was leaning against his doorjamb, wearing a pair of black satin boxer shorts and smoking a cigarette, looking mildly curious. The bellboy the weightlifter had abused was hurrying away from Rodriguez's room in the direction of the elevators, trying to tuck in his shirt and put his jacket on at the same time.

"This way," Tawny said, leading us down the hall away from Rodriguez, the elevators, and the atrium. I thought she was heading for the fire exit, but she turned right down the short hallway I'd seen earlier, then jogged left into terra incognita.

Shortly, we came to a small elevator.

"This goes down to the pool," she said, jabbing the down button.

There was a distant clunk as the elevator motor engaged. Shortly, the 1 above the door lit up. After several seconds that seemed like several minutes, the 1 went dark and the 2 lit up. It was a leisurely elevator, perfect for a resort, taking its time ascending to our floor.

"Come on, come on!" Tawny said.

I ran back to the corner and looked around. No one was in sight yet, but I could hear more voices in the main hallway, a loud, excited babble. The voices were coming closer.

Back at the elevator, the 4 was yellow. Then it went dark and the 5 blinked on and the door finally slid open. Tawny punched the button for the third floor and a lower one that said POOL.

"When you get off the elevator, go through the glass doors into the pool area and then go left," she said. "Go out the gate and follow the path that goes around this wing of the hotel. It will take you to the side parking lot."

The elevator stopped at three and Tawny got off.

"Thanks, babe," Reggie said.

She looked back at him. "If they find out I helped you, it's my job."

"They won't find out," I said.

"I'm in the book," she said to Reggie as the door slid shut, moving her head to keep him in view. "Tawny Pulaski."

CHAPTER SEVEN

Downstairs, the elevator opened into an empty hallway with squishy indoor/outdoor carpeting. Reggie tossed the bloody napkin in a corner and we went through double glass doors onto a concrete patio that overlooked the Oasis's pool complex. It's one of the largest and most elaborate in the desert, four sparkling pools connected by waterfalls and chutes, with a sand beach and a thatched-roof bar on an island that you can swim up to when you are ready for a drink.

The sun had sunk behind the black bulk of the Santa Rosa Mountains. Overhead, the desert sky was still a deep luminous blue brushed by the tops of swaying palm trees, but the valley was plunged into sudden twilight and the lounge chairs and pool decks were deserted. At the little tropical bar, a wrinkled woman in a white one-piece bathing suit sat hunched over a red drink with a yellow umbrella sticking out of it. The bartender was tidying up, getting ready to close.

There was a rack of fresh white towels beside the door we came out of and I grabbed one as we started down the concrete path to the gate, hotel rising to our left, swimming pool to our right. Beyond the gate, the path curved through a stand of California fan palm trees, past tennis courts and a maintenance building, then looped left around the back of the hotel.

The walkway ended at a set of concrete steps that dropped down to an asphalt parking lot full of valeted cars. The Seville was parked between a black BMW 720i and a silver Bentley, but the keys were at the valet station in front of the hotel.

Beyond the parking lot, a golf course lay green and hilly, charmed here and there by small lakes.

"Which way, bro?" Reggie said. His face and the front of his shirt were covered with his own blood. He had soaked up some of it with the napkin, but there was plenty left. My right hand and sleeve were stained with the weightlifter's blood and I had knots on my head where he hit me with the .45 and his big-knuckled fists. There was no way either one of us could go to the valet stand and get the car without attracting the wrong kind of attention, especially with the hotel in an uproar.

"This way," I said, walking straight across the parking lot toward the golf course.

"Where we going?"

"To that little lake over there to get you cleaned up, and then to the Hyatt."

The Oasis Palms is part of a resort complex that includes two golf courses and four hotels, the Oasis and Hyatt Regency Grand Champions on the north side of State Route 111, the Miramonte and the Indian Wells Resort Hotel, Ricky Ricardo's old place, on the south side of the palm-lined highway. The Hyatt was about a quarter of a mile away, hidden by a hill that was topped with a dense stand of elephant-ear plants.

"I ain't taking a bath in a lake," Reggie said.

"Why not?"

"Who knows what might be in the motherfucker—frogs and snakes and every other fucking thing."

"I don't want you to take a bath," I said. "But we can use the water to wipe the blood off your face so it doesn't look like you just killed a family."

There was a foursome playing far off on the other side of the course. Otherwise, the links were deserted as evening descended. We walked across the springy grass of a well-tended green, then down a sloping fairway to the edge of the water. Tree frogs were beginning to chirp as I knelt down and rinsed off my hands and forearms and folded my sleeves back to my elbows to hide the red cuff. Reggie took off his bloody shirt and hid it in some bushes. I dipped one end of the towel in the water and used it to wipe his arms and face. He used the other end to dry off with. His white T-shirt had a couple red spots where blood had soaked through, but it didn't look too bad. No one would notice at a distance.

We walked along the edge of the golf course in the shadow the Santa Rosa Mountains have cast each evening for millions of years to the top of the little man-made hill. From there, hidden among the elephant-ear plants, we could see the front of the Oasis and the back of the Hyatt, where a dozen or so people were scattered around a flagstone patio, eating dinner at glass-topped tables. The squeal of rubber on concrete made me look out toward Highway 111, where traffic was streaming by in both directions, a few cars with their headlights on, most without. A black-and-white had just skidded into the main entry drive shared by both hotels. A white Crown Victoria, the unmarked car of choice for cop shops from coast to coast, careened around the corner right behind it. At the Y, both cars veered right, racing up toward the Oasis's porte cochere.

"Little late, ain't they?" Reggie sneered. He was feeling better.

At the Hyatt, I left him sitting on a stone bench that overlooked the second hole and threaded my way through the diners on the patio, entering the hotel at the back side of the lobby. Crossing the quarry tile floor to the front desk, I was acutely conscious of the Beretta pressing against my belly.

I wanted to get a room where we could lie low until things settled down at the Oasis. We could have hid out on the darkening golf course for a couple hours, but it would have been uncomfortable, and the fairways were probably patrolled by resort rent-a-cops. The last thing I wanted was a confrontation with hotel security. Likewise, we could have spent the evening in the hotel bar, nursing drinks and watching golf reruns on TV, but Reggie would have stood out in his T-shirt and if the detectives in the Crown Vic were any good they would stroll through the resort bars, looking for suspects who fit whatever description they got from the snowbird and her pet husband. I wasn't worried about a description from Jimmy Z. With a mangled trachea and demolished nose, he wouldn't be talking to the cops until after surgery. Recalling the crunching sound his nose made, I felt a little sick. I had murder in my heart when I hit him and it's a poisonous emotion.

A room would be perfect. We'd be out of the public eye. We could shower and patch up our wounds and think about what to do next. But the leather chairs and couches grouped on Mexican rugs here and there around the lobby were filled with weary travelers waiting beside mounds of suitcases and golf-club bags, and there were four lines at the front desk. The hotel was almost certainly sold out.

I went to the end of the shortest line. When my turn at the counter came, ten minutes later, I smiled humbly at a young man behind a computer terminal who wore a white carnation in the lapel of his blue blazer and told him I needed a room and no I didn't have a reservation and yes I knew it was their busy time and that there was a golf tournament starting on Sunday but anything he could do would be appreciated.

He looked at his computer screen for a while, tapping keys and shaking his neatly barbered blond head, looking more and more mournful, despite the carnation. My head throbbed where the steel butt of the .45 had smashed into it and I felt half a dozen other twinges, aches, and sore spots coming into focus as the adrenaline of the fight and flight faded. A high-pressure stream of hot water pulsing from the kind of massaging shower-heads they have in luxe resorts would be heaven, but with each shake of the desk clerk's head, the prospect of a safe, comfortable room receded.

Then, suddenly, he brightened. "Well look at that!" he said. "You are in luck, sir. The hotel gods have smiled on us. We just had a cancellation come in this very moment. I can offer you a junior suite with a king and a fold-out couch if that is acceptable." He gave me a smile that was happy for both of us.

I paid cash, took the elevator up to the suite, and dropped off the black bag, then went back for Reggie, bringing him in a side entrance.

"I got dibs on the first bath," Reggie said, as we went into the suite.

It was a spacious room, segmented into sitting and sleeping areas by a louvered wooden screen. The carpet was thick, the furnishings luxurious. It looked like something a Hollywood set designer had concocted for a remake of *Grand Hotel*, and a few minor stars had probably slept in it.

"Fine," I said, "but before you get your rubber ducky out, I want to know what happened back there."

"What happened back there? At the hotel? Looked like you let that punk get the drop on you and we came away without the necklace."

"You're right. He did get the drop on me. What I want to know is how he got past you."

"I told you, he didn't get past me."

"Where the fuck did he come from, then?"

"He must of come up that back way."

"I don't think so. I think you were in a linen closet getting your dick rubbed and he did get past you."

Our relationship was like one between a grizzled staff sergeant and a younger first lieutenant. The lieutenant is in official command of the platoon but sometimes defers to the sergeant because of his longer experience in the service. Sometimes the sergeant may do something to show the lieutenant up because he thinks he should be in charge all the time. Power shifted back and forth between us, with Reggie willing to salute and take orders most of the time because I knew how to plan successful scores, but always trying to get his own way, too.

"It's a lucky thing Tawny did come up," he said belligerently. "She didn't want to make out by the elevators so we went down the hall and around a couple of corners. That's how come I saw that punk going into the room and went down and saved your ass."

I was pretty sure Jimmy Z had slipped past him while his eyes were rolled back in his head, but there was no point arguing about it. He had saved me from a psycho, for the second time in six months.

"I think you fucked up," I said, "but we won't fight about it right now. Go ahead and take your bath. I'm going to see if the resort shops are still open. If they are, I'll get us some new clothes. What size pants and shirt do you wear?"

"Forty-two waist, thirty length on the pants, extra-large shirt." He sounded mad, which made me think maybe he was telling the truth, but I couldn't be sure because he was a good actor when trying to cover his tracks. If you busted him cold in a lie, he would cop to it with a grin and shrug, but if he knew you weren't quite certain, he'd keep lying with his dying breath for the satisfaction of deceiving you.

The clock in the lobby said six-thirty. That shocked me. It seemed like it had been much more than two hours since we pulled up in front of the Oasis Palms. The Hyatt's main lobby shop was still open. It had everything from suntan lotion and postcards to romance novels and souvenir mugs, along with a fair selection of men's and women's resort wear. I bought Bactine, Band-Aids, and two complete outfits. Mine was khaki chinos and a yellow polo shirt, along with a fifty-dollar Panama hat and a pair of sunglasses. To aggravate Reggie, I bought him a big pair of brown plaid

Bermuda shorts, an oversize aloha shirt with red hibiscus on an orange background, and a pair of those leather sandals with crisscross straps that guys with white legs wear over black socks. Both of us would look completely different than when we arrived in Indian Wells.

Back in the suite, Reggie was lying on the bed with a towel wrapped around him watching a rerun of *Hawaii Five-O*, probably the worst TV cop show ever made, with laughable dialogue and acting, implausible plots, and bad guys with names like Big Chicken. Not coincidentally, considering the clichéd sensibilities of fin-de-siècle America, it was also the longest-running cop show in television history.

"What are you watching that shit for?" I asked him.

"Bikinis," he said. Onscreen, two Polynesian girls in skimpy swimming suits were having a giggly conversation with the former Disney actor who played Danno. Reggie had a point.

I took his new clothes from the bag and tossed them on the bed.

"Oh, no," he said when he saw the shorts. "I ain't wearing those stupid things."

"Yes you are," said the lieutenant, exerting his authority. "Think of it as a disguise. If anyone noticed you hanging around the Oasis lobby or saw us leaving the hotel, the cops will be looking for someone in long pants and a dark-blue shirt. They won't spot you in this getup."

"How come you ain't wearing short pants, then?"

"I don't want to look goofy."

CHAPTER EIGHT

When Reggie came out of the bathroom in his costume, I bit the inside of my cheek to keep from laughing.

"Fuck you," he said.

Except for his bushy beard, he looked like the original rube, a chunky wannabe who didn't have a clue that his clothes were clownish, not cool.

"You need a trim," I said.

I called housekeeping and asked them to send up a pair of scissors. A few minutes later there was a soft knock at the door. When I opened it, a slight young Mexican in a bellboy's uniform bobbed his head and held out a pair of shears, handle first.

"Thanks," I said, and handed him a five.

He bobbed his head again, grinned, and backed away from the door as I closed it.

Resort protocol requires a one-dollar tip for someone who brings a small item to your room, but most of the rich people who patronize fine hotels don't tip delivery boys at all, their gravitational attachment to their money having grown ever greater along with its mass. I gave the kid a five, not because I am a wonderful person, but, as with the valet, because it was an easy way to make someone smile, and because it made me another friend in Indian Wells.

Reggie grumbled but sat still with a towel draped over his shoulders while I trimmed his beard and hair to make him look more middle-class. He didn't like haircuts, and the fact that he let me shear him made me think he probably was guilty of abandoning his post after all. I used the Bactine and two small transparent adhesive strips to disinfect and close the gash at his hairline.

After I showered in the miniature marble palace of the suite's bathroom and changed into my crisp new clothes, we went down to dinner. I saw one woman in a turquoise St. John knit suit glance at Reggie and snicker. To the rest of the clowns with fat wallets and fairway dreams he looked like one of the crowd. Of course, none of them looked into his stony brown eyes. If they had, they would have clapped one hand on their wallets, the other over their mouths to keep from screaming, and hurried away at the speed of a golf cart driven by a defeated linksman racing for his first postgame martini.

Reggie had a whiskey sour and three Budweisers with his New York strip steak, enough to send him through a period of feeling good, during which he jollied up our waitress, and then make him sleepy. He didn't eat his asparagus. I had one O'Doul's with my slab of sautéed halibut and did eat my broccoli.

After dinner, Reggie went back up to the suite, while I strolled through the cool desert night to see what was happening at the Oasis Palms. There was a self-parking lot between the two hotels, built below grade and surrounded by philodendrons, banana plants, and elephant ear so that the limo set wouldn't have to see it. I walked across the neatly stripped asphalt to a concrete staircase that led up to the level of the porte cochere.

It was eight forty-five and there was activity at the hotel's gleaming entrance, people going to or returning from restaurants, movies, and pre-tournament parties. Normalcy had returned to the resort. Almost. The black-and-white was gone but the unmarked car was still parked near the valet stand.

I didn't like the idea of trying to retrieve the Caddie while detectives were still sniffing around. The valets were busy, and I might have to stand in plain sight in front of the hotel for five or ten minutes. We'd spend the night at the Hyatt.

I thought of circling around to the pool elevator and trying to get back into Evermore's room to search for the necklace, but it seemed too risky, more reckless than bold. She might be there. The detectives might be there. And the room had probably been searched, the necklace found, and put someplace secure.

When I got back to the suite, the lights were out. A cheerful plotless porno flick was writhing on the big-screen TV. Reggie was snoring on the bed. I watched the athletic sex for a few minutes, feeling voyeuristic in the dark, then switched it off and unfolded the Hide-Away bed. It was already made up, crisp and cool, with 300-thread-count sheets and a soft wool blanket. I found two goose-down pillows in the foyer closet.

Once I had the bed ready, I realized I wasn't sleepy and went out onto the balcony to soak up some of the mystic atmosphere of the desert night and think the situation over. Silver stars flickered above the date palms and a golden sliver of moon pulsed high up in the black sky. The Hyatt's pool complex was spread out below me. Surrounded by paving stones and native desert plants, the half dozen round and oval pools looked in the moonlight like natural, not man-made, features.

The Coachella Valley is the wettest desert in the West, with more swimming pools per capita than any other place in the country—not surprising since it routinely tops 110 Fahrenheit in the summer. There is abundant natural water, too. Away from sprinkler systems and maintained greenery, the valley floor is as dry and desolate as the most antisocial old prospector could hope for, but it is ringed by four mountain ranges—the Santa Rosas, the San Jacintos, the San Bernardinos, and the Little San Bernardinos, with the highest peaks over ten thousand feet. The mountains isolate the valley as surely as the sea isolates Catalina, giving it a far-off, Shangri-La feeling even though it is only a short drive from L.A. The rocky, pine-clad peaks also provide an infinite supply of water, snowmelt that runs down underground to fill aquifers below the sand. Valley place-names—Palm Springs, Desert Hot Springs, Indian Wells—testify to the availability of this ironic water. Another example of things often not being what they seem.

When I came to Southern California in 1992, I couldn't understand why people would go to the desert for a weekend trip or weeklong vacation when they had available to them mountain resorts like Arrowhead and Big Bear and one of the most dazzling seacoasts in the world, with 150 miles of bright, misty beach stretching from San Diego to Santa Barbara. Over the past four years, though, I had fallen under its spell. I loved the dramatic rise of the mountains from the dry seabed of the valley floor, the date palm groves, and the glittering resorts. I liked the desert nights especially, the stillness and mystery, but on that night I felt cut off emotionally from the world around me. Everything looked flat and mundane, the way it does when you are depressed.

The powerful charge of adrenaline that had gushed through me earlier in the evening as I burglarized the hotel room, fought with Jimmy Z, and then fled the scene had dissipated, leaving me listless as a speed freak crashing from a three-day run. I was depressed by the loss of the diamonds I had held in my hand, by Reggie's almost fatal negligence, and maybe by the aftereffects of steel striking my skull. I still faced the problem of retrieving the Cadillac and getting out of town without a police escort.

To revive myself, I tried a technique I learned from a medicine man I met in the Palm Valley on my first trip to the desert, several years before. The valley is a true oasis at the base of the San Jacinto Mountains, where a clear stream rushes down through fan palm groves before disappearing below the desert floor. The Agua Caliente band of the Cahuilla Indians has lived there for more than a thousand years. Sitting beside me on the bank of the stream, the medicine man showed me how to look at the whole width and thickness of the flowing water, not just the surface, getting inside it in a magical way. I felt energy pour into me when I connected with his concept, a tiny circuit closing in the infinite universe.

Since then I've found that the trick can work in any environment. Whenever I notice that the world has gone flat, the landscape looking like a mural painted on a factory wall, I know that I am too wrapped up in myself, cut off from the healing flow of reality around me. When that happens, I use my imagination to grasp the third dimension of depth, visualizing the twisting branches and twigs in each bushy treetop, seeing the shaped space between the leaves and the space between successive trees, and suddenly the world regains a subtle animation. In an urban environment, I visualize the texture of the bricks, the depth of the mortar lines, the segmented spaces inside the buildings and irregular spaces between them, and it has the same effect of pulling me out of myself and bringing the world back to life.

Looking at the nearest palm tree, I let the twenty-foot spread of the crown take shape in my mind, imagining how the raspy, sharp-edged leaflets attached to the stalks of the fronds, and how the fronds merged into the fibrous structure of the trunk. I thought about the roots branching into the sandy soil, drawing a steady stream of water molecules and minerals up through narrow ducts to feed the green fans and grow the sweet dates.

That was all it took to bring depth and dimension back to the desert night. I sensed the lively, shifting distances between the first palm, swaying slightly in the breeze, and those around it, felt myself in specific proximity to the black mountains resting their unimaginable weight on the earth and to the massive balls of burning hydrogen flickering far out across the universe.

The rose-tinted diamond earrings hidden in the hotel room behind me would fence for five or six thousand dollars. The thought of those beautiful gems with their highly compressed value lifted my mood further. I stood up and gripped the rail of the balcony, fully inflating my chest with cool night air.

There were things I didn't understand about the situation. Why was an elegant, wealthy woman like Evelyn Evermore traveling with a homicidal hood? Who was Baba Raba—one of the celebrity gurus California was famous for? Why had the lady carelessly left the necklace in an unlocked drawer, and where was it now? Why had Jimmy Z come back, and where had he left Evermore? They were the same questions that had been nagging me when I sat down, but now they were intriguing instead of unsettling, exciting instead of depressing.

I went to bed the way a criminal should, scheming.

CHAPTER NINE

The next morning, I was up in time to see the Santa Rosa Mountains stained red by the sun as it peeked over the Little San Bernardinos on the opposite side of the flat thirty-mile-wide Coachella Valley, horizontal rays skimming over the desert to fire the western peaks. While Reggie and I ate scrambled eggs with thick crispy strips of hickory-smoked bacon on the terrace overlooking the golf course, I leafed through the local newspaper. An account of the burglary and attempted theft of the diamond necklace was buried on page 6, where it wouldn't frighten the millionaires. The paper mentioned Evermore's name and reported that the jewels were worth half a million dollars. Any time the cops seize drugs or recover or prevent the theft of property, they inflate the value of the goods outrageously to make themselves look good. The article noted that the police were looking for two suspects. I hoped Tawny hadn't talked.

The paper also reported that James Zerotski, who was injured in the attempted robbery, had been taken to Eisenhower Medical Center, where he was in serious condition. It didn't mention the earrings.

I showed the article to Reggie. His lips moved silently as he read through it.

"Maybe we should go over an have a powwow with the punk," he said when he finished.

"About what?"

"Maybe he knows where the rocks are."

"I doubt it. He was out cold. It would be too risky, anyway."

"Whadaya wanna do, then?"

"I want to get the Caddie and get the hell out of town."

Back upstairs, I stuffed our bloody clothes and our shoes, which might have left identifiable footprints in blood or mud, into two plastic dry cleaning bags, then went down the back stairs and buried them in a Dumpster by the hotel kitchen.

At 8 a.m. we sallied out the main entrance of the Hyatt Grand Champions Resort and Spa like typical tourists with more cash than common sense, off to enjoy a day in wonderful wintertime Palm Springs. The front of the hotel was bustling with Saturday-morning arrivals and departures, bellboys wheeling suitcases into the lobby and hauling bags of golf clubs out to Mercedes idling with their trunks open.

"Have a grand day, gentlemen," the doorman said.

You don't get that at Motel 6, either.

A five-minute walk past hibiscus bushes with papery-red blossoms as big as dinner plates and flower beds full of yellow cannas and orange-flowering birds-of-paradise took us to the front of the Oasis, which was a mirror image of the busy Hyatt, cars two deep at the curb, laden luggage carts squeaking into and out of the hotel.

I spotted the kid with the pot-leaf tattoo coming through the oversize glass doors and went up to him.

"We're in a hurry," I said, trying to hand him the claim ticket and a ten-dollar bill. He was distracted, looking away from me at the line of cars to see how far it stretched.

"You have to go to the valet stand," he said, pushing the ticket and money back at me.

"We're in a hurry," I said again, putting something in my voice.

"So is everyone else," he said, annoyed, turning back toward me. When he recognized me, his expression changed from exasperated to dead serious in a flash. "Oh, it's you guys," he said, looking us over from top to bottom. "I didn't recognize you in those clothes." After glancing over at the valet stand, which was unoccupied, he jerked his head. "Follow me."

Reggie raised his eyebrows. I shrugged. We followed him. He led us behind a planter full of tropical greenery where we were hidden from the valet stand and most of the people in front of the hotel.

"The cops were asking about you guys," he said.

"What did they want to know?" I kept my voice calm and light despite the cold bolt of fear his words plunged in my gut.

"They—it wasn't just you, not at first—they were asking about everybody who valeted a car last night who wasn't registered here. They cross-checked our list against the front desk list and were looking for anyone who wasn't a guest. They found most of them in the restaurant and bar. It was just you and a couple of others they couldn't find, so they wanted to know more about you."

"Why were they asking questions?" I said. "What happened?"

The surfer shot me a sharp look from his hard blue eyes. "Some jerk-off with a bad attitude got beat up on the fifth floor. Someone tried to rob him or something."

"That's a shame," I said.

"Yeah," he said, keeping his eyes locked on mine. "You probably saw him. He pulled up with a foxy rich lady in a Town Car just about the same time you arrived. You were right behind him, in fact."

When I didn't say anything, he continued: "The cops were real interested in you and your car. They wanted to know what time you arrived and what you looked like and if anyone had seen you since then. They took down your license number and numbers of the other people they couldn't find. They said they were going to come back this morning to check on those cars."

I suddenly found myself standing on a razor's edge, thoughts flashing like tracers through my mind as I tried to decide how much danger we were in.

I always used stolen plates on my car during a job, and I had been lucky this time in a way that gave me some extra protection. Any stolen plate protects you in a situation where a victim or bystander writes down the number as you disappear around the corner. They give the number to the cops, the cops find out it is a stolen plate, and they can't identify the getaway car or its owner. But the protection vanishes if a squad car is cruising behind you and runs the number. There are computers in every police car nowadays, and it takes only a few moments to find out the type of car the plate goes with.

That's where I had rolled sevens. Cruising the parking lot at the Century City Mall on Friday morning, looking for a set of plates to steal, I spotted another new, dark-blue STS. It was the plates from that car that were on my Caddie now. If the cops ran the number the night before, it should have come back A-okay, except for the fact that Peter Blake wasn't the registered owner. But there is no law that says a friend couldn't drive the car and valet it in his name. The plates wouldn't have been reported as stolen because we replaced the ones we stripped off the parked Caddie with a spare set so the driver wouldn't notice his were missing.

Still, the cops were looking for us and had examined my car.

"Oh shit," the valet said, jerking my attention back into the moment.

"What is it?" I said.

"One of the cops that was here last night just pulled up."

I peeked around the foliage in the planter and saw a detective with white hair and a Marlboro Man face climbing out of a Crown Vic. He was wearing a tan suit with burgundy shoes, and his eyes were hidden by aviator sunglasses so I couldn't tell which way he was looking as he sauntered over to the valet stand. Finding it unoccupied—all the valets were busy parking or retrieving cars—he went into the lobby.

"Exit stage right," Reggie said, making saucer eyes.

"Agreed," I said, then to the surfer: "Can you get the car for us?"

He looked down at the ticket and the ten in my hand, closed his eyes briefly, and nodded. "I'll drive it around to the self-parking lot," he said. "Go down those steps over there." He pointed to the ones I'd come up the night before, when I was reconnoitering. "I'll meet you at the bottom in, like, five minutes."

Taking the ticket and the ten, leaving us behind the planter, he walked briskly to the valet stand, leaned over the counter, and snagged a set of keys from the pegboard and trotted out of sight.

Nonchalantly, bag of burglary tools hanging over my shoulder, pistol in my belt, I strolled over to the stairs. Reggie followed thirty feet behind. As I started down the steps, I glanced back to see the detective come out of the hotel with an annoyed-looking assistant manager type and go over to the valet stand.

We waited at the bottom of the steps for a very long couple of minutes, leaning against the concrete retaining wall that formed the end of the sunken parking lot. Several people came down the steps and walked past us to their cars, slightly hunched with embarrassment that they had been too cheap to valet-park. Reggie's eyebrows were up at his hairline.

"What if that kid turns us in," he said tersely, keeping his mouth still the way he did when he was in gangster mode. "Maybe we ought to car-jack one of these jokers."

"He won't turn us in," I said, and as I spoke my STS wheeled into sight and pulled up in front of us with a bark of rubber on asphalt.

"Thanks, bro," I said, handing the kid a hundred as he jumped out of the car.

He hesitated then pushed the money away. "You don't have to give me any more money," he said. "I hate the fucking cops. They are always hassling us about drinking and getting high at the beach. Just get the hell out of here before somebody sees you. I need this job."

"We're gone," I said. "Thanks again."

"Da nada."

By the time I closed the door and shifted into gear, he had disappeared up the steps.

As we pulled out of the parking lot onto the driveway that led to the highway, it seemed like we were in the clear. The tension that had stiffened my muscles began to dissolve. But there was a line of cars at the stop sign where the Oasis's drive merged with the drive from the Hyatt. As we edged toward the intersection, a blue Taurus with rental plates turned off the main drive, heading up to the hotel. The little man behind the wheel looked over at us as it passed. His fierce eyes swept over me without recognition, then snapped back. He slammed on his brakes and let out a yelp, made silent by two layers of auto glass, then bared his teeth at me. Beyond him, I saw his wife turn her big face in our direction.

We were at the stop sign by then, so I smiled and waved like they were old friends, and pushed the gas pedal toward the floor.

There are four ways out of Indian Wells and I took the least traveled, heading straight up into the San Jacinto Mountains on the Palms to Pines Highway. The Seville's power train pulled the car's four thousand pounds of metal and plastic, plus my and Reggie's combined four hundred pounds of muscle, bone, and memory, up the steep incline as easily as if gravity had been turned off. The RPMs stayed between two and three thousand, same as on a flat road, and the red temperature-gauge needle dozed at dead center, showing no strain on the engine.

At the first side road, I pulled over and ditched the stolen plates and put mine back on, then pointed the dark-blue nose of the car back toward the light-blue sky. Centrifugal force shifted us back and forth like slow windshield wipers as I navigated the sequence of hairpin curves that led to the top of the mountain, our torsos leaning one way and then the other. Indian Wells dropped away behind us, resorts, roads, and golf courses shrinking and flattening until the valley floor looked like the etched surface of a computer chip. Up among the pines, near the log-cabin Christmas village of Idyllwild, we ran into a snowstorm.

"Where'd this come from?" Reggie said.

"It's the elevation, man. Indian Wells isn't much above sea level. We're at seven thousand feet here." The dreamlike blend of environments—a wintry world in such close proximity to the palmy world of the desert—was one of the things I loved about Southern California.

"That's wild," Reggie said, an uncharacteristic note of wonder in his voice.

I looked over. "You want to stop and make a snowman?"

"Fuck you," he said. "What's your next great plan, anyway, since this was a bust? You got anything lined up, or are we shit out of luck?"

"I'm going to get that necklace."

"Oh, fuck," he said. "Here we go."

We took Highway 74 all the way to Orange County, over the top of the San Jacintos, down into and across the wide Moreno Valley, with its endless pastures and vast herds of dairy cattle, then up and over the southern part of the Santa Ana Mountains to hit I-5 at San Juan Capistrano. Ninety minutes later, at 1 p.m. on Saturday, we exited the interstate at Venice Boulevard and cruised seaward between the double row of royal palm trees that lined the avenue.

CHAPTER TEN

I parked in a gravel lot with a chain around it where I rented a space by the week. The skinny old black man who ran the lot nodded as we walked past his hut.

"Genamuns."

"How are you, Mr. Parker?" I said. He had an ironic name, too. He thought it was funnier than most of the people to whom he mentioned it repeatedly.

"Superior," he said. "It's a bee-*you*-tee-full day at the beach."

Which it was. Seventy-eight degrees with 45 percent humidity according to the static-filled weather update playing on his portable radio. The tangy breeze blowing in from the bay was soft as a cotton ball on the skin. Above us, the sun poured out an endless stream of radiance that bathed the toy buildings and tiny palm trees along the coast with cheerful photons. The snowy mountains had receded into dreamland.

The lot was at the corner of Horizon and Main, halfway between the Santa Monica and Venice piers, two blocks from the flophouse where we'd been staying for the past six weeks since leaving the Georgian Hotel. Walking to the house, I glimpsed a dark-blue slice of the Pacific sparking between two brick buildings and felt a glimmer of the excitement I always felt when I came to the edge of the continent.

The flophouse was one of two big frame structures sandwiched in between commercial buildings on the ocean side of Pacific Avenue, the main north-south drag in Venice Beach. They were worn-out Victorians built in the teens or twenties as private residences, later converted to boardinghouses.

Pacific Avenue ran parallel to the beach, a block inland from the boardwalk. It was a deep block, a world unto itself. The side streets that connected Pacific to the boardwalk had names like Zephyr, Wave Crest, and Sunset. They were packed with bars, tattoo parlors, hamburger stands, and souvenir shops selling seashells and funny T-shirts.

Venice was founded early in the twentieth century by a tobacco millionaire from back east named Abbot Kinney, who modeled it on the famous Italian city, with miles of canals cut into the salt marshes, and marketed it successfully as a beach vacation destination, the Coney Island of the West, with a 1,200-foot amusement pier and seafront hotels. Kinney was a brilliant entrepreneur, and the resort thrived during his lifetime but fell on hard times after he died in the 1920s. A fire destroyed the first pier, and most of the romantic canals were filled in and converted to streets during the 1930s and '40s. Beatniks descended in the 1950s, followed by hippies a decade later, both groups attracted by the cheap rents and quaint atmosphere. The city hit its nadir in the 1980s, when rival gangs took over poor neighborhoods, gunning one another down along streets lined with shabby bungalows.

Now Venice was on an upswing again. There was a Democrat in the White House and a bull market on Wall Street. Property values were rising as prosperity returned to Los Angeles in the wake of the post–Cold War recession. Gentrification was creeping down the beach from Santa Monica, old apartment buildings and arcades bulldozed to make way for luxury condos and cute boutiques.

The flophouse would disappear beneath the tide of redevelopment in the near future. In the meantime, we shared it with a triad of down-and-outers who occupied the first floor while we rented two furnished rooms and a bathroom at the top of a creaky wooden staircase. Two other big bed-rooms on the second floor were unoccupied.

Going through the front door into the living room, we found Pete lying on a broken-down couch, reading a library copy of *How to Win Friends and Influence People*, a good book that gave birth to an annoying industry of high-pressure happiness salesmen. There were empty wine bottles, beer cans, and fast-food containers scattered around the room, remnants of the usual Friday-night party that comprised card playing, drunk chicks, and arguments with the landlady.

"Back from the desert already?" he said, sitting up with his habitual abruptness and placing the book, front cover down, on the wooden packing crate that served as an end table. "Why you guys dressed like that?"

"Like what?" Reggie said, looking down at his vaudeville pants and sandals. I didn't say anything. I didn't recall telling Pete that we were going to the desert.

"Where's the other two stooges?" Reggie said.

Pete's face tightened. He didn't like Reggie's habit of referring to him and his roommates as the Three Stooges. Reggie knew it, which was why he kept doing it. It was part of his personality to always be stirring up a little trouble, whether there was a use for it or not.

"They're jacking off," Pete said.

Reggie made saucer eyes. "Together?"

"Negative. I don't allow any grab-ass in the house."

Pete was the Moe of the group. When they worked, which wasn't all that often, he was the one that organized the jobs, laboring at construction sites up the road or doing yard work in the canal district, a few blocks south, where expensive homes lined the few waterways that hadn't been filled in. He was five feet seven inches tall, about 150 pounds, with short brown hair and a neatly trimmed Fu Manchu mustache.

"How do you know they're jacking off?" I said.

"I saw Candyman heading for his berth with a stack of *Hustlers*."

"How about Budge?"

"That particular individual is always jacking off," Pete said. "Why you back so soon?"

He was full of questions.

"We got homesick," Reggie said.

Upstairs, I put the pink diamond earrings and the .32 in my stash, took a shower, and changed into Levis, black Reeboks, and a midnight-blue

T-shirt, the same color as my Seville. Our rooms were in the back of the house. The oversize double-hung window in my bedroom had admitted unobstructed sea breezes at one time. Now it held a view of the metal fire escape on the back of a run-down apartment building ten feet away, across an alley.

The house was a dump, lumpy plaster behind peeling wallpaper, Goodwill-store furniture. The bathroom smelled faintly of sewer gas and the kitchen was like a Club Med for rats. More than once, I'd heard them splashing around in the sink like drunk newlyweds in a hot tub. If you went down to the kitchen at night to get a snack and surprised them, they sat up on their haunches and gave you a dirty look. If their little arms had been long enough, I'm sure they would have put their paws on their hips.

It was a dismal contrast to the marble-floored resort we had just come from, and to the Georgian Hotel, where we had been staying before moving to the flop. The Georgian was an architectural gem, an intimate Art Deco hotel erected a few blocks north of the Santa Monica pier at the height of the Roaring Twenties. Clark Gable and Carole Lombard had an apartment there where they snuggled in secret, and most of the stars of the studio era had stayed there. The hotel faced Ocean Avenue, across from Palisades Park, the strip of green that runs along the bluff above the beach. We had a suite on the seventh floor that was furnished like a Fred Astaire movie and had a proprietary view that took in all of Santa Monica Bay from Point Dume to Rancho Palos Verdes. There was an excellent steak house with leather booths and dark wood paneling downstairs from the lobby. The staff was helpful and discreet.

It was a great place to hide out, and we still would have been there except for a Newport Beach detective named Burris who happened to see me coming out the front entrance one day in mid-December. I was on my way to the beach to take a walk and he was driving by, northbound on Ocean, with a woman and two kids in a Chevrolet sedan.

Probably his fucking family.

Our eyes locked for just a second, then he looked away, as if he hadn't noticed me. I went on down the steps of the hotel veranda and stood on the sidewalk until he was out of sight, then went back into the hotel, rousted Reggie from a six-pack nap, and checked out. Reggie had met Candyman on the boardwalk a couple of weeks before, so he knew about the flophouse. We could have moved to another luxe hotel, but I wanted to go someplace Burris wouldn't be likely to look for me.

Surveying my bedroom, I wished we had gone someplace else. I try to think of myself as a successful person, but here I was holed up in a rattrap that should have been condemned a long time ago, and no doubt would be soon. I had failed to snag the necklace and come perilously close to disaster. My partner was probably guilty of gross dereliction of duty. It was borderline depressing.

Southern California suited me down to the soles of my feet. Most mornings arrived as hopeful as a high school beauty queen getting off the bus at the Hollywood station and marching down a palm avenue toward the gates of the movie studios, one wicker suitcase full of enthusiasm, the other bulging with ambition. I was out the door early, looking for likely scores, squinting in the dazzling light, breathing the salt air deeply, friendly to acquaintances, helpful to strangers. At that moment in the musty room, though, optimism deserted me.

Losing the diamonds after holding them in my hand had left a bigger hole than I realized. Like an actor on the day after faltering in a big audition, I had an emotional hangover. You tell yourself it doesn't matter. You're a professional. Win some, lose some. But it hurts deep down. It screws with your self-image. Later, when you notice that you are feeling a little desolate and try to figure out why, it traces back to your failure.

Rolling across the landscape between Indian Wells and the ocean, over mountaintops and through valleys, the exhilaration of motion had distracted me from the bone-deep disappointment. As soon as the motion stopped and I was stationary within the moldering house, the sense of loss I had fought off on the balcony the previous night rose up around me.

But it wasn't just the lost necklace making the room look like an antechamber to despair. The close call in Indian Wells had dredged something else up into emotional view. When you are gliding along a smooth highway on cruise control toward a desirable destination, nagging background pain is easy to ignore. After a crash, underlying issues rise to the surface. There was something missing in my life. Besides the necklace. Besides my daughter. I had been in love the previous summer and lost that girl, too. That was part of it. A lot of it, maybe.

I had rescued Song—that was her name—from a rich psycho in Newport Beach who brought her to California from Vietnam to be his captive plaything. We were together for a while afterward, but, despite her exoticism, she turned out to be conventional at heart. After she left me for a Vietnamese doctor with a profitable practice in Westminster, I swore off caring, decided to just do my crimes and enjoy the cash without getting tangled up emotionally with people along the way.

Brilliant idea, huh?

Whatever was bothering me, I knew better than to wallow in it. I didn't have time. The house was a depressing dump. I was forty years old and pretty much alone in the world. But I had diamonds to find. Pink ones. And I needed to find them quickly. After the attempted theft in Indian Wells, whoever owned the necklace would be more careful. Our best bet for consummating the crime was to strike fast while the owner was still off balance, before new precautions could be devised and implemented.

There was a rap-tap at the bedroom door and Reggie walked in. He was wearing a white wife-beater, faded khakis, and the strap sandals, sans black socks.

"You need me for anything?" he said.

"Not right now, but stay available."

"I'll be around," he said. "I'm gonna go see what Chavi's doing. What are you gonna do?"

"I'm going to the library to see if there is anything about this Baba Raba character in the newspaper database. If the necklace really is his, we need to track him down fast. I'll look for you at Chavi's booth if anything turns up."

Reggie nodded and started back out the door.

"Hey," I said, "did you say anything to Pete about us going to the desert?"

"Negative," Reggie said, mocking the ex-sailor by using one of his characteristic responses.

CHAPTER ELEVEN

Downstairs, I found Budge flopped on the couch, reading a week-old copy of the *Santa Monica Daily Press*. He was a former high school defensive lineman who looked like the first Curley. Candyman had told me that he got his nickname from the coach at Venice High School, who always said that no one could budge him when he was dug in on the line. A big strong kid, he had played varsity his sophomore and junior years before dropping out of school to surf and work construction. At forty, his high school football career was still one of his two biggest claims to fame.

"Hi, Rob," he said gloomily, tossing the paper on the scarred pine floor with the rest of the debris and hauling himself up into a sitting position. He was wearing a pair of flowered board shorts and a T-shirt with the letters AWOL on the front.

"How's it going, Budge?"

He rubbed his fleshy face with large hands and shook his head. "I'm backed up," he said. Jolly most of the time, he became morose when he was constipated.

"You eat any of those apples I bought?"

"I cain't eat fruit, Rob. Gives me a stomachache. I'm gonna go down to Rite Aid here in a minute and get something to push all that old mess out of there."

I shrugged.

"Robby, mah man!" Candyman came into the living room from the hallway that led to the stooges' bedrooms. "You missed a first-rate affair lass night."

"What transpired?"

"We had us a couple of the cutest little surfer girls you ever seen—Mexican surfer girls, if you ever heard of some shit like that—and a whole case of strawberry wine. It was certifiably fine."

Candyman had been a major heroin dealer in Venice during the 1970s—Cadillac, fur coat, condo, and all. Cured off smack in the penitentiary, he confined himself now to sweet wine and marijuana. His main obsession was his ex-wife, who divorced him while he was in the pen. She lived nearby in a rent-controlled apartment in Santa Monica and the two of them maintained a complex love-hate relationship. Candyman was always on the verge of either suing her for something or getting back together with her.

"Heard from Shoshana?" I asked, to see which way the wind was blowing.

Candyman's coffee-colored face, which had been relaxed and wreathed in smiles, making him look like the young boulevardier he had been twenty years before, sharpened and shrunk into the visage of a bitter old man.

"That bitch," he said. "She s'pose to come over and take me to the doctor yesterday afternoon and never showed up. Same old shit with her. Always callin' a man no-count and shiftless if he don't do what she thinks he should, and have three jobs like her daddy always did, but she can do whatever she feel like. When you s'posed to take a man to the doctor to see about some medicine, you goddamn well ought to show up, right, Rob? Don't you think so?"

I nodded. "Sure."

"Not Shoshana. She call fifteen minutes before my 'pointment and say she can't make it 'cause her sister got a headache. What's her motherfuckin' sister's headache got to do with anything? I was thinking about getting back with her, but after that shit she pulled yesterday, she's gonna have to get by without my black ass. I mean, ain't that some bullshit, Rob? Say she gonna come for sure and then don't show up? She tell everyone else how to act but don't act right herself. She getting fat, too."

He had worked himself up into a state of righteous anger, striding back and forth in front of the couch where Budge was sitting, waving his arms and looking from one of us to the other. Then, when he could see that we were about to agree with him that Shoshana was a bad actor, he reversed himself completely. As usual.

"Course, you won't find a better woman," he said, stopping and looking at me with his eyes bulging as if I had asserted the contrary. "Do you know she sent me twenty dollars every week for six years I was in San Q so I could buy candy and cigarettes? And she's always takin' care of her family, her sister and her daddy." He shook his head and gave me another confrontational look. "She's a good woman, Rob. Bitch just don't know how to show up."

Conveniently, since there was no rational response to his remarks, Pete and our landlady, Mrs. Sharpnick, chose that moment to enter the room from opposite sides. Pete came in from the kitchen with half a sandwich in his hand and the other half in his mouth. He was two steps into the living room when Sharpnick burst through the front door. She was a tall, skeletal woman with a terrible temper who dressed in men's work clothes. Underneath it all, I'm sure she was a very nice woman. But it was way underneath. The only person I'd ever seen her be kind to was the street kid, Ozone Pacific, who she let camp in the house next door, which was too run-down to rent out. Pete wheeled and dodged back toward the kitchen as she came in, but she froze him with a harsh cry.

"Where's my rent check, you son of a bitch?"

CHAPTER TWELVE

Sharpnick addressed her inquiry to Pete, but Budge got a stricken look on his face. He had been homeless several times and dreaded going back on the streets.

Pete turned around, gulped down the wad of white bread and bologna in his mouth, and counterfeited a smile with his thin lips.

"Ahoy, Mrs. Sharpnick, I didn't see you come in. We'll have that particular check for you by the close of business on Monday." He handled the rent for the downstairs trio, keeping a portion of Budge's and Candyman's wages when they worked.

"It was due on the fifteenth," Mrs. Sharpnick said in a cold, threatening tone. "I want the money now."

"Negative," Pete said. "No can do. Don't have it. But you have my personal guarantee you'll get it on Monday."

"You're lying," she said. "I saw you going in Antonio's yesterday at dinnertime. A meal in there costs twenty. If you got the money to eat there, you got the money to pay me my rent."

Budge shifted his gaze from Sharpnick to Pete, his expression changing from fear to suspicion.

"I wasn't *eating* in there," Pete said, as if that was the most ridiculous suggestion he had ever heard. "I was talking to Gianni about some work he wants done. Reference to the rent you're requesting, we're still waiting to get paid for that demolition job we did last week. The man says he'll have our money on Monday for sure."

Mrs. Harriet Sharpnick did not answer. She had just noticed the mess in the living room and was swiveling her head slowly, taking in the details of the disarray with a furious expression on her face.

"What's this?" she said. "You dirty bums had another party, didn't you? What did I tell you about that?" She looked at Budge, who licked his lips and tried to grin.

"It whudn't a party, Miss Sharpnick, just a couple of—"

"This is a respectable house," she screamed, cutting him off. "And you bums have it looking like a pigsty. I've got the city on my back about this place twenty-four hours a day, complaining about the condition of the building, and you bindle stiffs go and make it worse."

"I don't know what they were thinking," Pete said, shaking his head. "You two know Mrs. Sharpnick doesn't allow any parties."

"Wait a minute, now . . ." Candyman started to object.

"Come on," Pete said, bustling around the room, picking up beer cans and empty wine bottles. "Let's get this place shipshape. Budge, look alive and help me clear the deck."

Pete's identity centered chiefly on his concept of himself as nononsense businessman and his supposed service in the U.S. Navy. He told me when we met that he had retired as a chief petty officer after twenty years at sea, but Candyman later contradicted that in a stage whisper, telling me that Pete had been dishonorably discharged for selling government supplies on the black market during his second term of enlistment.

Budge lumbered into action, picking up a full ashtray and the newspaper he had just thrown down and heading for the kitchen.

"Everything's under control, Mrs. Sharpnick," Pete said briskly, giving her a series of quick nods meant to drive her out of the room. "I'll have that check for you by seventeen hundred hours on Monday."

"You better," she said, then stalked out the front door, banging it shut behind her.

Pete went over to the front window and peeked through the curtains for a few seconds. When he turned around, the earnest expression he had used on the landlady was replaced by a contemptuous smirk. He dropped the beer can in his hand on the floor and walked over to the couch, where he flopped down, clasping his hands behind his head.

"That bag of bones is messing with the wrong seaman," he said, nodding. "She'll get what she's got coming to her before long."

"What do you mean by that?" I said.

"Nothing. It's just business."

"What kind of business?"

"Not yours," Pete said.

His rude remark surprised me. During most of the six weeks Reggie and I had been in the house, Pete had been friendly and respectful, always trying to buddy up and find out where our cash came from. But in the past week or so he had become more careless and self-confident, taking a higher hand with the other two stooges and showing less deference to me and Reggie. Now he was being downright confrontational.

"Aw, come on, Pete," Budge said. "She'll have a shit fit if we don't get it cleaned up before she comes back."

"That bitch ain't coming back," Pete said. "She's got three other houses to check on. We'll clean up when we're goddamn good and ready."

"You sure that eye-talian hadn't paid you yet?" Candyman said to Pete.

"What do you mean, am I sure? Didn't you hear me tell Sharpnick he's going to pay us on Monday?"

"I heard you all right. Like I heard you tell her me and Budge was the ones had a party you didn't know nothing about, when it was you pulled a case of wine off a liquor truck and got the whole thing started. Where'd you get the money to eat in Antonio's if you didn't collect that check?"

Reggie's nickname for our housemates caught the tricky blend of companionship and hostility that linked them. Like the original Stooges, Pete and his pals, while inseparable, were never far from bonking one another on the head with a monkey wrench or gouging an eye.

"I wasn't *eating* in there," Pete said. "I was conducting business, trying to keep you two swabbies off the streets. I only said that about the party to confuse the bitch. One of us has to stay on her good side or she might evict us."

"You're trying to confuse someone, all right," Candyman said. "I'm going with you to get that check on Monday."

"No problemo," Pete said.

CHAPTER THIRTEEN

I was thinking diamonds as I emerged into the sparkling seaside air.
Where were they? Would we be able to find them in time? What was the
next step if there was nothing about Baba Raba at the library?

I swung down to the boardwalk to get a Coke before heading inland,
hoping the effervescent sugar and caffeine would give me some chemical
inspiration. The boardwalk was not actually a walkway made of boards but
an asphalt path lined with stalls and storefronts and old hotels on the inland side. Street performers and artisans set up booths and spread blankets
to display their wares along the other side of the path, at the edge of the
sand that stretched down to the ocean. Heading south, drinking from my
twenty-ounce bottle of cola, I saw Ozone Pacific sitting cross-legged beneath his palm tree. It seemed like he was always around. I seldom went to
the beach without seeing his blond head bobbing in the crowd. He was
playing with his plastic gold coins, holding them in a stack in one hand

and then dribbling them into the open palm of the other. He had nice hands, unusual for a homeless guy. They looked like a girl's hands, with long shapely fingers and neatly trimmed nails. When he saw me, he waved and smiled.

"Hi, Rob!" he said when I walked over. "It's a beautiful day, isn't it?"

"Sure is."

"This would be a good day to get out into the country for a while, don't you think, Rob? Wouldn't you like to see all those animals? I just love cows and horses and all those other animals they have on farms."

He was dressed, as always, in filthy white sneakers, worn-out blue jeans, and a long-sleeved white-and-brown cowboy shirt with pearl buttons. He often talked about getting out into the country.

"Did you used to live in the country?" I asked him.

"I thought I did, but now I'm not too sure," he said, serious for a moment. "I know my mom used to tell me about it."

He was an exceptionally childlike young man, someone who had never grown up for some reason and probably never would. I wondered what had become of his family and how he had ended up here.

"Don't you love cows and horses and roosters and stuff?" he said, smiling again.

"I do, actually."

"Me, too," he said, smiling still more broadly in a way that made me smile with him.

"What are you in such a good mood about?"

"I'm rich," he said, ecstatic, dribbling his coins again and then tossing them up in the air so that they rained down around him.

I had an urge to practice some unlicensed reality therapy and point out to him that the coins were plastic, but I bit my tongue as he gathered them up. He was probably mildly retarded. If the plastic disks made him feel rich, what was the harm? He was no more deluded than people who bought into the artificial value of diamonds with thousands of real dollars or built their identities out of the fool's gold of brand names, department store clerks and Hollywood stars who wouldn't have been able to see themselves in the mirror if they weren't looking through Ray-Bans or to believe in their own reality if their bodies weren't wrapped in designer duds.

I took a long, searing drink of my Coke, the only kind of cola I ever buy, then screwed the top back on and held the half-full bottle out to Ozone.

"You want the rest of this?"

"Sure, Rob. Thanks!" He put the bottle in his Batman backpack.

"See you later," I said.

"Where you going?"

"To the library."

"Can I walk over that way with you?"

"Of course you can. What kind of books do you like?"

"Books about the country," he said. "Ones with pictures of cows and horses."

As we went south along the boardwalk toward the terminus of Venice Boulevard, where it stops, awestruck at the sight of the Pacific, shopkeepers and street performers shouted out friendly greetings to my companion. Some called him by his strange name, Ozone Pacific. Others called him Oz. Despite his limitations and lack of resources, or maybe because of those limitations, he was a popular character in the carnival world that clung to the edge of the continent. He seemed to know everyone.

"Have you ever heard of a guy named Baba Raba?" I asked him as we passed a body-piercing booth sandwiched in between a Thai takeout place and a shop that sold incense and statues of Buddha and Shiva.

"Do you know Baba Raba?" he said, excited.

"No. But I've heard of him. Do you know him?"

"Yes. He's a nice man. He talked to me before and made me feel better when I was sad."

"Really? Does he live around here?"

"He has an ash farm over that way." Ozone waved his rayon-clad arm toward the east, toward Lincoln Avenue and the 405 and the whole Los Angeles basin. "What is an ash farm, anyway, Rob?"

"It's not an ash farm, Oz, it's an ashram."

"What's that?"

We had come to Venice Boulevard and turned inland between the brightly painted fronts of the restaurants and bars that lined the block between the boardwalk and Pacific Avenue. The street was colorful as Bob Marley's cap, and reggae music blasted from speakers on a patio where people were eating rice and beans with jerk chicken.

"It's a place where people go to meditate and pray," I said. "Kind of like a church. Do you know where his ashram is? Is it near here?"

"I don't know, Rob."

"Do you know when he is going to be down here again?"

"No. I haven't seen him for a while. I wish he'd come back."

The soothing sound of the surf crumbling on the beige sand a hundred yards behind us gradually blended with the sound of traffic as we approached the intersection of Venice Boulevard and Pacific Avenue.

"Are you going to be seeing him, Rob?"

"I might be."

"Would you ask him if I can have my picture back?"

We were standing at the intersection, waiting for the light to change, surrounded by a mixed crowd of local hipsters, homeless people, and tourists.

"What picture?" I asked him, keeping an eye on the signal on the other side of the busy street. "The one of the lady?"

"Yes," he said.

Just then the light changed and the walk signal came on and I crossed the avenue with the herd.

"Why did he want the picture?" I said, stepping up onto the far sidewalk. When Ozone didn't answer, I stopped and looked back. He was waving to me from the other side of the street. "Come on," I called out, "cross before the light changes."

"You go on," he yelled over the sound of car engines idling. "I gotta get back down to the beach." He turned his small, cowboy-shirt-clad back and melted into the crowd.

CHAPTERFOURTEEN

The Abbot Kinney Memorial Library was six blocks straight ahead of me on Venice Boulevard, but I detoured a block south to walk along one of the city's remaining canals. Gentrification had hit hard in the canal district. Most of the antique Victorians and prewar bungalows that lined the waterways had been restored with newly milled gingerbread, stained-glass windows, and lavish applications of pastel paint. Here and there, a shack that had moldered beyond repair was being replaced with a bulky modern structure that filled every cubic inch of its lot and airspace. Evelyn Evermore's handsome yellow bungalow was two blocks farther south, along the Linnie Canal.

I was happy to discover that Baba Raba frequented the neighborhood. If the necklace belonged to him, as Jimmy Z said, it was critical to case him as quickly as possible, and I was starting to get a bead on him. He was in fact a guru of some kind with an ashram in the area. He was not a secretive spiritual teacher who stayed hidden from public view, meditating the day away within a cloud of incense smoke, safe from the troubles and temptations of society, but a classic California swami who liked to get out in the sunshine and mingle with homeless kids and millionaires. He had the power to make sad people feel better and perhaps to charm money out of the pocketbooks of lonely ladies. I wondered if he had found out about Evermore and her necklace from Ozone's picture, same as me, and if she had really given him the diamonds. And if so, why.

Ozone had showed me the picture less than three weeks before. If Baba had gotten his hands on it and wrangled a meeting with Evermore and managed to extract a twenty-six-carat donation from her in the short time since then, he must be one of the truly anointed, radiating the most inspirational energy imaginable. Or else a first-class charlatan.

There was nothing about the guru in the library's newspaper database, but there was a flyer on the cluttered bulletin board in the lobby announcing that free introductory meditation classes would be offered each Saturday night in January at the Murshid Center for Enlightened Beings, where seekers could bathe in the beneficent *darshan* of Baba Raba, head of the Magdalene Order, healer of the heartsick, frustrated, angry, confused, homeless, loveless, and depressed.

I'd fit right in.

If Baba stuck to his schedule, there would be a meditation class at eight o'clock that evening. The ashram was on Broadway between Sixth and Seventh, about ten blocks north of the library. I wrote down the address and phone number.

Back at the beach, I found Reggie building a fire in a concrete ring behind Chavi's fortune-telling stand. He was using a copy of the *Los Angeles Times* for tinder and a busted-up wooden chair for fuel. Nearby, on top of a Styrofoam cooler that undoubtedly contained cold Budweiser, there was a metal grill that could be laid across the fire ring and a stack of frozen T-bone steaks.

The fire was coming along nicely. It was hard to imagine now, looking at the fiftyish biker with scarred knuckles and tattooed forearms, but he had been a Boy Scout once, briefly, long ago. When his parents were still in the psuedo-sophisticated cocktails-and-dancing stage of their joint alcoholism, before the filthy fights and car wrecks and court appearances, his father had been a jolly troop leader who taught his oldest son the ancient art of building a fire.

"Hey, Rob," Reggie said as I walked up.

"Where'd you get the steaks?" I asked him.

"Meat truck," he said, nodding toward an alley that disappeared behind the boardwalk restaurants. "Stick around and I'll grill you up the best T-bone you ever tasted." In St. Louis, Reggie was famous for his barbequing skills.

"Deal," I said, and walked over to say hello to Chavi.

Draped in a flowing, multicolored robe, with a red scarf covering her thick black hair, she was holding the hand of a young Mexican woman who sat opposite her beneath the canvas roof of her booth, tracing the lines on the girl's palm with the tip of her index finger.

"For you," she said softly, "the path to spiritual fulfillment and happiness is through helping others."

The girl's eyes got wide. "How did you know that?"

"What?" Chavi said, looking up.

"I'm studying to be a social worker at City College. All I've ever wanted to do since I was a little girl is help children. My priest even told me that I have a calling. But I was thinking of quitting because the classes are so hard."

"Get a tutor to help you with math," Chavi said.

"How did you . . ."

"They have free tutors at the math lab at City College. You must never give up on your dream, darling. There are hurt children waiting for you to help them, some not yet born. You are on a beautiful path. Don't worry about anything. You will be fine."

"Thank you so much," the girl said, fumbling a ten-dollar bill out of her purse. Her eyes were full of tears.

"God bless you, and the little children through you," Chavi said. "Come back and see me soon."

"That was pretty good," I said as the girl walked away with a look of wonder on her face.

"Hello, Robert," Chavi said, slightly dazed.

"How did you know she is meant to help people?"

"Everyone is meant to help people," Chavi said. "Sometimes I see pictures when I look at their hands. Sometimes it is just a feeling. In her hand, I saw an image of the Virgin reaching out to save an abandoned soul. She really does have a calling, I think."

"How did you know she was having problems with math?"

Chavi spread her arms wide and tilted her head back, striking a pose.

"I yam of the Roma peepole. I yam geepsee," she said in her best mock-Romanian accent. "I see all!"

When I didn't say anything, she lowered her arms and smiled.

"Most kids at community college have problems with algebra," she said. "You don't need ESP to know that."

Chavi claimed to be the illegitimate daughter of Bela Lugosi and a raccoon-eyed B-movie actress who appeared in some of his later films. With her bright clothes, gold hoop earrings, and dramatic manner, she fit perfectly on a boardwalk crowded with theatrical characters.

On one side of her, there was a tall, skinny white guy dressed in classic hippie style with an embroidered Indian cotton shirt and granny glasses whose handicraft was mandalas he burned in scrap wood using sunlight focused through a magnifying glass. On the other was a diminutive Jamaican with a mouthful of crooked teeth who entertained the passing crowd by jumping off a stepladder into piles of broken glass in his bare feet while telling jokes or firing insults at people who stopped to watch his show and then walked on without putting a dollar in his cigar box. Beyond him was a heavyset, middle-aged white man who wheeled a battered piano out from someplace each morning and spent the day playing melodic jazz in return for money that people stuffed into a pickle jar. Beyond him was a chalk-portrait guy, then a woman selling wiki gear, then an Okie with an acoustic guitar and a Woody Guthrie twang in his voice.

The artists, hucksters, and entertainers stretched for more than a mile, from Venice Boulevard halfway to Santa Monica, creating a counterculture atmosphere and energy that attracted tourists from around the L.A. basin and the planet Earth. On that sunny Saturday afternoon, the boardwalk crowd was as colorful as the professional performers. Leather-clad bikers ogled elegant Latinas in spike heels and capris while bangers in thick plaid shirts and work pants held shop doors open for elderly ladies in flowered dresses; sophisticated international travelers looked down their aquiline noses at Iowa couples in JCPenney clothing who weaved like drunkards to avoid the beggars lurching out from behind palm trees rattling Starbucks cups. There were dreadlocks and flowing blond tresses, heartbreakingly beautiful bodies and ruined faces. Roller blades, skateboards, and bicycles; tight shorts, baggy jeans, and sweatpants; bodybuilders, businessmen, and mermaids. All mixed together in a murmur of mostly good-humored humanity flowing in two directions beside the shining sea.

North of us, up the boardwalk toward Santa Monica, something was creating a stir. The sound of the crowd changed, the multilingual buzz gaining density. People walking north began to go faster; those coming south toward Chavi's booth slowed down and looked back over their shoulders.

First in glimpses, then more clearly, I saw coming through the menagerie a figure that stood out even in that crazy seaside circus: a tall, rotund white man dressed only in a cotton dhoti, surrounded by a flock of young women in airy white robes who scattered red rose petals in his path. The man, who looked like he was in his fifties, and the girls, who were much younger, paused occasionally when someone stepped out from the line that had formed along the boardwalk and knelt to touch the man's bare feet or hand him a flower or piece of fruit. He greeted these devotees with loving smiles and graceful bows, hands pressed flat together in front of his barrel chest, fingertips pointing upward like a steeple, then came on majestically toward us, placing the soles of his feet on the silky petals strewn before him.

"Who's that?" Reggie said. He had come up beside me in front of Chavi's booth, attracted by the excitement of the crowd.

"It's Baba Raba," I heard a grade school voice say.

CHAPTER FIFTEEN

Turning, I saw that Ozone Pacific had come up behind me. He was gazing at the approaching guru with a look of awe and adoration.

"Why is he wearing a diaper?" Reggie asked.

"It's not a diaper," I said. "It's a dhoti. It's what Indian spiritual teachers wear to show their simplicity and detachment from society's expectations."

"Huh?"

As Baba Raba came to where we were standing, he turned his ponderous head toward Ozone and showed him the loving smile. It made me quiver a little bit even though it was directed a few feet to my right.

"How are you feeling today, my young friend?" Baba asked in a vibrant bass voice as he stopped in front of us.

Ozone Pacific nodded his head silently, returning the big man's smile with one that was equally loving but infinitely more childlike.

"Are you feeling better since our talk?"

"Yes, Baba," the boy said softly.

The guru was pear-shaped, with a huge ass that made his solid shoulders look narrow. He was six feet tall or a little better and probably weighed three hundred pounds. The hair on his cannonball head was cropped short in a gray crew cut. He had a wide mouth with thick, rubbery lips, a large nose, and big ears. A mat of dark hair grew on his chest and boulder belly. His short, thick legs were hairy, too.

His robed female attendants looked like children by comparison. Eyes downcast, they murmured among themselves, holding leftover holiday gift bags half full of rose petals. They ranged in looks from plain to pretty and in age from late teens to early thirties. One thing they had in common was nice bodies. There wasn't a fat chick among them.

Another girl stood close beside Baba on his right. She was a blond beauty who had undoubtedly been turning heads since junior high school, not that many years before. She wore white sneakers, tight white jeans, and a white T-shirt with a yellow OM symbol on the front. Her thick shoulder-length hair was a tawny golden color and her face had been sculpted by a slum dweller who dreamed of angels. She observed the crowd with an amused smile. The shape of her lips and arch of her eyebrows made my heart race.

"It looks like a diaper," Reggie said audibly, in the midst of a hush that had fallen as people waited to see if Baba Raba was going to say anything else.

Baba shifted his glittering black eyes from Ozone, who was to my right, across my face, to rest on Reggie, who was standing to my left, holding a spatula in one hand and a bottle of Worcestershire sauce in the other. He stared back at Baba.

"What's cooking?" Baba asked him after a few seconds.

"Um grilling T-bones," Reggie said. "Sorry there's not enough to go around."

Pity flowed into Baba's big-lipped smile slowly, like urine filling a specimen jar. He held his right hand out in front of him, thick index finger pointing up, and tick-tocked the finger back and forth, more or less in Reggie's face.

"It is not food that I would deign to eat," Baba said in his professional guru voice. "If you are wise, you will not eat it either. It is *tamasic*. Consuming dead animals feeds your animal nature and poisons your etheric body. It is unhealthy for your physical body, too."

"The hell you talking about?" Reggie said, offended. "Them are some prime T-bones."

The tick-tocking continued, and the pity in the smile overflowed.

"You are digging your grave with your teeth, my bearded friend."

"Um what?"

"You are digging. Your grave. With your teeth," Baba said slowly and distinctly, then bared his own horse teeth and tapped the top ones with his finger. He looked savage and a little crazy with his lips pulled back and his incisors showing.

"That's grade-A beef," Reggie said, his voice getting a little high. It had never crossed his mind that there might be someone who didn't relish a good steak.

Baba shook his head with heavy authority. "Innocent animals should be loved, not slaughtered. That bovine was full of hormones and antibiotics. It was terrified at the time of its death. Its adrenal terror flooded into its muscles and congealed there when it was killed. When you eat the steak, you eat the chemicals and the fear along with the rotting meat. You do not know when or where or how it was killed. It may have been dead and decaying for weeks. No, no. It is not good food. You are excited to have a nice juicy steak to chew and swallow, anticipating the taste of blood and flesh, but to me what you are cooking is as disgusting as a nice juicy piece of rat."

"Yeah, well, that's you, Bubba Rubba, not me," Reggie practically shouted. "What do you eat, seaweed and daisies?"

Baba shook his head again. "I am sorry I have offended you, my bearded friend." He gave the bow and the steeple. "I must speak the truth."

"Baba speaks the truth," the robed girls echoed. The crowd murmured assent.

Baba turned his luminous black eyes on me.

I forgot about Reggie and the steaks. And the blond girl. And the diamonds.

Looking into his eyes, I had the feeling that we had known each other in a previous lifetime. That we had been close companions for many years. That he remembered our time together clearly and was glad to have found me again. The feeling was one of overwhelming relief and gratitude. I recalled a first-person description I had read of the sensation a spiritual seeker felt when he met his guru for the first time, and I was pierced by the conviction that the same thing was happening to me late on a Saturday afternoon on the Venice boardwalk after forty years of wandering in the wilderness of the world. Behind me, I heard the surf rushing on the sand and flashed on the eternity of the sea and the mystery of life.

"How are you?" he asked me, and his words echoed inside my skull.

"I'm fine," I said. I felt warm and happy and safe to be there with him.

"Yes," he said. "You are fine. I can see that you are a strong, courageous man. Highly intelligent. But something troubles you."

The thought of my daughter rushed to the front of my mind like a prisoner rushing to the door of a cell when his lawyer arrives with word of his case. Her name was on my lips. I was on the verge of telling him about my loss and grief. But I caught myself.

Pulling my eyes loose from his, which was like pulling strong magnets from a block of iron, I took a step back and looked him up and down, from his well-tended size-twelve feet to the iron-gray bristles on top of his head. He looked ridiculous with his massive ass swaddled in a strip of Indian cotton and his big hairy belly sticking out, but he had tremendous physical and emotional presence, like a chief in a primitive land who contained in his well-fed person the collective wisdom of the tribe and wielded the power of life and death. His big hands, hanging at his sides, looked strong enough to tear a telephone directory in half. He would be a dangerous man to steal from.

The guru regarded me beneficently as I looked him over, getting mileage out of the loving smile.

The blonde was looking at me, too, her pretty smile tinged with contempt.

"He's good," I said to her. "He's really got something."

"Yeah," she said, mockingly, her blue eyes meeting mine. "I thought you were going to go."

I shook my head and smiled back at her, not mocking, friendly.

"I didn't."

"You almost did."

I shrugged, kept smiling. "He's got something."

"He's got lots of things," she said, moving her slim body closer to Baba and linking her arm through his gorilla appendage.

"Does he have them, too?" I said, nodding at the robed girls.

Her lip curled. "They don't even know where they are."

"So he's got them good."

Baba didn't like the turn the conversation was taking. His thick-lipped smile slowly morphed into a frown, like an iron bar being bent by a strong-man. In what looked like a warning, he clamped his hand over the girl's where she held his hairy forearm. His large fingernails were professionally manicured and coated with clear polish. Hers were bitten to the quick.

"Come and see me, my intelligent friend," he said.

"Why?"

"I can help you."

"With what?"

"Whatever you need."

"Like I said before, I'm fine."

"Come anyway," he said, unwavering. "We have most pleasant times." He rolled his eyes up and to the right as he said that, as if looking over his shoulder. I couldn't tell if he was feigning an ecstatic state or indicating the girls behind him.

"Maybe I will."

He gave me a final nod, heavy as a pail of quarters, and led the blond girl away, south along the boardwalk.

"Ya look like Baby Huey!" Reggie yelled after him.

A guy I hadn't noticed before who was walking behind the robed girls shot a hard look our way that Reggie didn't notice. He was dressed in de-signer jeans and athletic shoes. A short-sleeved black knit shirt was stretched tight across his muscular chest and shoulders. There were India-ink tattoos on his forearms. He reminded me of the inimitable Jimmy Z.

Chavi watched Baba and his entourage as they walked away, with Ozone drifting along in their wake.

"What's your take on that guy?" I asked Chavi.

She shrugged. "I don't know. His aura changes, so it's hard to see. He is either a saint or a devil."

She went back into her booth and began to spread out her tarot cards on a table draped in red cloth.

Reggie and I walked over to the fire ring, where he flipped the sizzling steaks and poured on Worcestershire sauce.

"I'll kick his fat rat ass if he's not careful," he said.

CHAPTER SIXTEEN

Two hours later, Reggie and I descended the wobbly wooden steps in front of the flophouse and walked north along Pacific Avenue. It had been dark for an hour and the neon-lit street was pleasantly lurid as the coast geared up for a Saturday night that would last till dawn on Sunday. Traffic was heavy, with some light horn honking and occasional catcalls and whistles. I just hoped they weren't whistling at us. Like all picturesque seaside cities, Venice and Santa Monica had a thriving gay community, evidence that homosexual men have good taste in real estate.

We crossed Pacific at Westminster and strolled inland along that quiet residential avenue.

"Whudaya think Baby Huey charges for a wrestling match with one of them chicks in the nightgowns?" Reggie said.

"You think he is pimping them out?"

Reggie gave me the half-exasperated, half-disgusted look. "Get real," he said. "You know good and well he is."

"They could be legitimate devotees."

"Yeah, and I could be the Lone Ranger's horse, but I'm not."

"Maybe you're right," I said. "Just remember, we aren't going over there to get laid. We are going to try and find out where those diamonds are so we can steal them, fence them, and stuff our pockets full of money."

At Sixth Street, we went two blocks north to Broadway, also residential, despite its glamorous name. The ashram, a converted Queen Anne mansion, was a block farther inland, at the corner of Broadway and Seventh Street. A fiftyish couple who looked like former hippies who had settled down to some lucrative artistic occupation came around the corner from Seventh and preceded us up the walk to the front door. It was standing open, pouring yellow light into the night.

It was forty-five degrees, cold for Los Angeles, and the foyer was cluttered with jackets and scarves hanging on pegs and piled on wooden benches along the side walls. Dozens of pairs of shoes were lined up beneath the benches. I sat down and pulled off my Reeboks. Reggie grumbled about the custom but took his boots off, too. Looking around to make sure no one was watching, he hid them in a corner beneath a red scarf.

"I don't want anyone heisting them," he explained.

Beyond the foyer, a wide hallway led to a staircase that went up to the second floor. A narrow hallway beside the staircase continued to the back of the house. To our left as we entered was a small bookstore and gift shop, where half a dozen people, including the prosperous hippies, were milling around, talking and laughing. Next to the shop was a library with closed French doors. Floor-to-ceiling shelves held hundreds of old books. A brown leather couch and two armchairs faced a cold fireplace.

I was still going back and forth in my mind about Baba Raba. When I saw the gowned girls on the boardwalk, I had the same thought as Reggie: temple prostitution, or something in that ZIP code. Many legitimate spiritual teachers have come to America from India, true holy men with more insight into the nature of reality and purpose of human life than a Hilton ballroom packed full of Baptist clergymen or Catholic bishops. But plenty of fakirs have come, too, and some of the good ones have succumbed to corruption in America, whirled up in a tornado of materialistic sensations and temptations that ashram life in India never prepared them for. And the corruption always seems to center on sex. So the sweet, submissive girls made me suspicious. But now I was having second thoughts.

The Murshid Center for Enlightened Beings had a cozy, spiritually comforting vibe that I recognized from other venerable ashrams I had visited. If Baba was a con man, he was not a fly-by-night. The collection of esoteric books in the library and the energy that hummed in the fiber of the building would have taken years to accumulate.

The meditation room was to our right as we entered. It had probably been the formal living room. Through the open French doors, I saw twenty-five or thirty people who had staked out their spots near the front, sitting with eyes shut on prayer rugs or cushions. One of them was Evelyn Evermore. She was wearing a white designer sweatsuit and had her hair tied back in a ponytail with a red ribbon. She sat in an unstrained lotus position with her spine straight and her shoulders relaxed. Baba Raba or someone else had given her good training. The palms of her lovely hands rested on her knees, thumbs pressed against the outside of her index fingers, other fingers extended upward, forming the *ahamkara mudra*, which counteracts fear and anxiety. I felt a twinge of fear myself at the sight of her, a guilty echo of the botched robbery at Indian Wells, but I was relieved to see her, too, since I didn't know for sure who had the diamonds.

"Check it out," Reggie said, nudging me with his elbow. I turned and saw the blond girl coming down the stairs, looking even more desirable than she had on the beach. Her hair was damp as if she had just bathed, and she was dressed in a white robe like the ones the flower girls had worn. As she came toward us down the hallway, it crossed my mind that she might not be wearing anything beneath the robe, an erotic supposition that she confirmed in part when she stooped to pick up a flyer that had fallen on the floor by the library door. The robe, which had buttons from navel to throat, was fastened only halfway up. As she bent gracefully to tidy up the ashram, I had a clear view of two white breasts with small dark nipples.

Glancing up, she caught both me and Reggie looking but didn't seem to mind too much. She gave us a half smile that was a delicious blend of tolerance and contempt as she brushed past us into the bookstore. I wondered if she had done it on purpose.

"He'll be down in ten minutes, Ganesha," she said to a young man who was sitting on a stool behind the cash register, reading a paperback copy of the Bhagavad Gita. "Let's close the shop and get everybody into the meditation room."

"Okay." He stood up from the stool. "It's time to go into the meditation room, folks. *Satsang* will begin shortly."

He was wearing the traditional orange robe of Indian monks that symbolizes the spiritual fire in which all worldly ambitions and attachments have been burnt up. But the longing gaze he bestowed on the girl as she turned away from him made me think a few pesky embers of desire were still glowing somewhere in his tofu-fed frame. As he herded the people out of the shop, the girl locked the cash register and put the key in a drawer behind the counter. Even with her as a distraction, I couldn't help noticing that she didn't lock the drawer.

"Did you see those nipples?" Reggie cackled in my ear, as the girl moved around the shop, snuffing out candles and turning off the lights. "She better not come close to me in that getup or I'll be snapping at those things like a trout at a mayfly." He had gone fishing when he was a Scout, too.

Stepping into the hallway, the girl turned her back to us to close the shop's glass-paned doors, showing us the shape of her cute little behind through the thin cotton cloth of her robe, giving me unspiritual urges.

Turning around, she looked me in the eye, as if she knew what I was thinking. Her blue irises sparkled and there was a hint of a smile. Two latecomers were taking off their shoes in the foyer. Behind me, someone rang a bell in the meditation room, a single pure note that lingered in the atmosphere like a color wash.

"What's the routine, babe?" Reggie said, thrusting himself into the situation.

The girl turned her head slightly and gave him a look that would have silenced most men. Reggie not only bore up under it but grinned through his grizzled beard and mustache.

"The routine?" she said, haughty.

"Yeah, we gonna sing hymns or square dance or what?"

"Baba will give a short talk from the Gita and then there will be forty-five minutes of silent meditation."

"That don't sound too exciting," Reggie said. "Why don't me and you go in the back parlor and you can give me some personal instructions."

"Hah," she gave a short, harsh, but not necessarily unfriendly laugh. "You don't beat around the bush, do you?"

"Depends on the bush," Reggie said.

He got another laugh. Though her features were delicate and she was making an effort to speak in a refined manner, there was something working-class about the girl's frankness and the way she held her body. She didn't seem to be offended by Reggie's crude approach.

"You have to come a couple of times before you get private lessons, pal," she said.

"How 'bout if I go out and come back in a couple of times?" Reggie said, lowering his voice to a growl. "That count?"

When the blonde laughed again, I figured Reggie was going to do what he usually did and snag the girl before I had a chance to make a move. Sometimes I hated the guy.

"Whudaya say, babe?" he said, taking a step toward her, as if to crowd her down the hallway. "Can a stranger get some lovin' in this church?"

"Whoa, big boy," the girl said, holding her arm straight out and putting her palm against his chest like a running back stiff-arming an opponent. "You can probably get some loving if you play your cards right, but not from me. Is that what you guys are here for?"

"That's what I'm everywhere for, sweetheart," Reggie said.

"Yeah, I see that. How about your friend? What's his story?" She nodded her head sideways, glancing over at me.

"Whudaya mean?" Reggie snapped, disconcerted to feel her attention shifting away from him.

"You two are completely different types," she said to me. "Why are you here?"

"Baba Raba invited me," I said. "Don't you remember?"

"I didn't think you'd come."

"I couldn't resist." We were looking into each other's eyes again and something between us dilated.

"I'm glad," she said, and I felt a warm glow in my cold heart. Then, as if catching herself, she added indifferently: "Baba will be pleased to see you."

"Shakti! It is time for *satsang*!" It was the lad in the orange robe, standing in the door of the meditation room. He sounded a little peeved, either because the girl was putting God behind schedule or because she was talking to us instead of sitting beside him on an embroidered cushion.

"Relax, Ganesha," the girl said. "I'm going to get him right now. And don't call me Shakti. My name is Mary, same as it's always been."

"Baba said you are called Shakti now," Ganesha whined. "He knows the best name for each of us."

"You and your friend need to go in and find a seat," the girl said to me, and then went down the hall toward the staircase. Reggie had been demoted. I was the primary and he was the secondary.

"Hurry up, you two," Ganesha said to us. "Everyone needs to be seated when Baba comes."

Reggie bumped the would-be swami with his shoulder as we went past him into the dim room.

"Watch where you're going," Ganesha said in an angry whisper.

"You watch it, or I'll stick one of those candles up your ass!" Reggie said.

CHAPTER SEVENTEEN

The lights had been dimmed and the air was mystic with the scent of sandalwood incense. The candles Reggie had made reference to were flickering on the altar. I took two small round pillows from a pile in the corner and sat down on them. It had been years since I practiced hatha yoga, but I was still able to contort my legs into a lotus position without actually screaming out loud. Sitting on two pillows took some of the strain off my knees.

"Where's the chairs?" Reggie asked in a stage whisper after watching me make a pretzel out of myself.

"They don't use them for meditation," I said. "Grab a couple of cushions and sit down."

People around us stirred and cleared their throats, giving us a subtle spiritual signal that we were disturbing them.

Reggie piled up three cushions and plopped down on them, sitting

American Indian–style, with his thick legs crossed but not locked into the lotus position.

Ganesha closed the double doors, which had cloth draped over the glass on the inside, and sat down on the floor by the wall, showing his relative enlightenment by not using a cushion.

I closed my eyes and began to take deep breaths, pushing my abdomen out so that the bottom of my lungs could fully inflate, then slowly pulling it back in to expel the air, taking twice as long to exhale as to inhale. It is the simplest form of breathing exercise and one of the simplest forms of meditation, very effective at dissolving negative emotions such as anxiety or sadness. Yoga has many complex breathing exercises with specific and startling psychic effects, but simple deep breathing is a surprisingly powerful technique. If you keep your attention focused on your breath, and breathe in and out steadily and slowly, it invariably calms the mind.

A feeling of peace had begun to stain me, spreading like blue dye from cell to cell, when there was a stir at the front of the room. Opening my eyes, I saw Baba Raba entering through a door at the far end. An attendant helped him up onto a low platform. It creaked beneath his barnyard weight as he walked forward and sat down cross-legged in front of the altar, facing the audience. The blonde, who came in with him, walked around and sat down on the floor in front of the platform, keeping her distance from a cluster of flower girls.

"Om namah shivayah," Baba Raba intoned.

"Om namah shivayah," the devotees responded with a single resonant voice.

"The purpose of meditation is to still the mind so that it can perceive the infinite peace within," Baba said. "The mind is like a curious little monkey. It is always running everywhere to look at everything, attracted first by one thing and then another, always trying to find something that will satisfy it. It sees a glittering jewel and wants that. But the jewel doesn't make it happy. So it wants a shiny new car. Or a big house. Or a beautiful girl or boy. Because it thinks those things will make it happy. But nothing satisfies it for long. Everything in the physical world dies or decays. By cultivating attachment to material things, the mind ensures its own misery. What the mind truly seeks, the only thing that can truly satisfy it, is already within each of us. The Bhagavad Gita teaches that we are all sat chit ananda. Every one of us. Young or old. Rich or poor. Man or woman. That is our essential, unchanging nature. *Sat chit ananda.* Infinite existence. Infinite consciousness. Infinite bliss."

Baba paused. The dark room, heady with the smell of sandalwood, was utterly still.

"This bliss, or *ananda,* is the peace that passeth understanding that Jesus spoke of. It is within each one of you right now, far brighter and vaster than the sun. You must train your mind to be still and look inward so that it can begin to perceive your spiritual reality. Everyone likes to come to Southern California because of the bright warm sunshine. Oh, it makes us very happy. The beautiful light. We love to go to the beach and lie in the sun and feel its warmth. If we get a nice tan, we will be beautiful, too. Everyone will want us. But you have a light inside you brighter than ten thousand suns and a beauty surpassing anything on earth. Still your mind through meditation and you will perceive it. Then you will not need jewels to make you happy. You will not need cars or houses. Or boys or girls. Or money or fame. You are happiness. You are joy. Plunge into meditation and the light within you will burn up all your pain and sorrow. All your shame and disappointment. Meditate. Meditate. Meditate."

Here, presumably following his own advice, Baba closed his eyes, lowered his chin to his hairy chest, and placed his hands together in his lap in *dhyana mudra,* the back of one hand resting in the palm of the other, thumbs touching. Again, I wondered if I was misjudging the big-butted guru. Spiritual truth is a tricky thing. In the mouth of someone who doesn't fully understand it, the truth becomes a lie. It is dead and empty. In Baba's mouth, it was thrilling and alive. His gloss of Vedanta's most essential principle was flawless.

Ganesha stood up by the door and bowed toward Baba with his hands steepled in front of his chest, then turned to the room.

"For those who are new to meditation, Gurudev recommends *tratakum.* This is a very simple meditation that anyone can do. While breathing slowly and deeply, fix your gaze on one of the candles on the altar near Gurudev. If you keep your gaze steady on the flame, it will still your mind. Each time you catch your mind wandering, gently bring your attention back to the candle flame. We will now meditate for forty-five minutes. Baba will answer questions in the library afterward."

I knew all about *tratakum.* Fixing your attention on a single object. It did indeed steady the mind. Continuing to take deep, slow breaths, flooding my blood with oxygen, I visualized the pink diamond necklace and waited for those around me to sink down into whatever meditative state they were capable of reaching.

After ten minutes or so, I opened my eyes and slowly swiveled my head to reconnoiter. To my right, Reggie was curled up like a giant baby in a fetal position with his head resting on two of the round cushions, snoring softly. He was holding the third cushion to his chest like a child holding a doll. Everyone else in the room seemed equally unconscious of their surroundings.

Ganesha had opened one of the French doors partway to let fresh air into the packed room, where fifty people were steadily inhaling and exhaling the atmosphere, extracting oxygen, adding carbon dioxide and moisture. Slowly, carefully, I unhooked my legs from the lotus position and stood up. My knees ached and my ass was numb. I did a dozen shallow knee bends to get the blood circulating, then tiptoed to the door, taking care not to bump anyone.

I watched Ganesha's face as I slipped out. He didn't stir. In the hallway, I resisted the delinquent impulse to rifle the cash register and headed straight for the stairs.

CHAPTER **EIGHTEEN**

Hallways went in two directions from the landing at the top of the stairs. Down one was a series of small, minimally furnished rooms, each with a bed, a chair, and a cheap dresser-and-mirror combo. The rooms were lit by white-glass globe ceiling fixtures that blinked on when I flipped the wall switch by the door. On one dresser there was a well-thumbed copy of the Kama Sutra. The drawers were empty.

The closets held bathrobes, flower-petal-strewing robes, scented oils, and a few miscellaneous devotional items such as velvet ropes and blindfolds. So. Baba was a rascal, after all—not that I thought sex was sinful or anything silly like that. But the context made me angry. In itself, Vedanta is pure good, the most accurate earthly map to enlightenment for those who seek it. The foolish prejudice it faces in the West comes mostly from people's fear of the unknown and the entrenched resistance of rival philosophies, both religious and secular. But sneaky fuckers like Baba hurt the cause, too, periodically giving yoga a black eye by screwing dopey chicks or absconding with the funds. I had never heard of a legitimate yoga ashram where women were for sale.

At least there were no whips or handcuffs.

Down the other hallway were three larger bedrooms set up like dormitories with four bunk beds apiece, so that eight people could sleep in each room. Two were cluttered with girl stuff and had female clothes in the closets and dressers. The flower girls. The third was less cluttered, had men's clothes in the closet.

A fourth bedroom, larger still, had a king-size bed and a view of the floodlit garden behind the house through tall casement windows that filled the exterior wall. Mary's white jeans had been tossed negligently on the orange bedspread and her flimsy white T-shirt was balled up on the floor. I wondered if the massive guru had been in the room when she peeled off her pants and panties, then shooed that thought away like a bird from a rail. You can't let your mind wander when you are perpetrating a cat burglary.

Aside from the evidence of Mary's desirable presence, Baba's lair wasn't debauched. There was a meditation nook with a dusty altar, complete with candle, incense burner, and bell, and a bookcase full of paperbacks by a bewildering variety of spiritual teachers, the top shelf packed with books by Chogyam Trungpa, the controversial crazy wisdom master who founded Naropa Institute. A foot-tall antique ceramic Buddha in a niche beside the bed radiated an aura of holiness so tangible that I had to resist an urge to bow down before it.

Set end to end along the length of the wall opposite the windows was an oak banker's desk, a computer desk with a new Macintosh, printer, and scanner, and a worktable piled with documents and blueprints. Some of the blueprints were street plans that showed the section of Pacific Avenue where Mrs. Sharpnick's flophouse was located and blocks north of there. Others were construction drawings for a large hotel.

The papers were a complex mix—minutes of Venice City Council meetings, construction and real estate documents written in dense legalese, sheaves of letters to and from various individuals and city and state entities. Two names appeared frequently: Herbert Finklestein and Anthony Discenza. The second name was familiar, but I couldn't think where I knew it from. Evidently, Finklestein and Discenza were principals in a limited liability partnership formed to develop a resort on the Venice shore, and that they were using the city's power of eminent domain to condemn and acquire property over the protests of landowners and neighborhood groups. There was litigation pending. The closing date for the financing was on Wednesday. If the money wasn't in place by then, the main twelve-acre parcel, which comprised more than half of the proposed resort, would fall out of escrow.

Turning from the worktable, I saw a small clock on the desk that showed eight forty-five. The position of the clock's hands shocked me like a bare wire. I had either lost track of the time during meditation or spent longer scanning the legal documents than I realized. *Satsang* would be over at nine o'clock. Only fifteen minutes remained to look for the diamonds and get back downstairs before the adepts opened their starry eyes and stretched and looked around to see if Krishna had materialized.

I searched the room as fast as I could without making noise or a mess. If I had been sure the necklace was there, I wouldn't have worried about the mess and could have worked more quickly. As it was, I didn't want to put Baba on guard, in case I needed to come back for another visit. I looked under the mattress, under the rugs, behind the pictures on the walls, in every container and drawer I could open, and in the tank of the toilet in the attached bathroom. No one ever hides anything in the toilet tank, but you are supposed to look anyway.

The clock kept ticking.

There were size-two girl's clothes in the closet along with an extensive selection of XXXL men's street clothes, including half a dozen suits from mid-level designers, Hugo Boss and Calvin Klein, along with one navy-blue, three-button Armani. There was also a flashy selection of shirts, ties, and shoes.

Baba had a dual existence going.

The right-hand desk drawers held office supplies and ashram files. The left-hand drawers were locked. There was also a locked oak file cabinet stained the same golden color as the desk. I couldn't find a key for the cabinet or desk and there wasn't enough time to run out for a crowbar to crack them open, so I took a sturdy steel letter opener and tried to pry the top-left drawer open with that.

The lock had a steel tab that extended up into a steel-lined niche on the top of the drawer frame. I pried down with the letter opener at the same time as I pulled out and down on the U-shaped drawer handle, trying to open up enough space between the drawer and frame so that the lock would slip. I had the tab almost out of the slot when the letter opener split the wood it was dug into. My hand shot forward, knocking a lamp onto the wooden floor with a loud crash.

I froze, stiff as an aviator in a glacier. Baba's room was in the back of the house. I didn't think they would be able to hear the crash in the meditation room, but I wasn't sure. After a few moments, I heard what sounded like feet pounding on a staircase. Quick as I could with shaky hands, I set the metal lamp back on the desk, then dodged into the bathroom, squeezing behind the door.

A few seconds later, the bedroom door was flung open and I heard someone breathing hard as if they had just run up a flight of stairs; then the door closed and aggressive footsteps went down the hall to the other bedrooms, more doors opening and closing.

When there was no more noise, I stepped out of the bathroom, holding the letter opener in my right hand, which hung down at my side, the tip of the dull blade pointing backward. It wasn't a good weapon, but it was a weapon.

I looked at the clock. Meditation would be over in another minute or two if it wasn't already. I had to get back downstairs. My hand was on the knob of the bedroom door when I heard voices in the hall.

CHAPTER**NINETEEN**

The voices were coming closer. One of them was Baba Raba's. The other was female. I started to retreat once more to the bathroom and then stopped. After an hour of meditation, the guru or his companion might need to use the facilities. The voices were right outside the door. Looking around wildly, I dove for the far side of the bed and wriggled under, same as sneak thieves and illicit lovers have been doing down through the dusty centuries since people first elevated their sleeping pallets to get away from crawling vermin. I felt a little silly hiding under the bed but, really, where are you going to go? The space beneath was clean and uncluttered. The bedspread hung down like a curtain to within a couple of inches of the floor.

I made it just in time. The orange fringe was still swinging when Baba came into the room. The floor shook as his big farm-boy feet plodded over and stood beside the bed, close enough to reach out and tickle. Facing him was a second pair of feet, much smaller and neater with red-painted toenails.

"I am sorry to take you away from the others," Baba said, "but I wanted to see how you are doing." His bedroom voice was less bombastic than his professional-guru voice. He sounded genuinely concerned. I wondered if his words were a prelude to hanky-panky and looked up to see how much clearance there was between me and the bottom of the bed. Not much. There was a box spring, but I didn't have confidence in it. If Baba started bouncing his washtub ass on the bed, the whole thing might collapse on me.

"That's all right," I heard Evelyn Evermore's cultivated voice say. "I want to talk to you, too." Happily, she didn't sound amorous. She sounded dismayed. Despite her fine meditative posture, she had not connected with her inner *ananda*.

"You don't seem well, my generous friend," Baba said. "You are upset by what happened in the desert."

"I'm upset about a number of things, Baba," Evermore said, the distress in her voice sharpening into anger. "I still want to know why you sent that disgusting man with me to Indian Wells. His manners were atrocious and he treated me like a prisoner."

"As I told you before you left, I sent him because I sensed you were in danger. Which turned out to be all too true. It is fortunate he was with you. Or the necklace would have been stolen."

"You are very interested in that necklace, aren't you?"

"Of course I am. It is essential for the work we are doing."

"So you say. But I am having doubts, Baba. That Jimmy character is a cretin. He put his hands on me. It was a horrible experience and it makes me question your judgment and intentions. Where in the world did you even meet someone like that?"

"The Hebrew teacher Jesus told the Pharisees that he did not come to save respectable people, but sinners," Baba said. "The Pharisees were rich and self-righteous and wanted to know why he spent time with barkeeps and prostitutes. He told them that people who are well do not need a doctor; only sick people need a doctor. Jimmy is a troubled young man and I am trying to help him. It is good for him to make himself useful in our work."

"So, you're Jesus now?" Evelyn said sarcastically.

"No, I am not Jesus. I am just one feeble and faltering man trying to do a little good in an unhappy world. And I can't do it alone. I need help. We all need help. Including you. I am sorry if Jimmy offended you. I will warn him about his behavior and make sure that he does not bother you again. He will apologize to you when he returns."

Evelyn's feet shifted restlessly and I heard her sigh. When she spoke, her voice wasn't as harsh: "I don't need an apology from him, and I don't mean to be judgmental. Jimmy Z is a real jerk, but we have all been jerks in our lives, and worse, I suppose. At least I have. Just keep him away from me." Her voice grew softer still. "Have you heard anything since the last time we talked?"

"Yes." Baba said, power and authority flowing back into his tone, crowding out the apologetic note. "She is still in Los Angeles and she wants to come home."

"How do you know? Have you found her?" Evermore's voice trembled. Baba had struck straight to her heart.

"The same way I knew about her father's sins," the guru said, getting sonorous. "The same way I knew about her love of riding and about all the things that happened to her when she was with you that I have told you about. I am in contact with those who have knowledge of her where-abouts, and I am seeking her in deep meditation. I am close to her now. We will find her soon."

"I want to believe you, Baba," the rich lady said. "And I want to help you in your work. I told you last week that you could have the necklace after Diamonds in the Desert, and I will follow through on that. I just hope you are not stringing me along. It has been six months since you said you would find her. I will do anything you want, but you have to find her soon. I can't stand this much longer."

Baba's big feet shuffled toward her and I could imagine his thick hairy arms stretching out to enfold her in a simian embrace. But she backed away, unwilling to be comforted against his beer keg of a belly.

"No. Keep your distance."

"What?" Baba said, sounding surprised and offended.

"We've been over this."

"I am only trying to comfort you, Evelyn," Baba said. "This is the time for faith. We will find her soon. I promise you that. Where is the necklace now?"

"The Indian Wells police have it, but my attorney is driving out on Monday afternoon to pick it up," Evermore said.

"Does he know that you are going to donate it to the center?"

"No. He is suspicious of you and I didn't want to argue with him, so I told him I need the necklace for a charity event I am attending later this week."

"Can we rely on him, Evelyn? It is essential that I have the diamonds in my possession by Tuesday afternoon."

"Of course I can rely on him. He has been my attorney for twenty years. He will take the necklace to the bank on Tuesday morning and put it in my safety deposit box. We can meet there in the afternoon."

"You are going to give it to me then?" For the first time in my brief acquaintance with him, I heard a quaver in Baba's big voice. I had a pretty good idea why.

"Yes. I will make out a receipt for you to sign and the necklace will be yours. I'll be glad to be rid of it."

"Do you think it is safe for the lawyer to transport it when thieves are after it?" Baba asked.

"He is taking an armed guard with him to the desert, and he has a safe at his office where he can keep it overnight. Is that what you wanted to talk to me about?"

"Yes. And to find out you how you are."

"Well, now you know. I am very unhappy." Talking about banks and attorneys, Evermore had recovered her moneyed poise. "You have a great deal of spiritual talent, Baba. I am in awe of you sometimes. Maybe you are exactly what you claim to be, exactly what I took you for when we met last summer. You helped me then. You gave me hope. But my patience is wearing out. I am wearing out. You said if I gave you the necklace you would be able to find Christina and bring her back to me. I am holding you to that. Find her soon, Baba. *Please.*"

Her bare feet turned quickly and flitted from the room. Baba stood silently until the sound of her steps faded. When she was gone, he took a deep breath, audibly sucking half the air in the room into his tremendous torso, then chanted the cosmic syllable *om* one time, drawing the resonant mantra out for a minute or more, filling the atmosphere with a vibration that raised goose bumps on my arms.

Drawing another breath, he began to chant *om* again, but halfway through, the chant morphed into a growl and then a terrifying roar. The roar ended with a crash followed by a series of temblors as Baba stomped out of the room. Sharp particles hit my face at the moment of the crash.

After Baba slammed the door and pounded down the hallway, I slithered out from under the bed and saw that he had smashed the Buddha on the floor. The jaggedly decapitated head was still intact, but there was a crack running from the bridge of the Aryan nose to the top of the skull. It looked like the merest tap would split it in two.

CHAPTER TWENTY

Shortly, I followed Baba downstairs. As I came to the bottom of the steps, the muscle I'd seen on the boardwalk came out of the hallway beside the staircase that led to the back of the house.

He went on point when he saw me. "What you doing up there?"

"Looking for the bathroom," I said. "Do you know where it is?"

"It's down here," he said, very unfriendly, jerking his thumb over his shoulder in the direction he had come from. "Don't go up there no more. That's for staff and clients, understand?"

"Sure. No sweat. How much do you bench, anyway?"

"Three-eighty."

"Wow," I said, giving him a wide-eyed look. "That's a lot. You're really strong."

"I get by," he said, slightly mollified.

"You work out down on Muscle Beach?"

"Yeah, I'm usually down there 'round four in the afternoon."

"Neat. Be careful no one drops a barbell on your throat tomorrow."

"Yer the one better be careful," he snarled.

I walked around him into the narrow hallway.

The bathroom was ten feet down on the left. I went in and locked the door behind me. There was a handwritten sign on the wall by the shower asking people to be considerate of others and not use an excessive amount of hot water, always a precious commodity in a crowded ashram. The sign by the toilet—there always is one—instructed residents and guests not to put paper towels, tampons, or anything but toilet paper in the commode because they would cause a clog.

I splashed cold water on my face and dried off with a damp towel. I shouldn't have antagonized Baba's tough guy, but I was irritable. I wasn't sure why. My upstairs adventure had been successful. I hadn't found the diamonds, but I had found out where they were and, more importantly, where they were going to be on Tuesday morning. That was big. I had also discovered Baba's alternate career and learned the nature of his hold on Evelyn. I should have been happy. But I wasn't.

The muscle was gone when I went back out into the hall and everybody else was in the library, so I decided to do some more exploring. The swinging door at the end of the hall opened into a big old-fashioned kitchen with white wooden cabinets and yellow linoleum.

The blond girl Baba was trying to rename, whose lithe limbs and sexy energy would have drawn the eyes of every man in the stands at a World Series game if she walked by when the count was three and two in the bottom of the ninth, was arranging some snacks on a wooden tray at the table. She looked up when I came in and smiled when she recognized me, a pleased smile, bright with surprise. It lasted only a couple of seconds before she tucked it away behind the bored, supercilious look that comes naturally to beautiful girls, but we both knew it had been smiled. The fact was added to our unique store of shared knowledge, things only she and I were aware of.

"What are you doing back here?" she asked in the same taunting tone she had used on the beach.

"Just looking around. What are you doing?"

"Making *prasad*."

"Can I help?"

She shrugged her small sturdy shoulders. "I don't see why not. Get those dates and the powdered sugar from the counter and bring them over here."

I took the wooden bowl of dates and cardboard box of sugar over to the table and sat down beside her. She smelled like castile soap. I resisted an impulse to bury my face in her shiny hair. I seemed to have a lot of impulses when she was around.

"Here." She handed me a paring knife. "Cut a slit in each date and put one of these almonds in, then arrange them in a circle on these little paper plates and sprinkle powdered sugar on them."

She was peeling oranges, tangerines, and grapefruits, arranging the segments in parallel rows on the wooden tray.

"That looks nice," I said.

"*Prasad* has to be really tasty and attractive," she said, primly. Then, giving me a sidelong look, "You probably don't even know what *prasad* is."

"Actually, I do."

"Oh, yeah? What is it?" Though she was obviously all grown up in the ways of the world, she had a childish pride and possessiveness about her knowledge of the esoteric. It made me like her that much more.

"It's food offered to a divinity like Krishna that takes on divine energy in the process. It is then shared among the god's devotees as a way of receiving his blessing."

"Wow," she said, her attitude changing easily from superiority to admiration. "That's pretty good. I never heard anyone say it so simple before. I mean, I kind of knew that's what it was, but I couldn't have put it so neatly."

I shrugged. "How long have you lived here?"

"I've only been here a couple of months, but I've lived in other ashrams before. I really groove on Hinduism and yoga, you know?"

"Yeah, Vedanta is a cool religion. What brought you to this ashram?"

"My roommate graduated last semester—I go to City College—and I couldn't afford the rent, so Baba let me move in here. I help out with karma yoga and he doesn't make me pay anything. He's pretty cool."

"What all does karma yoga include?"

"Mostly working in the kitchen," she said flatly. "But I kind of help manage the place, too. What about you? What do you do? How do you know about Vedanta?"

"I studied it years ago when I lived in Florida." I didn't mention that my scholarship took place in a prison library in between card games and yard fights. "I spent some time with Muktananda when he was in Miami." That was after prison, when I was a dewy-eyed spiritual seeker, through forever with lying and stealing and all forms of dishonesty.

"Wow! You met Muktananda? He was one of the great teachers of this age."

"Yeah, he was. Maybe I can tell you about him sometime."

"What do you do now?" she said, slightly cooler, sensing a spiritual come-on.

"I own a construction company."

That was the cover story I'd used for the past several years. I had business cards, stationery, sample cases, and a phone number that was answered by a professional-sounding woman who always said the same thing: "Coast Construction. No, Mr. Rivers is out on a bid. If you leave your number, I'll have him call you."

"A construction company? Really?" Mary sounded skeptical. "You have a job going down on the beach?"

"No," I laughed. "I'm on vacation."

"Let me see your hands."

I held my right hand out to her. She took it and turned it over in a businesslike way, unself-conscious about her raw fingertips. "No calluses," she said, looking up from my palm. Her bright blue eyes were fringed with exceptionally long, exceptionally light eyelashes that gave her a fairy-like appearance.

"I'm an executive, not a carpenter."

"I doubt it," she said, letting go of my hand. "That cat you are with is some kind of player, for sure. I think you are, too."

"Why?"

"Female intuition. I grew up around players and I know one when I see one. For my money, you are some kind of naughty fellow. Maybe a con man or a bank robber. Tell the truth—I'm right, aren't I?"

I was flattered by her estimate of my criminal standing. Bank robbery—not walking in with a scrawled note in a trembling hand, but planning and executing a major heist—is a high-class crime. Those guys get a lot of respect in the joint. At the same time, her flash of insight caught me off guard. To distract her from further speculation, and because I could hardly help myself, I scooted my chair closer to her and put my right arm around her.

"You're projecting," I said, taking a chance and lightly nuzzling her neck. She got still when I touched her, but didn't shy away. "I think you are the naughty one. I'm not a bank robber, but I make plenty of cash in construction, and I wouldn't mind spending some of it on you."

I didn't know if she was a temple prostitute like the other gowned girls or just an easygoing ashram lass who believed in free love, but she had showed us her breasts and I was getting such a warm and lively vibe from her that I thought there was at least an outside chance she would let me slide my hand between her thighs and lay her on the table while everyone else in the building talked about ultimate truth and spiritual transformation.

"I'm not for sale," she said, placing her left hand against my ribs and pushing me away with calm, steady strength.

"I didn't mean to imply that you are," I said, backing off a little. "I just meant I'd like to take you out sometime and get to know you."

"That's sweet," she said, sardonically but thoughtfully, too. "I'm flattered. But I don't even know you. Maybe if you came around and took some yoga classes we'd have a chance to get acquainted."

"We have a chance right now." I leaned toward her again and tried to turn her head so that I could kiss her red lips. I don't know why I was being so aggressive. It wasn't like me. Maybe it was because she hadn't seemed to mind Reggie's direct approach in the hallway and because I wanted to cut him off before he got another chance with her. Maybe because sex was in the air in the ashram and she radiated an intoxicating female energy that stirred me to my core. I wanted to put my tongue in her mouth, to taste her and touch her intimately.

"Stop," she said sharply, jerking her head away. "I can't. You seem like an interesting guy and all, but I'm with Baba now. I can't fool around with you."

That chilled me. I saw the tangled jeans on the orange bedspread again and knew why I had felt irritated when I came downstairs.

"So—what? You're part of his string? You let him rent you out in those nice little rooms upstairs?"

"Screw you, pal. No one turns me out. No one ever has and no one ever will. Why don't you get the hell out of here?"

"I'm sorry," I said quickly. "I shouldn't have said that. I just don't understand why a gorgeous girl like you would waste your time with an overgrown fakir like Baba. He's got to be at least twice your age and three times your weight. And you can't tell me that he isn't pimping those other girls out."

"You don't know what you're talking about," she said, reverting to a bored tone. Her anger had faded as fast as it came. Calling her gorgeous hadn't hurt. "Baba's not a Boy Scout, but he is a real guru. There are people at this ashram who have seen him levitate during meditation. He helps people, too. I've seen him do it. Like that kid who was with you on the beach—we found him bawling his eyes out on the boardwalk one day and after Baba talked to him for a few minutes he was all happy and smiling. Could you do that for someone?"

"Why was he crying?" I asked.

"I don't know. I think he said his mom was supposed to meet him and didn't show up, or something like that. But Baba made him feel better. That's the point. And it's not like you think with the other girls. They do it with the guys Baba tells them to do it with, sure, but it's, like, tantra, you know? It has a spiritual purpose."

"Yeah, and I bet it puts a lot of spiritual dough in Baba's dhoti, too."

"So what? Money makes the world go round, pal. He uses it to keep the center open so people can learn about yoga and enlightenment."

Ganesha chose that moment to hurry into the kitchen from the hall. He practically skidded to a stop when he saw me sitting with the blonde. Confusion, anger, jealousy, and sorrow played across his transparent face. He took refuge in the anger.

"You aren't supposed to be back here," he said to me, angrily.

"It's okay," Mary said. "He's helping he make *prasad*."

"It's not okay," he said, helplessly turning his anger on her. "You don't run this ashram, Shakti. You have to follow the rules, same as everyone else. Only staff are allowed in the kitchen. Your *friend* has to leave." He put some stink on the word "friend."

"You should try not being an asshole sometime, Ganesha," the girl said. "You might like it."

Her contempt wobbled the boy's knees.

"It's not a problem," I said, standing up. "I have to go anyway." I didn't want to provoke a conflict that would draw attention. "Maybe I'll come back and try one of those yoga classes. When are they?"

"There's a schedule in the rack by the front door," the girl said in her default tone of indifference.

"You should take up meditation, bro," I said to Ganesha as I walked past him. "It would help you relax."

"Hey," the girl said as I was going out the door. "We're having a karma yoga day tomorrow if you want to come. Starts after morning mediation, and there's a free lunch for everyone who helps. I'm cooking."

"I'll think about it," I said, matching her indifference.

"Hurry up with *prasad*," I heard the boy's thwarted voice say as the door swung shut behind me. "Baba is waiting for it."

"I bet he is," I said to myself. "The fat bastard."

Looking into the library as I passed, I saw twenty or so people sitting on the couch and floor, gazing raptly at Baba, who was enthroned like a tribal god in a big chair by the fireplace, where flames now crackled. He was staring balefully at a young woman with round glasses who was perched on an arm of the couch with an expectant look on her face.

"That is so basic," he said angrily. "How many times do I have to answer the same question for you people? Atman and Brahman are one and the same. That is the essence of Advaita Vedanta. If you can't grasp that simple principle, I am wasting my time with you."

The girl looked like she might start crying, but Baba didn't seem to notice. He shook his head in disgust and called on the next questioner.

Reggie was sitting on the front steps.

"It's about time," he said. "Where were you?"

"Prospecting."

"Find any gold?"

"A nugget as big as your thumb."

CHAPTER TWENTY-ONE

I had two short days to plan the robbery. Everything would have to be in place by Monday night if we were going to pounce on Tuesday morning. In the next forty-eight hours, I had to find out where Evermore's financial institution was and pick a spot to intercept the lawyer before he took the necklace into the high-security environment inside the bank. To do that, I would have to find out his name and locate his office. It would help to know what he looked like, the kind of car he drove, and the route he would be following to the bank.

If I could track him to his office, that might actually be a better place to do the robbery than a bank. If he was driving out to the desert on Monday afternoon and returning late that evening, he would have to keep the necklace someplace overnight. Evermore said he would keep it at his office, but it was possible he wouldn't want the jewels out of his sight and might take them to his house. Both scenarios offered possibilities. I liked the idea of robbing him in a leafy suburb or burglarizing an empty office building on Monday night much better than pulling an armed robbery in a bank parking lot on a busy weekday morning.

"Well?" Reggie said, irritated. "Whud you find out?" It was the second time he had asked the question. We were halfway back to Pacific Avenue. The temperature had dropped a few degrees and the offshore breeze had picked up, tossing the tops of the tall palm trees and blowing trash along the street. It was an uneasy combination. The Santa Anas usually brought warmer temperatures.

"Sorry," I said. "I was trying to sort some things out. I found out where the diamonds are."

Reggie made saucer eyes. "Where?"

"They're still in Indian Wells, but Evermore's attorney is bringing them back here Monday night. Depending on how things shape up, we'll hit Monday or midmorning on Tuesday."

"Stickup?" He made a gun out of his hand to illustrate his question.

"Could go either way. We might be able to burgle them or it might be strong-arm. The lawyer will be traveling with a security guard."

"Rent-a-cops ain't shit," Reggie said. "I'll take care of 'em."

"I'm not worried about the junior G-man. If it's a stickup we'll come down on him like a brick chimney."

Somewhere to the south, I heard a siren drifting toward us. As we came to the juncture of Westminster and Pacific, a medium-size engine honked its way through the busy intersection. Looking north, in the direction it was going, I saw a storefront with flames boiling out the front. Another fire engine was coming down Pacific from Santa Monica. As we walked the four blocks south to Sharpnick's, I looked back several times. The fire seemed to be spreading.

When we were half a block from the flophouse, the front door flew open and a jolly-looking girl who could not accurately have been described as petite scampered out onto the porch, shrieking. She was wearing a pair of plaid boxer shorts and nothing else. Her melon-size breasts flopped as she ran. Budge came out right behind her. He was wearing the same flowered board shorts he'd had on earlier and was topless like the girl. His breasts and belly jiggled, too. The pair of them ran around the side of the house into the backyard, laughing like lunatics.

"Looks like the party's started," Reggie said, putting some giddyap in his short-legged stride. A series of motorcycle accidents had left one of his legs two inches shorter than the other. His boot was built up to compensate for the differential, but he still limped. If you were trying to get him to go someplace on foot that he thought was too far to walk, he would exaggerate the limp, hobbling like Chester on *Gunsmoke* and bitching until you agreed to go back and get your car or hire a cab. But he could stump along at high speed if he wanted to, and the topless girl had piqued his interest. He enjoyed the company of drunk chicks.

We entered the house, leaning forward against a blast of soul music pouring out into the windy night. Two black guys I'd seen around and a Mexican who worked at the café where I ate breakfast were shooting dice against one wall. Candyman was curled up on the couch, necking with a white girl who could have been the twin of Budge's quarry. Two black women who looked like part-time hookers were sitting by the stereo, laughing and drinking wine from paper cups, bobbing their heads and swaying their shoulders in time to the music.

"Look! It's Reggie and the other guy," one of the black girls said. "Come 'ere an gimme some sugar, Reggie." She stretched out her arms toward him and wiggled her fingers.

"I got something sweet for you, all right," Reggie growled, heading her way.

Swaggering across the living room, he narrowly missed a collision with the topless girl, who charged in from the kitchen, followed by Budge, who was still laughing in the explosive, staccato style that possessed him when he was drunk.

"Ha-ha-ha-ha-ha-ha-ha-ha-ha!" he laughed loudly, spotting the girl. It sounded like the laugh of a maniac but was so good-humored that it was hilarious instead of threatening. He could keep it up for minutes at a time, pausing for a quick breath every dozen or so "ha"s.

The girl had stopped in the middle of the room. Looking back over her shoulder at her pursuer, she wiggled her plaid behind, then scampered with small steps and upraised arms into the bedroom hallway. Budge was winding up, Jackie Gleason style, to race after her when he saw me standing by the door.

"Hey, brother!" he shouted over the music, "come on in and join the party!"

Roused from his clinch by Budge's shout, Candyman looked up and gave me a lazy wave, a blissful smile, and a slurred, "Rob, mah man!" before being tugged back down by his inamorata.

"Hey, Budge, who you say this is singing?" the black woman not necking with Reggie yelled. She was barefoot, wearing purple capris and a yellow tank top. Her hair was teased up into an impressive Angela Davis–type 'fro.

"My girl, Teena Marie," Budge shouted ecstatically. "The queen of blue-eyed soul!"

Before hooking up with Rick James and becoming the only white female soul singer to have a number-one record, Teena Marie had been a student at Venice High School in the same class as Budge. His second claim to fame was that he had taken her to the prom their junior year. It was 1973 and the Gondoliers had had a good season the previous fall. He was a popular athlete and she was a wild beauty already flaunting her irresistible voice in area talent shows, looking for a way out of her parents' world. The way he told it, they made out on the beach afterward and she let him get his fingers wet rubbing her through her panties. For some reason, in a house full of tall tales, everyone believed him. Maybe it was because he had every record she had ever made, knew the title of every song, and still talked about her on a daily basis even though five presidents had been elected and twenty-three Southern California springs had come and gone since the two of them walked barefoot in the sand listening to the surf crash in the darkness.

"That's some swinging shit," the woman said, doing a sexy little double-clutch frug in front of the stereo while her girlfriend slurped on my partner.

Budge came over to me grinning. "I got a girl in the bedroom," he whispered.

"Yeah, I saw her. She looks nice."

"Gonna get my knob polished!"

"That should be fun," I said. "Listen, I'm going to turn the music down a little bit so Sharpnick doesn't get wind of the party. You don't want her swooping in on her broomstick and spoiling all the fun."

"Aw—screw her," he said with drunken courage. "She ain't nothing but a walking skeleton. Pete knows how to handle her."

As if on cue, Pete entered the room from the kitchen, wearing his peacoat with the collar turned up. I assumed he had come into the house through the back door, same as Budge and his girl. He stopped just inside the living room and glanced around with darting eyes.

"Hey, look, it's Party Pete!" Budge yelled, drawing everyone's attention to the ex-sailor.

Squaring his shoulders and sticking out his chest, Pete marched over to the stereo and turned the volume down to a conversational level.

"Negative," he said. "I'm not partying tonight. Got an oh-six-hundred wakeup mañana. So let's keep the noise down. We don't want the shore patrol showing up."

"Loosen up, Moe," Reggie said, coming up for air. "It's only ten-thirty."

"Yeah, man, it's Saturday night!" Budge said. "Time for a party! Grab a girl and join in."

"What you mean you ain't partying tonight?" Reggie's hottie said, sniffing. "You smell like you just put one out."

"You're crazy," Pete said, backing away. "You better keep the noise down, if you know what's good for you."

He glared at Reggie and the girl for a few seconds, then turned on his heel and marched down the hall and into his bedroom, slamming the door behind him. He had completely dropped all pretense of respect or friendship toward me and Reggie.

"You see that shit?" Candyman said. He was sitting up on the couch with a disgusted look on his face.

"I know," Budge said, his jolly mood punctured. "If Pete don't want to party, he don't want nobody else to party either."

"Nah," Candyman said, shaking his head in an anti-Shoshana manner.

"What?" Budge said.

"That little sumbitch wearing new boots."

"Whurd he get money for new kicks?" Budge said.

"That's what I want to know," Candyman said, angrily. "Look like Wolverines. Hundred bucks a pair."

CHAPTER TWENTY-TWO

The next morning was crystalline. The wind blowing down from the mountains had cleared every particle of pollution from the air before it died down to a light breeze in the night, making the world look clean and new, like an aquarium after the water has been changed. When I left the snoring house a few minutes past seven, the fronds on the palm trees along Pacific were fluttering like tinsel in the early sunlight. A block away, the jade-green sea was full to the brim, stretching in a sparkling sheet to the razor-line of the horizon.

I was thinking diamonds as I walked north along the deserted boardwalk to Santa Monica, watching the Ferris wheel grow from the size of a quarter to a structure that loomed high above me. In the restaurant at the end of the pier, I ate pancakes and sausage, washing the meal down with a glass of milk and finishing up with two cups of strong black coffee. Afterward, chemically exhilarated, I strolled inland on Colorado, past the homeless encampments in Palisades Park, to Lincoln, which I followed south to Broadway. Grim-faced churchgoers in expensive cars made up most of the traffic. Their eyes darted as they drove, looking for sinners. I came under suspicion. It was justified.

When I arrived at Baba's Hindu church, the place was bustling with volunteer workers. There were cheery old ladies in overalls weeding the flowerbeds and hippies on stepladders washing windows. Along the Seventh Street side of the hulking Queen Anne, a dozen or so men and women were standing by a pile of extension ladders and aluminum walk planks, looking as clueless as Eskimos in Acapulco.

Ganesha seemed to be in charge, his ocher robe moving back and forth between groups as he offered encouragement and answered questions. I didn't see Mary or Baba Raba, but Evelyn Evermore, whom I had hoped to encounter, was among the group by the extension ladders. She was wearing Jordache jeans that fit her just right, showing her shape but not constricting her movement, and a brown-and-gold Pendleton shirt with the cuffs turned back neatly to her elbows, exposing downy forearms. Her thick platinum hair was tied back in a ponytail with a yellow ribbon.

Ganesha walked briskly up to Evelyn's group just as I joined it.

"Does anyone here know roofing?" he asked hopefully, looking up from his clipboard.

I waited to see if anyone else was going to say anything, but they just looked at one another with the silly smiles and shrugs of the spiritually inclined but mechanically inept.

Karma yoga has a magical allure for most meditation students because washing the dishes or weeding the garden is actually a lot easier than concentrating on a candle flame, and the results are more apparent to others. Honest swamis often are on a shoestring budget. They need volunteer workers to keep their ashrams afloat on the cosmic tide and tend to dole out effusive praise for minor tasks.

So everyone wants to help. And that works out fine with weeds and dirty dishes. Problems rear when skilled labor is required. Turn most of these proto-yogis loose on a task more complicated than painting a door and you're courting disaster. Give them a simple plumbing job, for instance, and hot water will soon be coming out of the cold tap while the lights blink off when you flush the toilet. If the group Ganesha was addressing tackled the roof without supervision, you'd be able to take a shower in the living room next time it rained.

"I know something about it," I said.

He turned toward me eagerly, recoiled slightly when he recognized me, then suppressed that reaction with a determined nod.

"Okay, you will be in charge, then. What's your name?"

"Robert Rivers," I said. "What are we doing?"

He was writing my name down on the top sheet on his clipboard, which I didn't like. When he finished, he flipped to the third page and scanned it.

"You see that part of the roof up there?" he said, pointing. "That part that slopes down?" Since every section of the roof sloped down, his description wasn't particularly acute.

"That shed roof over the bump-out?" I asked, following the beam of his index finger.

"Is that what it's called?"

"Yes."

"Well—it's leaking somewhere and Baba wants to put these new shingles on it." He pointed to some bundles of asphalt singles stacked on the sidewalk. "Are you sure you know how to do it?" He was familiar with the "can-do" attitude that actually can't.

"Yeah, no problem."

"Do you know how to set this . . . stuff up?" he asked, gesturing toward the ladders, ladder jacks, and walk planks. No doubt he had many precise Sanskrit terms for psychic states stored away in his perceptive young mind, but he didn't have much terminology when it came to construction equipment.

"I'll take care of everything," I said. "But I am not going to need all these people. If you have the right quantity of shingles over there, we're only reroofing about three hundred square feet. Why don't you four help me?" I extended my arm to separate Evermore, the artistic guy I'd seen the previous night, and two other able-bodied men from the rest of the group.

"All right, thanks," Ganesha said. "The rest of you can come with me and help clean up the backyard."

Asphalt shingles come thirty-three square feet to a bundle, each kraft-paper-wrapped package weighing between seventy and ninety pounds, depending on the thickness of the shingles. There were ten bundles stacked on the sidewalk with a gallon of tar and a five-pound box of galvanized roofing nails on top. Hammers and nail pouches lay on the grass.

After we introduced ourselves, I showed the men how to set the ladders and ladder jacks up to position the walk plank at a comfortable height, so that the edge of the roof was at waist level when we stood on the plank.

It was a simple job. The section of roof that was disturbing Baba's nirvana was an unobstructed rectangle, twenty-four feet wide by fourteen feet deep, which meant a minimum of cutting and fitting. The shallow six-in-one slope would be easy and safe for amateurs to work on.

While the able-bodied guys started carrying the heavy bundles up and spreading them out on the roof where they would be handy as we progressed, I helped Evelyn and the artistic guy, whose name was Walt, run a starter course, then showed them how to place and nail down the shingles. When the laborers had caught their breath, I got them going too, each person working a six-foot-wide section, lacing their shingles in with those laid to their right.

We put the new shingles down on top of the existing ones. With the old shingles to guide them, my helpers did reasonably good work. It wasn't the neatest job I'd ever seen, but I was confident the living room would stay dry. When Evelyn started to lag behind, I went over and helped her. Squeezing past her on the narrow walk plank, the front of my body was in full contact with the back of hers. She didn't seem to mind the intimacy.

Standing to one side, watching me work, she wiped her forehead with a bandana and smiled.

"How did you learn to do roofing?" she asked.

"Funny story," I said. "I had just gone into the remodeling business in St. Louis, doing carpentry and concrete work, when there were two hellacious hail storms that knocked out about a third of the roofs in the city. Big roofing companies were giving people three-month waits just to get an estimate. I had never nailed down a shingle before but I had an alcoholic friend who knew the trade, and he showed me how. Within a month I had three full-time crews working and more jobs coming in from referrals than I could handle. By the time the season was over, I pretty much knew the business."

"Weren't you worried about learning the trade from an alcoholic?"

"I didn't really have a choice," I said. "All roofers are alcoholics."

"Really?" she laughed.

"Really."

"That's a great story. You were fated to be a roofer. And you know carpentry, too. It must feel good to have all those skills."

I wasn't a hundred percent sure, but it seemed like she was flirting with me. That opened up possibilities.

"What about you?" I said. "You look like someone with a lot of skills. What do you do?"

"Oh, I golf and play tennis quite a bit. I used to surf, but I stopped after I hurt my back. I still ski and ride. I have two horses at a little stable up in the valley."

"Do you work?"

She made a wry face. "I guess you could say I am a philanthropist."

"That's a noble calling. Do you help support the ashram?"

"Yes," she said, briefly. "I help out a little bit. What's your connection to the center? I don't remember seeing you before. Do you take classes?"

"I am thinking about taking some," I said. "How 'bout you? Do you take classes?"

"Yes, since last summer."

"How do you like it?"

"It's good," she said, without conviction.

"Do you live in the area?"

"I just moved into a house in the canal district, as a matter of fact. It needs quite a bit of work, but I think it will be a great place once it is fixed up."

"What kind of work?"

"Quite a bit of carpentry work, actually." She paused. "Are you still in that business?"

"Yes, I am." I took one of my Coast Construction cards out of my wallet and handed it to her. I'd worked in remodeling for ten years in St. Louis during my laughable attempt to fit into straight society, five years sober and five years drunk, so I knew enough to make the cover story stick.

"Would you have time to come by and take a look at the house and tell me what you think?"

"Be glad to," I said, keeping my voice light and conversational. "I'll get your address and phone number when we are done."

"Wonderful." She gave me a nice smile.

When we had shingled as much of the roof as we could reach from the walk plank, we climbed up onto the roof, kneeling on the shingles we had just nailed down, working our way up the slope to the wall where the shed roof ended. I flashed the final row of shingles to the wooden siding with roofing cement and membrane, using a putty knife someone had thoughtfully sent out with the materials.

When I was finished, one of the able-bodied guys helped me take the scaffolding down. He was a cowboyish kid named Johnny dressed in Levis and a jean jacket, about twenty-five.

"It's nice to see someone around here who knows what they're doing," he said, when the equipment was stacked and the trash picked up.

"Are there some issues with competency?" I asked.

"You could say that. This used to be a super place when Swami Sankarananda was running it, but it's gone downhill since the big guy took over."

"In what way?"

"Seems more like a singles bar than an ashram nowadays. Those girls of Baba's are always trying to cozy up. I told them I'm married and trying to live a clean life, but they don't seem to get the message. I know it's supposed to be spiritual union and everything, but it rubs me the wrong way. I come here to meditate and get my head straight, not get laid. I'm about ready to switch to the Ramakrishna Center. It's farther from where I live, but at least those guys stay down on the farm."

"How did Baba happen to take over?"

"No one seems to know. Maybe Ganesha knows, but he's not saying. Baba's not even from the same order as Sankarananda. From what I hear, he came out of the Naropa Institute, and that place got to be a real can of worms. Everybody was fucking everybody and a bunch of them died of AIDS. You can call that tantra if you want to, but I don't want any part of it."

"Me either," I said.

"Really?" He cocked his head and gave me a look. "What about Evelyn?"

"What about her?"

"Nothing." He held up his hands at shoulder height with his palms toward me like someone surrendering. "She's a cool lady. And foxy, too, for her age. I'm just saying she gets around."

"Oh, really?"

"Yeah. She pretty much goes with the new flow. I know three or four guys she's taken home. I guess she's pretty hot. One of the guys got hung up on her, but she told him she doesn't want anything serious. Just likes to play around. Which is great. More power to her. It's a free country. I just don't reckon this is the place for it, necessarily."

Ganesha came around the corner from the backyard and walked toward us.

Seeing him, Johnny stuck out his hand, which I shook. He had a firm grip.

"Good working with you, man," he said. "Don't tell Evelyn or Ganesha I said anything. I like both of them. I just don't agree with the way this place is being run."

CHAPTER TWENTY-THREE

"Did everything go okay?" Ganesha asked when he came up to me, holding his clipboard to his chest.

"It won't leak anymore," I said.

"Thank you for your help," he said, and made a pained face. "I'm sorry if I was rude yesterday. It's just that there has been so much going on around here lately, and we had some problems yesterday . . . but that's no excuse. I was at fault and I apologize. It's nice of you to help. We'll be having lunch in a few minutes if you would like to join us."

"I'd like to," I said. "Have you seen Mary around?"

"She's fixing the food," he said, a different kind of pain on his face. "You'll see her at lunch. Thanks again for your help."

He turned abruptly and strode toward the front of the house. I went in the opposite direction, along the side of the house and through a gate into the backyard.

An old brick wall enclosed the yard on the Seventh Street side, shielding it from the view of passersby. A hedge of lilac bushes divided it from the yard next door and the one behind it. At the back of the enclosed space was a rose garden with a bench facing a blue-and-white statue of the Virgin Mary. Near the house, several picnic benches had been pushed together, end to end, and the flower girls, now dressed in work clothes, were going in and out the back door, carrying food from the kitchen to the tables. Several volunteer workers were washing their hands and faces with a garden hose while others stood in groups, waiting for the dinner bell. It had warmed up and most people had shed their jackets and sweaters.

I saw Mary's face at the kitchen window, looking out at the preparations, and waved to her. She didn't seem to see me, so I went up the back steps into the kitchen.

She was standing by the sink, filling a pitcher with water.

"Hi," I said. "What can I do to help?"

"Nothing," she said. "Everything is under control. We'll be eating in a few minutes."

She was wearing flip-flops with a rainbow strap, pink shorts that lived up to the name, showing all but the last and most provocative inch of her slim thighs, and a neat little white sleeveless blouse that buttoned up the front. If she had looked any sexier, I would have done an involuntary back flip with my head spinning around on my shoulders. As it was, I felt impulses. Strong, shameful impulses.

Taking a deep breath to constrict my pounding heart, I walked over and stood beside her. "Why don't we go to the beach after lunch," I said, taking a shot. "It's turned into a real bluebird day out there. We could walk over to the Santa Monica pier and ride the Ferris wheel. It's so clear, I bet we could see the Channel Islands from the top."

"No," she said, turning to look at me with no expression. "I don't want to do that. Please wait outside. Only staff are allowed in the kitchen."

"Why so cold?" I said, but she ignored me and handed the pitcher to one of the flower girls.

"Put some ice in this and take it out," she told the girl, as if I had not spoken.

Going back down the steps into the sunny yard, I cursed myself for being too critical of Baba the night before. That was probably what had offended her. If she was invested in his worldview, she couldn't afford to see him as a phony.

I sat down at one of the picnic tables, feeling angry and unhappy. The Sunday *Los Angeles Times* was scattered across the red-and-white-checked tablecloth, and a headline in the California section caught my eye: DISCENZA SAYS PACIFIC CITY LAND ACQUISITION NEAR COMPLETE.

I remembered then where I had seen Discenza's name prior to reading the documents in Baba's bedroom. He was an often-investigated member of the Venice City Council, allied with the old-school mayor and two other councilmen against a triad of reformers. The article identified him as managing partner of the LLC developing Pacific City and said he had recused himself from voting on matters connected with it. The project had nevertheless been approved at every phase, in spite of strong neighborhood opposition. According to the city charter, when there was a tie vote on the city council, the final decision was left to the mayor. Because he was a voting member of the council, every vote had been a tie, and he had used his extra ounce of authority to nudge the city's decision in the developer's favor at each stage. There was no mention of Finklestein or Baba Raba in the article. Since the construction documents were in the public record, Finklestein's name would be known to reporters and activists, but probably not his local identity as an XXXL guru. The last paragraph noted that there would be an on-site protest against the development later that afternoon.

"Are you reading the rest of the paper?" one of the cheery old ladies asked, looking at me brightly from where she was standing on the other side of the table.

"No," I said.

"I'm going to move it out of the way so people can sit down to eat."

Briskly, she gathered up the real estate, classified, news, and travel sections and marched away.

Baba was providing a nice lunch for his karma yogis. Arranged at one end of the long, rectangular table were big bowls of cole slaw, potato salad, and a green salad with romaine lettuce, tomatoes, cucumbers, black olives, and feta cheese; platters of cheddar and Swiss cheese sandwiches made with thick whole-wheat bread and garnished with avocado, tomato, and bean sprouts; bowls of fresh fruit and shelled nuts; a big tray of some kind of baked whole-grain desert; and pitchers of water, lemonade, and sassafras tea.

When Mary came down the wooden steps with another tray of dessert, the eyes of every man in the yard followed her, some openly, with approving smiles and nudges, others surreptitiously, glancing and looking away and glancing again, trying to capture her image in their minds or hearts or groins.

"Where is Baba?" Ganesha asked her as she set the tray down.

"How should I know?" Mary said. "I don't run the ashram."

Ganesha made his pained, apologetic face once more. "Would you please see if he is going to come down? Everyone is hungry."

Mary walked away without a word, across the yard and back up the steps into the kitchen. So it wasn't just me she was being rude to.

The people in the backyard eyed the food while carrying on conversations about yoga, yard maintenance, and local politics that rose from murmur to emphatic discussion and died down again, punctuated by bursts of laughter.

After about ten minutes, Walt called out from across the yard, "Ganesha, we're starving, man. When do we eat?"

Ganesha looked at the kitchen door, then up at the second-floor windows of Baba's bedroom and shook his head.

"Right now," he said decisively. "I guess Gurudev is occupied. Let's gather around the table and join hands."

As the group encircled the table, Johnny came up on my left side, Evelyn on my right. I had no consciousness of Johnny's hand, concentrating on the touch of the fine feminine instrument I had first noticed in the lobby of the Oasis Palms Resort Hotel. Even as it rested quietly in mine, returning gentle pressure with gentle pressure, Evelyn's hand was articulate and exciting.

Of one accord, everyone bowed their heads and closed their eyes. Ganesha chanted the sacred syllable *om*, drawing it out for thirty seconds or so as everyone joined in. Twice more the welded circle chanted with a single resonant voice the sound that is said to have ten thousand meanings. Afterward, we stood in silence for another minute, ears ringing, before a simultaneous squeeze of hands signaled the end of the meditation.

When I opened my eyes, I saw that everyone else was grinning, too.

"Dig in," Ganesha said. "You've earned it."

As people formed a line to get at the groceries, Mary came out the kitchen door and down the steps, looking angry. As she stalked past me, I reached out and snagged her, grasping her bare arm with my hand, which was still glowing from the eloquent touch of Evermore's smooth skin.

Mary jerked her arm away, whirling to face me, then calming slightly when she saw who I was.

"Sorry," I said. "Didn't mean to startle you. I was just going to say you can cut in line in front of me if you want to."

"That's all right," she said. I couldn't tell if that meant "No thanks, I don't want to join you in line" or "No problem, I don't mind that you touched me."

As I watched her face for a clue, she looked up at the back of the house. Following her azure gaze, I saw Baba Raba looking down from one of his bedroom windows. The casement window was cranked open and he was visible from the middle of his thick hairy thighs on up, wearing his dhoti and a bent iron frown.

Mary lowered her eyes to mine, smiled, and then slid into line in front of me. There were additional impulses but I kept my hands to myself as we edged forward. When we had our food, she linked her arm though mine and led me to the bench in the rose garden, glancing up once at Baba, who still loomed like a dark demigod above the picnic. I wondered if he recognized me and regretted his invitation.

"You still want to take me to the beach?" Mary asked when we sat down.

"I sure do."

I didn't care if she was using me to make a point with the guru. It gave me an opportunity to sit close beside her, with our thighs touching. When we came to dessert, she let me feed her a piece of the coarse sweet cake, taking it from my fork delicately with her lips and tongue, chewing it slowly while looking me in the eye, occasionally blinking her fairy eyelashes. When I tried to feed her a second piece, she laughed and pushed my hand away.

"That's enough of that," she said. "Let's get this place cleaned up, then we'll go."

Everyone pitched in to straighten up the yard and put the food away, with Ganesha and Mary supervising.

"You're really having a good day, man," Johnny said as we moved one of the picnic tables back where it belonged.

After lunch, some of the volunteers left and some returned to the jobs they had been doing, scraping paint or pulling weeds. I was waiting for Mary by the kitchen steps when Evermore walked up and handed me a card with her name and address written on it.

"When do you think you can come by and take a look?"

"I'm booked up next week," I said. "But I could stop by tonight if you are going to be home."

"Super!" she said. "Make it around six-thirty."

"I'll see you then."

CHAPTER TWENTY-FOUR

Mary kept me waiting for fifteen minutes, either because she was tied up with Baba or to test her power over me. When she finally came back out, her subtle smile made up for the wait. I don't know if she was truly beautiful or just very pretty, but I sure liked her looks. Her body was perfect from my point of view, occupying the midpoint between a too-skinny fashion model and a too-voluptuous *Playboy* bunny. She looked as wholesome as the girl who lives next door on Sycamore Street and sings in the church choir, raising a soprano hosanna to the heavens, and as experienced as the girl who sleeps with the prime minister when his wife is in the country.

"What are you grinning at?" she said, giving me a little shove.

"Take a guess," I said.

As we walked down Broadway toward the ocean, I tried to sort out my mixed motives toward Baba's delectable blonde. I was powerfully attracted to her, so much so that I was in danger of thinking more about how to get into her pink pants than how to find the pink diamonds. At the same time, when I reminded myself that the necklace was the true object of my *tratakum*, the thing I should be focused on as if it were a blip on a radar screen on the eve of Armageddon, she seemed like a good potential source of intelligence, someone who could fill me in on Baba's operation, if I could gain her confidence.

"Did you know these streets used to be canals?" I asked her.

"What do you mean?"

"Where we are walking right now was water sixty years ago. All the streets in this area were canals until they filled them in during the nineteen thirties and forties."

"Why did they fill them in?"

"Lack of imagination," I said. "They were silting in and overgrown with weeds. It was simpler and cheaper for city hall to turn them into streets than to repair and maintain them."

"Wow, that's interesting. I never heard anyone mention that before. You know a lot of stuff, don't you?"

"I pay attention," I said.

"I bet you do."

Whatever Baba had done to annoy her had shifted her attitude toward me to some degree. She was trying on a girlfriend persona, seeing what it would be like if I were her man, feeling for where my buttons were.

"Ganesha told me you fixed the roof," she said after a little while. "He said it seemed like you knew what you were doing. It's cool that you know how to do stuff like that. So, are you really in the construction business?"

"Kind of," I said, not wanting to lie to her any more than I had to. She let the ambiguity pass.

The boardwalk was packed with a typical Sunday-afternoon crowd out to enjoy the atmosphere and entertainment. A "silver man," wandered down from the Santa Monica Promenade, was doing his robot impression in exchange for dollar bills proffered by wide-eyed little kids pushed forward by their parents. A gang of hip-hop acrobats was bouncing and spinning and flipping in front of a suitcase-size boom box that made my chest reverberate as we strolled by. A man in a harlequin costume was swallowing swords.

The breeze had shifted quarters and was now blowing inland off the splashing water, carrying the exhilarating scent of the sea and seeming to impart the energy of the ocean to everything along the shore, putting a three-dimensional kaleidoscope into motion. Palm trees stirred, sparrows twittered and hopped, basketballs thumped and banged on the courts, boys and girls whizzed past on wheeled devices, pennants flapped, seagulls skimmed, and the homeless shook their silvery cups. Cappuccino machines hissed as sweet foam boiled up like the waves where they curled and creamed on the beach.

We stopped at a counter along the boardwalk to have Cokes.

"Oh, that is so good!" Mary said. "I know it's not healthy, but I love soda. It is one of the things I miss living in the ashram."

We were sitting on old-fashioned stools with metal bases and round vinyl-covered tops, sipping our Cokes through straws like two high school kids on a first date.

"So Baba allows prostitution at the ashram, but not soda?"

"Lighten up," she said. "It's not prostitution, not exactly."

"What is it, exactly?"

"Have you ever heard of the Magdalene Order?"

"No."

"You know what tantra is, though, right?"

"You bet."

"Okay, what is it, then?" She used her taunting tone as if she didn't believe me, but I think she just wanted to hear my definition before continuing her explanation.

"You tell me," I said.

"It's fucking for God," she said.

I laughed out loud, and a Sikh drinking tea at the other end of the counter turned his turbaned head to look at us.

"What?" she said. "Isn't that what it is?"

"Yes, that is a great definition. I kind of knew that's what it was, but I couldn't have put it so neat."

She gave me a dazzling smile then, young and happy. I reached out to put my hand on hers, but she pulled her hands back into her lap before I could touch her.

"Let's hear your definition," she said.

"Tantra is when a man and a woman engage in sexual intercourse to achieve a sense or state of union," I said, looking deep into her fairy eyes. "Instead of making love selfishly for physical pleasure and to gratify the ego the way people usually do, tantric lovers do it to transcend the ego. Becoming one with the other person is like practice for becoming one with God. Just what you said. It is a way of breaking out of the bounds of the little, socially constructed self and becoming part of something larger and better."

"You really know this stuff, don't you?" she said, trying out the admiring-girlfriend mode again.

I shrugged. "So, where does the Magdalene Order come in?"

"Mary Magdalene was the chick in the Bible that Jesus saved from being stoned to death for sleeping around," she said. "Baba says she wasn't a hooker because she was a bad person but because she was full of love and didn't know what to do with it. He says everyone is like that underneath, but society suppresses it and makes it into something bad if people express it without permission. Jesus saw all the love that Mary had inside her and chose her for his companion. Then she found the right focus for her love and helped Jesus do his thing." She spoke in an excited enthusiastic manner, proud of her esoteric knowledge and something more.

"How did she help him?"

"Through tantra."

"You mean she slept with him?"

"Yeah. She helped him find God, like what you were saying."

"This is what Baba teaches?"

"Sure. I know it's not what they say in Sunday school, but it kind of makes sense, you know?"

"And that's what the girls at the ashram do?"

"Kind of. Baba says most of the men that come to the ashram aren't ready to find God, but that the girls are helping them by healing their hearts. He says everyone is wounded because they haven't received the love they need and deserve and that that's what's wrong with the world. That's why people are so angry and mean. He says the Magdalenes' unconditional love helps the johns feel better about themselves and become better people."

"But it's not unconditional."

"What do you mean?"

"Don't the men have to pay to have sex with the girls?"

"Yeah, but they have plenty of money. They are all important people, big businessmen and politicians. I've seen some of them in the newspaper. And Baba uses the money for a good cause."

"Where does he get the girls?"

"I don't know. They were all there when I came."

"What do they get out of it?"

"Baba says they grow spiritually by giving love."

"Does he have sex with them?"

"Why are you asking so many questions about this? Are you trying to figure out how to get laid up there? Because it's not hard if that's what you want."

"I'm not trying to figure out how to get laid. I'm just trying to figure out what's going on over there. Operating a string of call girls out of an ashram, no matter what you call them, doesn't fit with what I know about Vedanta. I don't want to start taking classes there if it is really just a whorehouse."

"So what if they are whores?" She spit the word back at me angrily. "What's so bad about that? Isn't everyone a whore in one way or another?"

"I'm sorry," I said. "You aren't part of the order, are you?"

"No," she said, calmer. "Baba wants me to join, but I won't do it."

"Why not, if it's such a good thing?"

"Like I told you," she said in a tough tone, "no one turns me out. And there is something strange about those girls. It's like they are on something."

"You think he is feeding them drugs?"

"No," she laughed. "I don't think he'd do that. He is really not as bad as you think. It is more like he is using tantra and psychic powers to control them. He has some kick-ass *siddhis*. I've seen him do some amazing things. Like with you at the beach yesterday. He really turned up the juice on you. I know you felt it." She paused, giving me a curious look. "Why is he interested in you?"

"I'm an interesting person," I said lightly, but her question made me uneasy. Why had he focused on me? I didn't like the idea of his mental powers probing my subconscious when it contained a crystalline image he would be quick to recognize. "Did Baba start the Magdalene Order, or does it exist in other places?"

"I'm not sure."

"Do men call and make dates or do they join a tantra yoga class or what?" I was counterprobing.

"There's no class. It's more like private lessons. I'm not sure how they set up the appointments. There are a couple of guys that run the girls for Baba, a creep named Jimmy, and some other muscle-bound jerk who goes by Namo. I can't stand either one of them. Can we talk about something else now?"

"Sure," I said. "Why don't you tell me something about yourself?"

Instead of answering, she noisily sucked the last of the Coke from her vase-shaped glass, then rattled the ice and tilted the glass to her lips to get another drop or two. I could tell she came from a lower-middle-class background, same as me. Soda is one of our favorite things.

"Let's keep walking," she said, standing up. "I've never ridden on that Ferris wheel before. Might be fun."

As we continued north on the boardwalk I looked back and caught the Sikh sneaking a peek at the pink shorts and shook my finger at him.

CHAPTER TWENTY-FIVE

It was a bright, breezy three-quarters of a mile from the snack stand to the pier where the Ferris wheel was revolving slowly against the backdrop of the Santa Monica Mountains. I took the hint and didn't ask Mary anything else about herself. As a reward, she gave me the Cliffs Notes version of her life story.

She was twenty-four, a Gemini born in May 1971, as I was stumbling through the second semester of my drug-blurred freshman year at Hazelwood High School. She grew up in a two-bedroom, one-bath tract house in Anaheim half a mile from Disneyland. Her mother, like mine, was an alcoholic. Her father was a mindless Catholic churchgoer who beat her when she started getting interested in boys. She ran away from home in her early teens and had always been with older men, starting with a thirty-year-old pot dealer when she was fourteen. After that it was a little vague. She had traveled, worked at different things. She had quit drugs and alcohol two years earlier when she got interested in Eastern religion, gone back to school fifteen months before, in the fall of 1994, after passing the GED test.

Her personality, which she complimented me by displaying freely, was a blend of sunny optimism, fatalistic cynicism, and fierce self-determination. She was intellectually ambitious, though not terribly well informed. She was a bit of a snob about some things, little-girl curious about others.

As we walked down the sloping causeway onto the Santa Monica pier, she let me take her hand, which made me ridiculously happy. When we came to the amusement rides, I impressed not just her but myself and the concessionaire by slamming the big wooden mallet down hard enough to ring the bell atop the thirty-foot tower of the high striker. Mary clapped and laughed, and the concessionaire made a "Well, what do you know about that?" face.

I am six-two and weigh about 175 pounds, which makes me look skinny. But I am a lot stronger than I look, and years in construction taught me a thing or two about leverage and swinging hammers.

I don't know if she was doing it to mess with me or not, but Mary said she wanted a popsicle. So I bought her a cylinder of cherry ice. She licked it contentedly as we waited in the line for the Ferris wheel. When she put it in her mouth the first time to suck on it, she looked up frankly into my eyes, saw some of what was going on there, and then burst out laughing, bending over and slapping her thigh with her free hand, leaving a red mark.

"Naughty boy," she said.

"What do you expect after all that talk about tantra?" I said, my face the color of the popsicle.

"It's okay," she said, still laughing, reaching out to punch my arm. "I know how you guys are."

When we made it to the front of the line, a five-foot-tall carnie with four-foot-long arms took our tickets and opened the gate on our seat.

"Here we go," Mary said, excited.

We sat down side by side and I put my arm around her, cupping her bare shoulder with my right hand. We were facing northwest, toward Malibu. When the huge wheel lurched into motion, carrying us back and up, the sea-bright world expanded swiftly around us, getting vaster and grander as we came up to and over the exhilarating top, then shrinking again as we sailed downward, then expanding again, wider and brighter and bluer, the

Channel Islands swimming into view, misty and green, as we were lifted skyward again. Round and round we went, half a dozen times, then stopped at the very top, 120 feet above the water, as the carnie began unloading and reloading the cars.

"Wow!" Mary said. "This is beautiful. What islands are those?"

"The closest one is Santa Cruz. The one beyond that is Santa Rosa."

"How far away are they?"

"Sixty or seventy miles."

"Awesome!"

"Look back this way," I said, turning to the south. "That's Catalina. The island beyond it is San Clemente."

"Cool! I love Catalina. Saul and I used to go there for the weekend."

"Who is Saul?"

"He's the man I was with for a couple of years, until he died last year. Let's not talk about him."

"All right."

The wheel jerked forward as the carnie brought another car to the loading platform.

"Thank you for bringing me here," Mary said, her voice quiet and close to me in the infinite space of the heavens. "It was a cool idea."

Her eyes were liquid and sleepy. I leaned over and kissed her, feeling her soft lips for the first time. She rewarded me for my good idea by kissing me back. She kept her mouth closed, but she put her hand on the back of my head. When I put my hand on her breast, feeling her hard nipple press against the center of my palm, she pulled away.

"Don't," she said.

"Why not?" I begged.

"I'm going through a lot of changes right now," she said sincerely. "I feel like my body is the only thing I have control over, and that's important to me. I don't want to do it with every guy that comes along. Baba has been after me since I moved in to do tantra with him, but I feel stronger when I say no."

"You mean you aren't sleeping with him?" I said, and I guess my voice gave me away.

"Does it matter that much to you?" she said softly.

"Yes."

"You're awful sensitive for a criminal." Her eyes were sparkling. "I think it's sweet."

She put her lips to mine and her cherry-flavored tongue went briefly but generously into my mouth. After a blissful moment, I pulled away.

"Was he bothering you today?"

"I don't know. He walked in on me while I was taking a shower, but he said he didn't mean to."

"He meant to," I said, and the wheel lurched, lowering us toward earth.

"You don't know that. He's good guy in a lot of ways. He's taught me tons about Vedanta, and he lets me stay there rent-free. He does a lot of good in the community." She paused and matter-of-factly put a barrier between us: "I may end up doing tantra with him. I haven't decided yet. He has a way of looking at me that makes me feel really amazing. Maybe I could find God that way, you know?"

"Come on, Mary. You know the guy is off the reservation."

"I'm still making up my mind," she said firmly. "I have to make my own decision about him. If he pushes me too hard, I'll leave. But in the meantime, as long as I am staying with him, I owe him some loyalty. Who knows? Maybe all this stuff that seems bad is just a test of faith."

She was groping for integrity and a worldview of her own, separate from that of the men who desired her. At the same time she may have been rationalizing a little bit, because the ashram was a good deal for her and she wanted to keep staying there.

The wheel jerked into motion once more, bellying out and dropping us back down to the loading platform.

"I just don't want him to do to you what he has done to those other girls," I said.

"He won't," she said. "Let's not argue about it. We're having a fun day at the beach. Let's just enjoy ourselves." She reached over and took my hand as we walked back along the pier toward the shore. But her hand felt cool and impersonal, more casual than intimate.

CHAPTER TWENTY-SIX

As we walked south on the crowded boardwalk, it seemed to me that we were drifting apart. The bulky guru had wormed his way between us. What Mary had said about her preference for older men was a gift to me, but it also made her easy prey for Baba, a father figure who praised sex and made a good case for its spiritual potential, in contrast to her biological father, who had viewed her stirring sexuality as a threat.

Baba had a huge advantage over me because Mary lived with him and was an eager student of Vedanta, which he was a true master of in some respects, while I had to concentrate on stealing the necklace that he believed was his. Whether that led to a direct confrontation or not, I wouldn't be hanging around the ashram after I got the diamonds and so wouldn't have the chance to try and win Mary over. It seemed like our kiss in the big blue California sky might be the high point of our relationship. We had touched and tasted each other but nothing would come of it.

Then I got lucky.

Two of the hip-hoppers we'd seen earlier were walking toward us. The big one was black, about my height but thirty pounds heavier. The smaller one was a wiry white guy who had been acting as the group's mouthpiece, rounding up the crowd and badgering people for money. As they approached, he threw his hands out to his sides and shifted his head back and forth like a Balinese dancer, ogling Mary.

"Goddamn, girl! You're too fine for the wintertime. Where'd you get those pink pants? Why don't me an' you do the dirty dance?" He hopped back and forth, grinning.

His clowning brought a lewd smile to the face of his friend.

"Fuck off," I said harshly, before Mary could respond.

The grins dropped off both their faces.

"You talking to me, bitch?" the mouthpiece said.

"I must be," I said, giving Mary a hard shove toward the sand to get her clear. "You're the only loudmouth piece of shit I see."

The little guy did an impressive back flip and landed in a crouch, cocked and ready for action. The big guy took a step toward me.

"Whud you wanna do?"

I paused as if reconsidering and raised my hands to shoulder level, palms toward them.

"I'm not going to do anything," I said. "You guys look too tough. Let's let this cop handle it."

As I said that, I extended my left hand, pointing off to the side and behind them. At the same time, I shifted my hips so that my weight rested heavily on my flexed right leg and my right hand hung down to the level of my knee.

Both sets of eyes followed my left hand as it pointed, and both heads swiveled to look for the cop. As the big guy's head turned away from me, I brought my right fist up from way down low in a good old-fashioned roundhouse, pivoting my hips and hitting him in the temple as hard as I have ever hit anyone.

He dropped like a sack of cement.

When the white guy turned back toward me, responding to the thunk of my fist on his friend's skull, I was following through, swinging my right leg forward and planting it, toes toward him, holding my left fist low behind me and my right forearm upright in front of me, guarding my solar plexus and my face.

As the little guy charged me, I snapped a back fist in his face to throw him off balance and pivoted again, opposite, stepping forward with my left foot and swinging my left fist in a second roundhouse that was a country cousin of the first one.

He was quick and ducked to one side so that I only hit him a glancing blow, but it still knocked him down. When he bounced back up, he jumped sideways like a jackrabbit, put two dirty fingers in his mouth, and gave a piercing whistle. Immediately an answering whistle came from the crowd to the south and the other three acrobats came running.

Two were black, one Asian. All three were muscular and, after they saw their boy down, mad as hell. For a bad moment I thought I might get my ass stomped in front of the girl. But we were next to the weight pens, and two big lifters who had witnessed the altercation ran over and took flanking positions on either side of me.

"Beat feet, niggers," the biggest one said. His naked pecs were the size of dinner plates, his biceps like thighs. The hip-hop boys didn't want any part of him. They helped their friend up and retreated.

"We'll get you, motherfucker!" the mouthpiece said when he and his crew were at a safe distance, pointing at me with a look of fury on his rat face.

"Thanks, guys, you saved me," I said to the lifters.

"Anytime, bro," Humongo said. "I don't like those guys, anyway. Thur always causing trouble around here."

"Nice moves," the other one said, giving me a thick-necked nod of approval before rocking back into the weight pen.

I looked around for Mary and saw her standing by a palm tree at the edge of the sand with her hand over her mouth. Her eyes were wide.

"You okay?" I said, walking toward her.

"Yeah," she said, coming to meet me. "Man! You really laid that guy out!"

"Just a lucky punch," I said, playing it to the hilt.

"I don't think so," she said, looping her arm through mine and walking close beside me as we continued south. Most girls like guys who will fight for their honor, especially when they win, and it felt intimate again between us. But I knew Baba was still lurking in the background, exerting his mystic gravity on the girl.

Ahead of us to our right, a crowd was gathered on the beach, facing a man standing on a temporary stage who was speaking into a microphone.

The crowd's back was to the ocean, the speaker's to the boardwalk. As we came closer, the sound of his amplified voice clarified into words.

". . . lose essential housing and see rents on what's left go through the roof. It will change our neighborhood so completely that we won't recognize it anymore. And for what? So a corrupt city councilman and some greedy out-of-town developers can make a killing and rich people can have another fancy hotel to stay at on the weekend? There are plenty of fancy hotels, but not nearly enough affordable housing."

The speaker was Walt, the artistic Baby Boomer from the ashram. This was the protest I'd read about in the paper. Clearly, Baba Raba's role in the development was not known or the aging hippie would not have been doing karma yoga for him that morning.

"Hey, that's Walt," Mary said.

"Let's hear what he has to say."

I stopped beside a concrete wall that bordered the sand and half-leaned, half-sat on top of it with my feet wide enough apart for Mary to stand between my legs. When she leaned back against me, into my arms, I had one of those moments of supreme happiness that Vedanta offers, not just through the channel of meditation but through the aperture of love, a sense of true *ananda*, escape from the boundaries of both time and self. The feeling made me think of Kim Henner, my first girlfriend, who I was crazy about in fifth grade. I remembered the first time I held her and gave her a tentative kiss out behind the shed in her backyard. That was my earliest taste of the magic that can be in the union of male and female. I had not thought about that moment in many years, but it turned out I had not forgotten it, either.

When I wrapped my arms around Mary, pulling her closer, she snuggled against me, pushing her buttocks into my groin. A dizzy wave of desire washed through me as all the blood in my body rushed to the spot. It felt like my genitals were about to explode. Her sensitive ass felt the change and she turned her head to look back at me over her shoulder, smiling.

"Easy, big boy," she said.

"Sorry," I said. "Can't help it."

"It's okay," she said, shifting her butt slightly from side to side, rubbing it against me. "I like to know a guy has a strong drive."

". . . tax breaks that make it a bad deal for the city, any way you add it up," Walt was saying as I tuned back in to his exhortation. "The city council is in their pocket. If we don't organize to stop this, we are going to lose our shops, our homes, and our way of life. Do you want that?"

"No! No! Fuck them! Boo!" the crowd shouted. There were at least a hundred angry people standing in front of the stage, all of them potential opponents of Baba if his role in the resort deal should happen to somehow mysteriously leak out.

One particularly booming boo caught my attention and I looked over to see Budge standing at the edge of the boardwalk. He was wearing his AWOL shirt and carrying a Rite Aid bag.

As Walt resumed his speech, Budge turned away from the platform and saw me. We exchanged a nod and he trudged over.

"Hey, Rob," he said. He looked hungover.

"Hi, Budge. What's going on here?"

"They're trying to fuck up the surfing, same as always," he said. "Build a big hotel with a marina. Walt's trying to stop it."

"How did last night turn out?" I asked him.

He shook his head mournfully. "It got purty drunk out."

"Your girlfriend spend the night?"

"Was I with a girl?"

"Yes," I laughed.

"She musta gone home. Who's this?" His bloodshot eyes had been darting quick looks at Mary while we talked, starting with her ankles and working up to her alert face.

"This is Mary," I said. "Mary, this is Budge."

"Hullo, Mary," he said.

"What are you AWOL from?" she asked.

"It don't mean 'absent without leave,'" he said. "Means 'always west of Lincoln.' Lot of us down here don't like to go too far from the shore. Everything we need is right here."

"Really?" I said. "You don't go past Lincoln?" That busy avenue was only eight or nine blocks inland. The ashram was just within that boundary.

Budge shrugged. "I might go as far as the 405 a couple of times a year, but that's about it, bro. There ain't no point. Everyone in the world wants to come here, and we're already here."

Mary saw a girl she knew passing by and went over to say hello. Budge watched her going.

"Damn, Rob," he said. "Where'd you snag that little hottie? I thought Reggie was the ladies' man."

"I get lucky every once in a while," I said. "What's in the bag?"

He closed his eyes and shook his head, holding his free hand over his abdomen. "Laxative," he said.

"Problems?"

He nodded very slightly, like a headwaiter acknowledging a bribe. "I ain't shit in three days," he whispered.

When Mary came back, she had Ozone Pacific with her.

CHAPTER TWENTY-SEVEN

"Look who I found," Mary said, putting her hand on Oz's shoulder.

"Hey, little buddy," Budge said, exchanging his constipated grimace for an affectionate grin. "What you up to today?"

"Hi, Budge. Hi, Rob," Oz said, giving us his trademark smile. "I was thinking about taking a bus out to the country today to visit a farm or something. Do they have farms like that, Rob? Where you can see cows and horses and stuff and ride on a tractor?"

"They probably do," I said. "I'll find out for you. How's everything else going?"

"Great," he said. "It's a bee-*you*-tee-full day at the beach!"

"I see you've been hanging with Mr. Parker," I said.

Oz nodded happily. The old parking lot attendant sometimes bought the boy dinner after he knocked off for the day. I had seen the two of them sitting at the counter where Mary and I had Cokes, Ozone devouring a hamburger and french fries while Mr. Parker explained the finer points of backing big cars into tight places and removing scratches with rubbing compound.

"Where'd you get those cock boots?" Budge asked Oz. The boy's ragged tennis shoes had been supplanted by a pair of brown cowboy boots with black stitching. They were a little bit run-down at the heels but still in good shape overall. The color matched the brown of his two-tone cowboy shirt.

"Mr. Parker gave them to me," Oz said. "They were his grandson's but he got too big for them. He's a six-footer."

"They're really nice," Mary said. "Those are just what you'll need for a trip to the country." Then, in a gentler voice, she asked: "Did your mom ever show up?"

The smile fell from Oz's face, leaving it looking haggard and aged, like the face of a famine victim.

"No," he said. "She didn't come. I walked all the way down to Ozone looking for her, but I couldn't find her. I waited all day but she never came back."

The street he mentioned intersected the boardwalk a mile north of the palm tree where he hung out.

"Ozone isn't that far," I said, with false heartiness, trying to counter his mood.

"It sure seemed far," he said in a small voice.

"Aw, cheer up, little buddy," Budge said, slapping him on the back. "Maybe she'll come see you next weekend."

Ozone's wide eyes were amazed and hopeful. "Do you think so, Budge?"

"Never can tell," Budge said. "Come on, let's walk back down to the house and get something to eat. You going that way, Rob?"

"No, I'm going to walk Mary back to the ashram."

"Do you live at the ash farm?" Oz asked Mary.

"Yeah, for right now," Mary said.

"Do you know when Baba Raba is coming back to the beach?"

"He'll probably be down here in the next day or two. Why?"

"I just want to ask him about something"

"We're gonna get going," Budge said. "Come on, Oz."

"Let's walk with them," Mary said, taking my arm in hers. "It's such a pretty afternoon, I don't feel like going back yet. Evening meditation isn't for another couple of hours."

"No argument here."

"I shouldn't have asked about his mother," she said as Oz and Budge went on ahead. "It upset him."

"Don't worry about it." I squeezed her hand. "He'll be fine. She'll show up one of these days."

The four of us strolled leisurely southward, Oz telling Budge how beautiful the country was, Mary and I stopping occasionally to look at the vendors' wares. I bought her a mood ring, and when she put it on it glowed bright green.

"That means a romantic feeling," said the old woman selling the rings.

"Oh, really?" Mary said. She held her hand out in front of her to look at the ring, then looked over at me, smiling. "Maybe there's hope for you, pal."

Before long, we came to Wave Crest. Antonio's restaurant was halfway between the boardwalk and Pacific Avenue. Two men were talking by the entrance. The older one, about sixty, was dressed like a waiter, in black pants and a white shirt. He had thick, wavy gray hair and a drooping mustache. The second man looked even more Italian than the first, with an aquiline nose, olive complexion, and dyed black hair slicked straight back. He was wearing a dark, expensive-looking suit. When he smiled, his capped teeth and shark's eyes looked familiar.

"Who are those guys," I asked Budge.

"The old guy is Gianni," Budge said. "The other guy is that crook Discenza. He's the s.o.b. behind that hotel and marina they're trying to build."

"What's he doing down here?"

"He owns Antonio's," Budge said. "You guys go on without me. I want to ask Gianni something. I'll catch up with you."

Mary, Oz, and I walked a few blocks farther south to Westminster.

"We're going to peel off here," I said to Ozone. "You want to walk back to the ashram with us and see if you can talk to Baba?"

"No, I'll wait for Budge," Ozone said. "If you see Mr. Baba, tell him I said hello."

After we crossed Pacific Avenue, I looked back and saw Ozone standing at the curb on the west side, waving to us like a passenger at the rail of a cruise ship, setting sail on a voyage from which he would never return.

"Bye, Rob. Bye, Mary."

"Bye, Oz."

"Goodbye!" Mary waved back at him.

At the ashram, we went along the side of the house into the backyard. At first I thought all the karma yogis were gone, but then I noticed Johnny sitting on the bench where Mary and I had sat, facing the statue of the Virgin Mary. He was leaning forward with his elbows on his knees and his head bowed.

At the bottom of the kitchen steps, Mary turned and kissed the corner of my mouth and looked up at me with her eyes sparkling.

"Thank you so-o-o-o much, Robert," she said. "I had a wonderful time!"

Then, before I could answer or ask her for another date, she ran up the steps and disappeared into the sanctuary of the kitchen. It was a slick maneuver by an experienced girl who knew how to avoid entanglements. I was frustrated by her swift withdrawal but happy about the warmth in her voice and smile. She had enjoyed being with me and I thought I could probably coax her out again and maybe get her to try some tantra with me if time allowed.

As I turned to go, my mind was already shifting back into crime mode, looking ahead to the meeting with Evermore and what I needed to learn there. Johnny was standing by the bench, facing the house. He raised his hand in greeting and we walked toward each other.

"What's up?" I said.

"Just saying goodbye to the Lady." He nodded his head toward the statue. His eyes were red.

"Goodbye?"

"Yeah, I'm through with this place."

"What happened?"

"Baba and Ganesha got in a big fight. It was pretty ugly."

"What were they fighting about?"

"Baba had that girl Gopi up in his room doing something to her and she started screaming and Ganesha went in there to see what was wrong. Then him and Baba started yelling at each other and Gopi ran out crying."

"Which one is Gopi?"

"She is that tall skinny chick who wears her hair in a long braid that hangs down to her butt. She has black hair."

"What did Ganesha say to Baba?"

"I couldn't hear everything. I was fixing a leak in the bathroom sink down the hall and the bedroom door was closed part of the time, but from what I heard, Baba was bawling Ganesha out for coming into his room while he was doing tantra with Gopi and Ganesha said that it wasn't tantra, it was sadism. Baba went nuts then. It was scary. He was snarling like an animal. He threatened to expel Ganesha from the ashram and said he would use his *siddhis* to destroy him spiritually, some shit like that. It was a real mess."

He looked around at the garden. "I love this place. It's kind of like I found God here. When Swami Sankarananda was alive, it was a little bit of heaven on earth. But that shit today was too much for me. There is something wrong with Baba. He sounded crazy. He scares me. I don't want to tell you what to do, but if I was you, I'd find some other place to learn yoga."

How'd it end up?"

"Ganesha sounded pretty shaken up, but he stood his ground. He told Baba that unless he stopped his left-handed practices and returned to true Vedanta he was going to call the swamis in New York and tell them what was going on out here."

"What did Baba say to that?"

"That took the wind out his sails. He quit yelling and started trying to convince Ganesha that nothing wrong was going on and that he was going to get himself in trouble if he called New York. He said that he was an enlightened master and that Ganesha was supposed to obey him and something about Gopi's ego consciousness and attachment to her body, that it had to be reduced for her to advance spiritually. Sounded like a crock to me. One of them shut the door after that and I didn't hear anything else."

"What are you going to do?"

"I guess I'll try the Ramakrishnas. They have a pretty nice place in Hollywood, right by the freeway."

"Good luck." We shook hands. "Thanks for filling me in."

"Take care, man."

As he disappeared around the corner of the house, the backdoor opened and one of the flower girls came down the steps. She was wearing tight black stretch pants, a red blouse, and red high heels, clothes more suitable for clubbing than meditation. She gave me an empty look as she went along the flagstone path into the side yard. Her pupils were huge.

I waited a few moments, then went to the corner and peeked around in time to see her walking up to a gleaming XJ16, the most expensive Jaguar on the road. The tough guy I'd met the night before was leaning against the red car with his back toward me, talking to the driver through his open window. The driver was wearing a real estate salesman's blue blazer and a black toupee. He handed some cash out the window. While Namo counted the money, the driver stared at the girl getting into his car with a look of lust so naked that his face took on the raw lividity of a skinned animal.

So the girls did outcalls as well as in-calls in the little rooms upstairs. I was surprised to see the operation so out in the open. Either Baba was getting reckless or he had police protection. Even if he had protection, his world was starting to wobble. His patroness was losing patience with him, his aide-de-camp was threatening to turn him over to the spiritual authorities, and I was closing in on his two most valuable possessions.

CHAPTER TWENTY-EIGHT

I could hear Candyman and Pete arguing as I went up the front steps. When I pushed the door open, they were squared off in the middle of the shabby living room, on the verge of physical violence. Budge was standing to one side with a grim look on his face.

"I want my goddamn money I worked for!" Candyman shouted.

"Negative!" Pete shouted back, belligerent, looking up at his taller housemate. "I told you we haven't been paid for that particular job yet."

"Then where you get the money for them new boots, huh?"

"An old shipmate came into port and paid me back some money he owed me."

"Bullshit! No old shipmate of yours would have anything to do with your sneaky ass. Where'd you get the money to eat in Antonio's?"

"All that dope you did must of eat up your brain," Pete said. "How many times I got to tell you? I wasn't eating in there. I was talking business with Gianni, trying to find some work for you two swabbies so you don't end up on the streets."

"No you wasn't," Budge said.

Pete and Candyman swiveled their heads to look at him.

"I asked Gianni if he had any work for us. Said I was following up for you. He didn't know what I was talking about, Pete. He said his cousin Carmen does all his work."

"The old wop must be getting senile," Pete said. "He told me he was taking bids for a new patio."

Candyman took a half step toward Pete and leaned down, nose to nose. His coffee-colored hands were balled up at his sides.

"Gimme my goddamn money," he said.

"Take it easy, guys," I said. I didn't want a blood-spattering brawl.

Pete gnawed on his lower lip, looking into Candyman's bloodshot eyes for several tense seconds, then flinched.

"You want your money? I'll give you your money, all right." His face was red and furious. He yanked his wallet out and pulled out a thick sheaf of bills. Candyman's eyes bulged. Pete peeled off five fifties and slapped them into the ex-junkie's hand. Candy counted them quickly and shook his head.

"Thirty more," he said. "Budge and me both worked thirty-five hours at eight. That's two-eighty apiece."

"I don't pay for beer breaks," Pete said.

"Where'd you get all that money?" Budge said, awed. From where I stood it looked like the compact ex-sailor had a couple of thousand dollars in his hand.

"I'm moving up in the world," he said. "Too bad you won't be going with me."

"Don't be mad, Pete," Budge pleaded. "We just want our money. There's nothing wrong with that, is there? We got bills to pay, too."

"Here's your money, you big corked-up bastard," Pete said viciously, handing Budge some bills. "It's the last you'll get from me. You like talking to people so much, you can find your own work from here on out. The both of you are off my crew."

"Don't be calling me names, man," Budge said, thrusting out his big chest. "Um not gonna be a bastard, now." His macho football player self had overcome his economic fear.

"I don't give a shit what you are," Pete said. "I'm through with you. I'm moving out of this dump on the fifteenth. You sink or swim on your own."

"Where you moving?" Budge said, surprised.

"That particular information ain't your business," Pete said. "But you better be looking for a new place, too."

"Why?" Budge asked.

"Take my word for it," Pete said, maliciously. "You're all going to be in the street." He looked at me. "That includes you and your smart-ass side-kick."

"How do you know?" I said.

He sneered. "I got my sources. You aren't the only smart guy around here."

"You pay this month's rent?" Candyman demanded.

"I'll give the bitch the money tomorrow."

"You better."

Pete stalked out of the living room into the kitchen. A moment later the back door slammed, stirring the rats in the cupboards.

"He's full of shit," Candyman said, counting his fifties again. "He don't know what's gonna happen. He ain't nuthin' but a bum like the rest of us."

"Yeah," Budge said, still stung by the "bastard" remark. "He's always riding us to keep the place shipshape but he's the biggest slob in the house. He don't even flush the toilet after he goes. I went in the head the other day after he came out and there was a turd as long as your arm floatin' in the can."

"You don't think he knows what he's talkin' 'bout, do you, Rob?" Candyman said.

"I guess we'll find out."

Upstairs, I took a quick shower and put on clean clothes: gray slacks, a long-sleeve white pima-cotton dress shirt, black leather walking shoes that were comfortable but looked dressy, and my black leather jacket. The meeting with Evermore was critical. Time was running out. The lawyer would be bringing the diamonds back from the desert in a little more than twenty-four hours and our base of operations seemed to be getting shaky. I didn't know exactly what to make of Pete's mysterious malevolence and threatening prediction about the house, but they added to my sense of urgency.

I glanced in Reggie's room on my way back downstairs but there was no sign of him. The living room was empty too. Budge and Candyman were either on their way to the liquor store or just now sitting down on a couple of stools at Mulligan's on the boardwalk. By the time an hour went by, all their problems would be dissolved in the solvent of ethyl alcohol.

They would roar with laughter and nuzzle whatever warm female flesh was next to them. Tomorrow morning, their problems would be back with an extra set of horns, but tonight they would be blissful as two of Kerouac's beatnik Buddhas, huffing a joint in the alley behind the bar with blurry companions, rejoicing in selfless oblivion.

I didn't have that luxury.

Traffic on Pacific Avenue was lighter than it had been the night before, when Reggie and I had walked to the ashram, but there were still plenty of merrymakers going to and fro in the blended light of neon and stars. I covered the dozen blocks to Evelyn Evermore's house at a rapid pace, arriving right at six-thirty.

The front of her two-story bungalow was in good shape from what I could see in the light from the streetlamp and her porch light. The yellow shiplap siding looked sound. The steps and veranda, railed with a white balustrade, didn't sag or creak.

Evermore opened the door the instant I knocked, as if she had been waiting inside with her hand on the knob. She was wearing the red satin outfit she had worn on Friday night, which jarred me a little bit. There was a fruity tang of alcohol on her breath when she spoke.

"Right on time," she said with a glowing smile. "I like that."

Behind her I could see an entry hall and living room with dark-stained oak flooring, both empty. Her new home was unfurnished.

"I hate to be late," I said. "It makes me feel incompetent."

"Oh, no," she said, stepping out onto the porch. "You strike me as very competent. The timing isn't actually so great, though. I wasn't thinking when we spoke earlier, but most of the work is on the outside. I don't know if you will be able to see enough in the dark to give me a bid."

"Let's take a look. If I have to come back in the daytime, that's not a problem."

"Are you sure? It wasn't very good thinking on my part."

"I'm sure." I couldn't be certain that I would find out everything that evening I needed to know for the robbery and I liked having the option of a return visit the next day open up like a photo album in front of me. "What needs to be done?"

She walked me around the house, using a small silver flashlight to point out several areas where bushes had grown against the house, holding moisture and rotting some of the siding. I leaned on the wall at the third place she showed me, feeling it flex inward.

"Part of the frame is bad, too," I said.

"Is that a big job?"

"Depends on how much of the structure needs to be replaced. No way of telling for sure until the siding is removed."

In the back, we walked up onto a wooden deck that ran the width of the house and overlooked the Linnie Canal. It was surrounded by the remains of a balustrade like the one that enclosed the front veranda. Some of the balusters had rotted at the top and bottom and fallen out. Others were leaning. The whole structure was uneven and wobbly.

"This is probably the biggest job," she said. "What do you think it would cost to tear all this out and build a new deck and dock?"

"I'll have to see it in the daytime."

"I'm embarrassed to have anyone over the way it is now," she said. "But I think it will be a beautiful place to entertain when it's fixed up. I just love these old canals."

Strands of twinkle lights, stretched across neighboring docks and patios, reflected brightly in the black water. Canoes and paddleboats bobbed gently, and a mother duck with half a dozen yellow ducklings paddled past en route to some reeds where they would spend the night. A couple of houses down, a white wooden footbridge arched over the canal, adding to the storybook atmosphere.

"It is a beautiful spot," I said. "Is there anything else that needs to be done? Anything inside?" I was itching to root through a drawer or two while she got me a glass of water or used the bathroom.

"There are a few small jobs inside," she said. "But the main stuff is all outside. After the repairs, the house will need to be painted and it may need a new roof, too—one of your specialties. It's silly to try and look at that in the dark, though. I should have asked you come earlier, while it was still daylight."

"I don't mind coming back," I said again.

"I know," she said, softening her voice and standing close to me so that her breasts just touched my chest. "I just hate to waste your time. Could I possibly make it up to you by taking you out to dinner? If you're not busy, I mean. I'm sick of ashram food. I would really love a good piece of fish."

I wondered if this was what she had in mind all along. Not that I cared. Taking her out to dinner, having a chance to talk, was perfect for me.

"I'd love to go to dinner," I said. "But you'll have to drive. I walked over from where I'm staying at the beach, so I don't have my car."

"That's no problem," she said, putting her hand on my upper arm and giving it a squeeze. "We can take mine."

The back door was locked, so we walked around to the front. She went in to get her keys and a wrap, while I stepped back and looked at the house from the curb. Sometimes I wished I still was in the remodeling business. I missed the pleasures of carpentry and concrete work, of analyzing and repairing structures so that they were better-looking and stronger than they had been to begin with.

Evermore's white Lincoln was parked on the street, two houses down.

"Do you mind driving?" she said as we walked to the car.

"Not at all." Taking the keys from her manicured hand, I unlocked the passenger door and held it open while she got in, then walked around and slid in beneath the oversize wheel, taking the spot Jimmy Z had occupied two days before on the journey to Indian Wells. The bench seat was light-blue leather, soft and smooth and well conditioned. When I turned the key, the electronic dash display lit up like a video game and the Bose stereo popped on, playing saxophone jazz full of tender emotion. The intimate air was scented with Evelyn's lilac perfume.

Lincolns don't drive worth a shit, but they are nice inside.

CHAPTER **TWENTY-NINE**

She wanted to go to the Chart House in Malibu. I swung over to Pacific Avenue and followed it a mile north to where it changed names, becoming Nelson Way and then Ocean Boulevard. A block south of Colorado Avenue, we swooped down onto the Coast Highway, passing beneath the antique structure of the Santa Monica Pier with a light stream of Beemers, Mercedeses, and middle-aged rich guys on Harleys returning to their straitjacketed lives after a weekend of desperate play in the Southern California sun.

Past the little ghetto of multimillion-dollar shacks that sits on the sand below Palisades Park, the world opened up to our left. Beyond its white fringe, the black ocean stretched in a long shallow arc to lace the beaches of Oahu and Japan. To our right, ragged bluffs rose up against the starry sky, hugging the road as it unspooled along the curve of the coast.

At the seaside restaurant an aging valet crept away in the Lincoln while

I escorted Evelyn inside with my right hand in the silky small of her back. The maître d' addressed her by name with a warm smile and a half bow. We were promptly escorted to a window table with a white cloth and candle. Just beyond the plate glass, ten feet below us, the nighttime surf, always exciting, crashed against a boulder breakwater. Farther out, but still within range of the restaurant's spotlights, smaller rocks were bobbing and diving like seals in the heaving water.

"Where are you staying at the beach?" Evelyn asked after the waiter brought her a beaded glass of chardonnay.

"With friends," I said, briefly. I was drinking O'Doul's. "How long have you lived in Venice?"

"I bought the house in November," she said, and took a pretty good slug of the wine.

"What made you want to move there?"

She looked at me with her eyes liquid, deep, slightly blurred by alcohol. I wondered how much wine she'd had before I arrived at her house. "It's a long story," she said.

"We have all night."

She kept her shining eyes on mine for a few more seconds, then shook her head. "You don't want to hear about my problems."

"I'd be happy to listen," I said. "But I don't want to pry." She was either going to open up or she wasn't.

"I appreciate that." She placed her hand on mine. I wasn't sure if she meant my willingness to listen, my discretion, or both.

The food was ambrosial. We started with crisp Caesar salads and crusty bread. She had sautéed Dover sole. I had grilled swordfish. We split a delectable side dish of creamed spinach with baked crumbs on top. She had two more glasses of chardonnay, amber and sparkling in the candlelight.

"I know it's just a chain restaurant," she said as we were finishing, "but I love this spot." She was looking out the window, through our shared reflection, at the waves breaking on the beach beyond the boulders. Two sea lions had swum in and flopped on the sand. "The ocean is so wild and beautiful here."

"It's a great restaurant," I said conversationally. "That was the best meal I've had in weeks."

She didn't look at me when I spoke, continuing to gaze out the window.

"My daughter was conceived on that beach down there where the sea lions are," she said quietly, more as if reminding herself than informing me. When I didn't say anything, she looked over at me. "It was the most beautiful day of my life. There was nothing out here then, just the sea and sky. We spread our blanket where the rocks sheltered us from the road and made love naked in the sun. His family was one of the biggest landowners in the Central Valley, and my grandfather Phelan was mayor of San Francisco at the turn of the century and a United States senator after that, and there we were, screwing like two peasants on the seashore." She laughed, a bit drunkenly. "I hope I'm not embarrassing you."

"Not at all," I said. "When was that? When was your daughter conceived?"

"It was Indian summer," she said, getting dreamy again. "September 1960. We were married that June, after Terry graduated from Stanford. I had just finished my freshman year. We had a huge wedding at Grace Cathedral. It was the talk of the town. We went right around the world on our honeymoon. We spent two weeks in Hawaii at the Royal Hawaiian on Waikiki. Went to Japan and India and Iran and Egypt. Spent two weeks in Paris and two weeks in London. We were presented at court to Queen Elizabeth.

"That spring, when I was a schoolgirl at Stanford, I would have died before having sex outdoors in a public place. But by the time we got back from that trip, I was a different person." She paused for a moment, remembering, then went on: "That's when I first got interested in yoga. In India, on our honeymoon. We went up to the headwaters of the Ganges, where the famous ashrams are. Everyone said the atmosphere was so pure up there you could hear *om* in the air all the time, and you could!

"Everything about life seemed exciting and magical then. Christina was born the following June, on our first wedding anniversary. That was a miracle to me. I was happier than I had ever been before. Holding her when she was a little baby was like being in heaven. And I loved Terrence so much. He made me feel like the luckiest woman in the world."

"Sounds like a wonderful life."

She had been smiling wistfully, drifting in a drinker's nostalgic haze, but her face changed when I spoke, turning grim. "It didn't last," she said. "I caught him with a typist from his office that Christmas. It was downhill from there. We still had some good times and I hung on to hope as long as I could. But he wouldn't stop. I finally divorced him . . . too late. Because of him, I lost my daughter . . . my Christina."

"What happened to her?"

"She disappeared."

"When?"

She shook her head. "Let's get out of here. If you are really interested, I'll tell you about it, but not here. Take me home."

She reached for her purse when the waiter brought the check, but I took the leather folder from his hand and paid in cash, then led her out of the restaurant into the cool California night. She was wobbly from all the wine. The looks that I got from the maître d' and valets ranged from sly to sympathetic to suspicious.

She was so quiet on the drive back to her house that I was afraid she had passed out. But when I looked over I saw that her eyes were open, staring out at the ocean. When I helped her from the car, she leaned her breasts against me and breathed alcohol fumes in my face. Inside, she dropped her wrap on the floor by the door.

"I'm sorry the place is so bare," she said, gesturing at the empty living room through an archway to our left. "I rented out my house in Bel Air furnished, and I haven't gotten around to buying new stuff for this place."

When I prompted her, she resumed her story, first in the kitchen, where she got a bottle of wine and two glasses, then upstairs in her bedroom. It was the usual. After the first affair, her dream of an ideal life was shattered, but there was still a lot to hang on to. Terrence worked his way up rapidly in the Prudential Insurance Company, where he had family and fraternity connections, becoming a vice president in his early thirties. They moved into a series of steadily larger houses, drove ever more expensive cars, and went on elaborate vacations. There were apologies and promises and special gifts each time she discovered a new affair.

She spent her time swimming, golfing, playing tennis, and attending country club dinners and charity dances, consoling herself with increasing amounts of alcohol as the privileged years played out. She doted on her daughter, with whom she rode in Golden Gate Park and at her in-laws' sprawling ranch.

The ranch, in the picturesque territory above Visalia, sloped down from forested Sierra foothills to cover a vast swath of the flat valley floor. There were extensive orchards, square mile after square mile of field crops, herds of cattle, and horses.

"It was Christina's favorite place when she was a little girl," Evelyn told me, sitting on the edge of her bed. "She loved to ride her horse and work in the farmyard. She fed the chickens and ducks and helped with the dairy cattle. She won every award you can think of for her riding. Her grandfather called her the best little cowgirl in the West."

It was a queen-size bed covered with a white chenille spread. The only other furniture in the echoing room was the armchair where I was sitting, a nightstand, and a small maple desk with matching spindle-back chair. The desk was piled with disordered papers, and there were open moving boxes full of books and clothes in a far corner. The windows that flanked the bed's white wooden headboard overlooked the black canal.

"She and I used to spend a month at the ranch each summer," Evermore said. "In the winter we would go to plays and movies and recitals. She was a wonderful little ballet dancer and swimmer. We were closer than any other mother and daughter in our circle. The other mothers were all jealous of our relationship."

Things changed when Christina was eleven. She lost interest in her activities and grew distant from Evelyn. Her grades faltered and she started getting in trouble at school. But the problems ebbed and flowed. After an unpleasant scene, the girl would calm down and revert to her sweet, quiet self. Evelyn would take her to a matinee and then to the Top of the Mark for a late lunch, where the daughter would drink Shirley Temples while she consumed Manhattans, applauding the piano player more loudly as afternoon wore into evening and lights blinked on in the neighborhoods spread out below them.

The more wine Evermore drank, the more freely she talked and the more emotional she became, pouring out her heart to a stranger the way drunks have since some cat in a loincloth first sampled spoiled grape juice and made a sour face, then a happy one. People usually try to get away from loquacious drunks, but I was acutely interested in what she had to say.

The family tragedy surfaced in December 1975 when Evelyn came home early from a trip to Paris with her older sister and found Terrence and Christina asleep together, naked, in her and Terrence's bed. Terrence swore it was the first time. He begged and pleaded and rationalized and promised that it would never happen again, that there would be no more affairs, that he would get counseling. Evelyn, befuddled by alcoholism, dreading scandal, struggled to believe him. That Christmas he gave her the pink diamond necklace to seal the deal.

It had been created at Tiffany and Company in New York in the 1930s as a gift for the actress Marion Burns from her director Raoul Walsh and was made of color-coordinated stones, starting out deep rose at the bottom of the pendant, shifting to light pink at the top. Evelyn had cherished and despised it, telling herself that it was a token of renewed affection and faithfulness, showing it off to her envious friends, all the while knowing that it was a bribe to buy her silence about her husband's crime.

Terrence behaved himself during the bright, bracing month of January, but in February Evelyn discovered that Christina was pregnant, and that the incest had been going on intermittently for several years, whenever Terrence was driven by his demon and the opportunity arose. She left her husband then, taking Christina and moving into the Fairmont Hotel, on Nob Hill, across the park from the cathedral where she was married.

That spring, after several months of tears, fights, threats, denials, detectives, and escalating family drama, she fled San Francisco to get away from Terrence and his influence, moving into her sister's home in Bel Air while divorce proceedings went forward.

Christina's child was born at Cedars-Sinai in July 1976, a bicentennial baby. A few months later, before the divorce was final, Terrence drowned at the Monterey marina after drinking a bottle of scotch and falling off his yacht in the middle of the night. Evelyn inherited their Pacific Heights mansion and a multimillion-dollar portfolio of stocks and bonds. There was also a million-dollar life insurance policy that Prudential paid off on without a murmur.

Evelyn bought a house in Bel Air near her sister and tried to start over. She enrolled Christina as an eighth-grader at Sea Winds Middle School, where the girl promptly hooked up with a dark-clothed, drug-using crowd. She dyed her blond hair black, played hooky, and got in trouble with the police for vandalism and underage drinking. The following April, during spring break, she wanted to go to Mexico with her friends. When Evelyn refused, backed up by her sister, whom she called on for advice, Christina took her nine-month-old baby and ran away.

"That was the last time I saw her or little Kelly."

"Her baby?"

"Yes."

"Where did they go?"

"She went to Mexico with those kids, then to a commune in the San Bernardino Mountains with a man she met in Oaxaca. I hired a detective and he traced her to the commune. But by the time he found it, she was gone."

The loss of her daughter sent Evelyn tumbling down a steep staircase of drunkenness and promiscuity. After her family intervened and had her hospitalized, she got sober and began the life she had lived ever since — of upper-class sports, charity work, and Eastern spirituality. She had kept a series of detectives on the case through all the years since Christina's disappearance, spending large sums to follow up leads in San Francisco, Santa Fe, Las Vegas, Mexico City, Miami, and many other cities. When Baba contacted her out of the blue the previous summer and told her that he had word of her daughter, his call had sent a thrill through her because the last message she had ever had from Christina was a postcard years before asking for five thousand dollars to be sent to her, general delivery, at the Venice Beach Post Office.

CHAPTER THIRTY

When Evermore went to see Baba Raba at the Murshid Center for Enlightened Beings, he told her that he had met someone who knew her daughter. He said Christina had been living in Venice earlier that year and that the man who knew her didn't want to come forward because he was a drug dealer who had sold Christina marijuana and cocaine. Baba told Evermore that the dealer would track Christina down if she would give him ten thousand dollars to pay off a pressing debt. During their first conversation, the guru mentioned several things about Christina's past that he said the dealer had told him. The accurate personal details made Evelyn believe the offer might be legitimate. She wanted to get a private detective involved, but Baba said that would spook the dealer, so she left the matter in his hands, along with a cashier's check for ten grand.

Through the late summer and early fall, a pattern had developed. Each time it seemed that they were on the verge of making contact with

Christina, there would be some hitch that required another chunk of cash to smooth over. The amounts had increased to $15,000 and then $25,000. Under the stress of anticipation and repeated disappointment, Evermore began to drink again, which made it easier for Baba to manipulate her. Each time she got upset about the delays, Baba doled out a few more intimate facts about Christina that could only have come from her or someone who knew her well. He was aware of the incest and told Evermore things about Christina's relationship with her father that even she didn't know but which nevertheless rang true.

In early January, he had asked about the necklace. She wasn't sure how he found out about it, but when she revealed the circumstances in which she had received the diamonds, he told her that she must get rid of them if she wanted her daughter back.

"He said a lot of stuff about crystals, how they focus and magnify psychic energy," Evermore told me. "It didn't make sense to me at first, but after I did some research, I understood what he was talking about. Crystals are very powerful and mysterious. They really are. That is how early radios worked, you know, with crystals that sent energy waves through space."

Baba told her that the diamonds were contaminated with negative energy because she had taken them in exchange for her daughter's innocence, and that the crystals were broadcasting a kind of force field that was keeping the girl away. That was why all their plans had fallen through and all the money gone to waste. He said that the best thing would be to give the necklace to him so that he could sell it and use the money in a worthy cause. That would destroy the force field and allow Christina to return.

"I know it sounds crazy," Evermore said, "but I told him he could have the necklace after I wore it to this big charity bash we have out in the desert every winter."

"How much is the necklace worth?" I asked her.

"I don't know, exactly. It was valued at a quarter of a million the last time it was appraised for the insurance rider, but a jeweler who cleaned it several years ago told me it was worth twice that."

"That's quite a gift to give someone you've only known six months."

"My sister would kill me if she found out."

"I can see her point," I said. "Has it ever occurred to you that Baba is conning you?"

"Of course it has!" Evelyn said sharply, with a flash of alcoholic anger. "I wonder about it almost every day. But I have to believe him. If he is lying it means I will never get her back. I couldn't live with that now, not after coming so close. And he must be telling the truth. How else could he know all those things about her? He knew the name of her horse and the kinds of trees that grew along the trails we rode on at the ranch. He knew which suite we stayed in that winter at the Fairmont and the names of the kids she ran away with. He even gave me a picture of her and little Kelly that he got from one of those people. I'll show you."

Half leaning, half falling sideways, propping herself up on her elbow, she opened the nightstand drawer and took out a snapshot. It was a photo of the girl whose pictures I had seen in the jewelry box at the Oasis Palms. The girl was holding a baby dressed in pink footsie pajamas and smiling toothlessly at the camera.

"Baba's psychic powers could explain some of what he knows about Christina, but not this picture. I took it myself the Christmas before she ran away." Evelyn paused, looking down at the creased photograph. "Those pajama's were Christina's when she was little. She dressed the baby in them for the picture. We had a wonderful time that day. Everyone was happy. Look at the way little Kelly is smiling! Christina kept the picture in a frame on her dresser, and she took it with her when she ran away. It could only have come to Baba through someone who knows my daughter."

"What kind of psychic powers does he have?" I asked, still worried about him rummaging around in my neurons.

"They're called *siddhis* in yoga," Evermore said. "He can tell what you are thinking sometimes, and he knows about things that are going to happen ahead of time. He sent a kind of a bodyguard to the desert with me because he sensed danger. I told him it was silly, but he insisted, and it turned out he was right. Someone broke into my hotel room and tried to steal the necklace. They would have gotten away with it, too, if the guard hadn't gone back to my room."

"Why did he go back?"

"When we were on our way to dinner, he asked me if I had put the necklace in the room safe. When I told him no, he got angry and turned around and went back to the hotel. That's when he caught the burglar in the room and got beat up. He is still in the hospital out there."

"Where were you when he went back up?"

"In my car in front of the hotel, why?"

"It's just lucky you didn't go up, too," I said. "You could have been hurt."

If she was in her car in front, Jimmy must have gone in through the lobby as I suspected and slipped past my partner.

"Were you able to wear the necklace at your charity event?" I asked.

"No. I was too upset to go. The Indian Wells police have it now. My lawyer is driving out to get it tomorrow afternoon so Baba can have it appraised on Tuesday."

"Why is he having it appraised?"

"So he can use it as equity in a real estate deal. He and Councilman Discenza are planning to build a resort down at the beach. That is his worthy cause. He says he is going to use the money he makes on the deal to fund yoga centers all over the world."

"Who is your lawyer?" I asked casually.

"Armand Hildebrand."

"Where's his office?"

"In Santa Monica," she said, looking befuddled. "Why are you asking all these questions?"

"I need to find a good lawyer up here to help me set up a limited liability partnership," I said. "Does Hildebrand handle that kind of work?"

"I'm not sure. Probably."

"Where does Baba have to take the necklace to get it appraised?"

"I don't know and I don't care," she said, suddenly weary, retreating into the arms of intoxication. She had been talking lucidly for someone with at least two bottles of wine in her, the way drunk people often do when booze dissolves mental barriers and lubricates the hesitant tongue. But the emotional pressure driving her confession had run down when I steered the conversation to business details. She finished her chardonnay, set the glass on the floor, and looked at me, blinking slowly. "I don't care about the jewels or the money. I have more money than I can ever spend. I just want my daughter back. I'm lonely, Robert. I need someone to love, someone to love me."

We were looking into each other's eyes and the look became intense and expansive, with that feeling of falling into the other person's irises.

"Could you love me?" She mouthed the words silently.

I moved from the chair and sat beside her on the bed, putting my arm around her as she leaned heavily against me, turning her face to mine. I felt more compassion than lust as I kissed her the first time, a sense of sharing in her loss that was so like my own. But when she took my hand and placed it on her breast, a chakra well below my heart chakra began to whirl.

We merged in a second deep wine-flavored kiss while I felt her breasts, thumbing the nipples stiff through red satin. Rubbing against Mary at the beach had stirred me up. The latent sexual charge that had gathered while we walked and touched and talked about tantra surged back to the forefront now, urging me toward Evelyn.

Besides being amorous, I was angry at Mary for not giving in to me. She had known that she was driving me wild and had played hard to get, in part because of the globular guru, in part for other reasons of her own. Now I had a lovely woman in my arms, another of Baba's victims, who wanted to give me the gift that Mary had withheld and I was tempted to take her not just for the physical pleasure but as a form of revenge.

When Evelyn reached for my genitals, though, I pulled away. She was too drunk. She wanted sex now, but when she woke up tomorrow she might feel degraded. I didn't want that. Also, surprisingly, despite my resentment toward Mary, I couldn't bring myself to betray the connection I felt between us.

I lifted Evelyn's hand and kissed it, then kissed her lips again, lightly, and stood up.

"You've had a lot to drink," I said. "I don't want you to do anything you'll regret."

"Please," she begged. "I know what I'm doing. I don't want to be alone tonight."

In her pleading face I saw early signs of the decay that would overtake her if she kept drinking. Another year or two on the polish would transform her from a svelte middle-aged siren to a flabby old woman. And it was Baba who was driving her to drink.

"I'll stay until you go to sleep."

"Will you lie down with me and hold me?"

"Yes. I'll wait in the hall while you get ready for bed."

"Don't bother. I can sleep in what I have on. I'm too tired—too drunk—to change. I just need to use the restroom."

She walked unsteadily into the adjoining bathroom and closed the door. After a few minutes I heard water running. A little while later the toilet flushed. She came back out with her hair brushed and her lilac perfume reinforced. I peeled the bedspread and top sheet back so that she could lie down, then sat on the edge of the bed to take off my shoes.

"Thank you for being so nice," she said, placing her hand flat against my back, with her fingers spread.

That stung.

I lay down beside her, still dressed in gray slacks and white dress shirt, and put my arms around her. She laid her head on my chest and snuggled against me. I was glad she had given the necklace to the guru, because I didn't think I could have stolen it from her after hearing her story.

When she started to snore softly, I slipped out of bed and put my shoes and jacket on and searched her desk. The seashell jewelry box was in the top-right drawer, along with her wallet and checkbook. Her bank, where the necklace would be dropped off on Tuesday morning, was the B of A on Wilshire in Santa Monica.

In the jumble of papers on top of the desk, I found one of her lawyer's cards paper-clipped to a note she had written him about the lease on her Bel Air property. Her handwriting was as elegant as her hands, expressing a private-school education in the 1950s.

I wrote the address of the Bel Air mansion on the back of the embossed card, stuck it in my pocket, and headed for the exit, passing through bare room after bare room, leaving Evelyn all alone in her empty house.

Outside, the brisk sea air revived me. Walking back to the flop through quiet streets, I tried to bring Baba and the situation into clearer focus. I had found out a lot about him, but he was still surrounded by a dangerous mystery. I now knew how he had convinced Evelyn to give him the necklace and when and where he was supposed to take possession of it. That seemed to give me the upper hand. But the wild card of psychic powers was still in the deck.

Anyone who doesn't believe in some type of ESP isn't paying attention. Even if they are unaware of it, everyone has had premonitions, not necessarily clear or of cosmic significance, but to some degree accurate. I'd had many such glimpses. The ability to see around existential corners was as much a part of my stock-in-trade as a cheerful smile and a loaded gun. Sometimes that meant carefully thinking through the likely stages of a scenario, action and reaction seen several steps ahead, as in chess or politics. Other times, though, it was a flash of insight, a visual or emotional sense that there was danger behind a locked door or something well worth risking danger for in a darkened building.

And I knew from my study of yoga years before that spiritual masters often have a second sight far more penetrating than my blurry guesses, the ability to perceive both past and future and to divine people's inner thoughts and intentions. That's what worried me about Baba.

The con job he was running on Evelyn made his spiritual stature doubtful. No true guru would exploit a mother's grief for personal gain. But it was possible he had developed *siddhis* through sincere spiritual striving and then succumbed to the temptations that came with them.

According to the ancient texts, exceptional spiritual development instills tremendous charisma. Baba's stroll along the boardwalk the previous evening showed how people flock to the spiritually electric, ready to surrender themselves body, mind, and soul. Gaining complete power over people sometimes revives a guru's lower self, presenting one of the last and most insidious challenges on the path to enlightenment. Those destined to merge with God resist the temptation and use their powers selflessly for the good of humanity. Others succumb and begin to gratify the ego's hunger, exploiting disciples for sex or money or influence behind a cloak of rationalizations.

Baba was hard to figure. The only thing I knew for sure as I felt the loose boards of the flophouse steps beneath my feet was that a battle with him was coming. We were both reaching for the same prize piece of merchandise, and one of us was going to get his fingers broken.

CHAPTER THIRTY-ONE

Up early on Monday, I met Chavi in the hall as I headed downstairs. She was on her barefoot way back to Reggie's room after using the bathroom. Her face was glowing and I knew that Reggie wouldn't have to worry about doing his own laundry for the next week or so and that he would probably be coming in for a new shirt or pair of pants.

Chavi smiled when she saw me.

"Who is the lucky lady?" she said.

"What do you mean?"

She held my chin and turned my head, her eyes roving over my face.

"You look like someone who is falling in love."

"You're good," I said. "What do you and Reggie have planned today?"

"I'll be at my booth," Chavi said. "We both know what Reggie will be doing." She shrugged, smiled good luck with the girl, goodbye, and see you later, then went on down the hall.

The Santa Anas had blown again during the night, whisking away the smut of expended sighs and sad memories, leaving the seaside world sparkling. It was still windy, palm trees thrashing. The front door of the abandoned house next door had blown open. I stepped into the littered living room and called Ozone Pacific's name. I wanted to ask him something. When he didn't answer, I went down the hall to the room where he camped out, following an orange extension cord that Budge had run over from the flophouse and spliced to an old mechanic's drop light that he hung from the ceiling. The light operated with a pull string and held a forty-watt bulb, bright enough for Oz to see what he was doing after dark.

His sleeping bag was empty. Already out panhandling. The lining of the child-size bag was decorated with cactuses, bucking broncos, and cowboys with whirling lariats. His conglomeration of homeless-person junk—magazines, a few old books, some canned goods, and a gallon container of water—was piled in a corner. Looking at his living quarters, I wondered again how he had ended up this way. He had been an infant once, held in someone's loving arms. There had been people who cherished him and dreamed of a different future for him than the one he had found. Or maybe not. Maybe he had been born unlucky to someone who didn't want a child or who lacked the emotional or financial resources to raise one.

A short walk down Pacific Avenue, lively with people plunging into the workweek after the fantasy of the weekend, took me to the lot where the Seville had been parked since our return from Indian Wells.

Mr. Parker had a young black guy in a double-breasted beige suit cornered by his shack.

"Parking lot 'tendant," he said to the young man, scanning his face for any sign of amusement. "Mr. Parker. Get it?"

"Oh, yeah, that's funny," said the guy, who looked like the manager of a men's boutique or a small hotel. "I'll see you this evening, then."

"Some people got no sense of humor," Mr. Parker said as I walked up.

"Nice car, though," I said, nodding at the gleaming black Maxima pulled up in front of the shack.

"Yes, sir!" Mr. Parker said, forgetting his disappointment at the man's failure to appreciate his perennial joke. "She's slick all right. Not as slick as your Caddie, though. You need your keys?"

"Yes, please."

"Nice day for a drive," he said when he came back out of the shack.

"This wind dies down in a little while it'll be another bee-*you*-tee-ful day at our beach."

"Sure will," I said. "Have you seen that kid Oz this morning?"

"Not this mornin'. That young man don't come this far over. I only see him afternoons when I eat lunch, or evenings after I close the lot."

"What do you mean he doesn't come over this far?"

"Don't you know 'bout him?"

"No."

"He don't come this side of Pacific or go beyond Ozone, up yonder. That's how he got his name, you know? Ozone Pacific? He stay right on the beach."

"Why?"

If Mr. Parker was right, Ozone was confined to a strip of real estate no more than a quarter-mile wide and at most two miles long, if he ranged all the way south to the Marina del Rey channel, where Venice Beach ended.

"Guess he juss like it down there."

"How long has he been there?"

"Ain't sure, Mr. Rivers. I don't like to pry too much 'bout a man's bidnis. He was hanging 'round down by that palm tree of his when I opened my lot eight years ago."

"He hasn't crossed Pacific Avenue in eight years?"

"Not that I heard of."

I wheeled the Caddie out onto Horizon, jogged through the neighborhood to Lincoln, then took Lincoln north to Wilshire. When I thought of Ozone trapped in his tiny world I felt pity as sharp as panic and turned my mind away from his strange plight, focusing on the present moment, a remedy for mental and emotional distress recommended by spiritual teachers in all traditions.

I was on my way to an exciting meeting. It *was* a beautiful morning, if a little windy, and I was driving a new Cadillac. With its smooth leather, silky ride, and rocket-ship power, the Seville made every trip a pleasure, and I relaxed into the sensation of piloting the car along Wilshire through Brentwood and Westwood, past sidewalks crowded with UCLA coeds, serious and sexy, to the ultimate name-brand city of Beverly Hills. A bronze Bentley pulled away from the curb on Crescent Drive just as I turned off Wilshire, and I slid into the convenient spot. Most of the stores along Beverly and Rodeo wouldn't open for another hour or two, but I knew Fahim would be in his shop.

When I rapped on the glass door at the corner of Beverly and Brighton, he looked up from a catalogue and came around from behind the glass case to let me in.

"Sabaah al-kheir," he said. *The morning is good.*

"Sabaah an-noor," I replied as he had taught me. *The morning is light.*

He was a Lebanese immigrant jeweler in his fifties with whom I had been doing business for several years. Medium height and build, short gray hair, gray goatee and rimless glasses.

"What can I do for you, Robert, my friend?" he asked, his gray eyes sparkling.

"Let's go in the back."

When he saw the pink diamond earrings his face shone.

"You always bring quality, Robert," he said, inclining his handsome head. Dressed impeccably in Brooks Brothers threads, possessed of the excellent manners typical of Middle Easterners educated in Europe, he was a pleasure to do business with. He had plenty of legitimate customers, but he took special pleasure in illicit deals, partly because of the Bedouin currents deep in his blood, partly because those deals were the most profitable.

Fahim examined the diamonds lovingly, using a loupe, a microscope, and some kind of scanner to make sure their rare rose color had not been enhanced by radiation or heat. After his technology had backed up his jeweler's eye and intuition, we haggled for a few minutes for form's sake, arriving at the price he had in mind all along. He paid me in cash, six bank-banded packets of crisp hundreds, a neat and generous 30 percent of the likely retail value of the two stones. I wasn't sure what he did with the jewels he fenced but suspected that he sold them overseas through family connections, eliminating the chance of any blowback from the local cops.

At the door, he laid his neatly manicured hand on my shoulder. "Go in safety, Robert," he said in his formal way. "Return soon."

"Back at you, bro," I said, getting him to grin.

I cruised toward the ocean on Wilshire, cutting over to Santa Monica Boulevard at Twentieth Street and continuing west to the address on the card I had taken from Evelyn's desk. Her lawyer was ensconced in a small 1950s-vintage office building. It was three stories, with a handsome limestone-and-glass veneer. Two flourishing date palms at the corners added a tropical touch.

I parked down the street and walked back along the alley behind the building. There were steel bars over the ground-floor windows and a metal fire escape with the first set of steps retracted. Around front, I walked in the entrance and looked at the directory in the unattended lobby. The offices of Hildebrand & Hildebrand took up the entire third floor. Apparently the nepotistic bastard had taken his son into business with him.

Access to the third floor was by a tiny four-person elevator and a set of service stairs. The building's front and back doors were both alarmed. The lawyer's office door would be, too. It would be tricky ghosting through multiple alarm systems without disturbing the doughnut eaters but we could probably do it. Jail time for breaking and entering an unoccupied building is much less than for armed robbery, and in a burglary you don't have to worry about hero complexes and heart patients.

Back in the alley, I took another look at the fire escape. If we pulled the retracted steps down, it would get us to the third floor. From there, we could climb onto the roof, using the short steel ladder that was bolted to the wall to give maintenance workers access to the top of the building.

I liked it. Going through the roof, we would avoid the alarm systems. There might be a vent opening large enough to squeeze through once the cover was pried off. If not, I could use a cordless reciprocating saw to enlarge a smaller opening.

Buildings like this one weren't constructed with security in mind. The roof was nothing but tar and plywood atop two-by-eight or two-by-ten joists with lath and plaster underneath. The saw would be noisy for twenty or thirty seconds, but it was a commercial district. There wouldn't be anybody around at 2 a.m. We could find a place to watch from, wait till the cops did their midnight drive-by, then drop down into the lawyer's office with a pack of safecracking tools.

If the safe stymied us, we could put on masks and jump the lawyer when he showed up the next morning. Heroically self-sacrificing attorneys are as rare as virgins in Vegas, and I didn't think it would take too many light taps on the forehead with a pry bar to convince Hildebrand, junior or senior, to cough up the combination. Once we had the diamonds, we could tie up the lawyer, his security guard, and any of the office staff who came in early, then take the elevator down to the lobby. If we brought our tools into the building in a couple of sturdy shoulder bags, we could carry them out the front door without attracting attention. All we needed was a place to park the car that wasn't too far away and wouldn't attract the attention of the police.

Well-dressed pedestrians passed in both directions on the sidewalk in front of the building. The boulevard was busy with cabs, passenger cars, and local delivery trucks. Looking up and down the street, I saw a Norm's one block west of the lawyer's building. Norm's restaurants, scattered across Los Angeles and Orange County, are all-night eateries that bustle until two or three o'clock in the morning. It was a gift.

I walked down to the diner-style eatery, got the morning paper from a machine, and went inside and sat down at a booth by the front window. Looking through the plate glass, I had a clear view of the lawyer's Eisenhower-era office building. When the uniformed waitress slouched over, I ordered a western omelet with rye toast and hash browns, feeling cozy and in control.

There was an article in the paper about the fire on Pacific Avenue that we had seen on Saturday night. Three structures had been badly damaged and would have to be demolished. The fire chief was quoted as saying that the buildings had been unoccupied and dilapidated and that tearing them down would help clear the way for new development. The cause of the fire was unknown — to the authorities, at least.

CHAPTER THIRTY-TWO

I took Santa Monica west to Ocean Boulevard and turned south, driving along the edge of Palisades Park above the Pacific. The choppy blue water was frosted with whitecaps, the blustery beach deserted. Turning left at Westminster, away from the water, I made my way to Mr. Parker's lot.

When I walked through the front door of the flophouse a few minutes later, Budge and Candyman were standing by the kitchen door with worried expressions, talking to a Asian man with a clipboard who glanced over at me as I came in.

"What's all that mean?" Candyman said with a touch of belligerence.

"All these violations have to be corrected or the house will be condemned," the man said patiently. He wore thick glasses with heavy black frames. His blue suit looked like it had come off the rack at Sears.

"How long we got to fix 'em?" Budge asked in a frightened voice.

"Fourteen days."

"Fourteen days!" Candyman said. "How we s'posed to fix all that in just two weeks?"

"It will be very difficult," the city inspector said.

"What's going on?" I said. All three of them looked over at me.

"They're gonna condemn the house, Rob," Budge wailed.

"Are you a resident here?" the inspector asked me.

"I live upstairs."

He nodded. "Acting on a tip from a concerned citizen, I inspected the premises with these gentlemen's permission and found numerous serious violations of the housing code, starting with the plumbing and electrical systems and including the structural integrity of the building. There's also a serious health hazard from rodent infestation. If the violations aren't corrected within fourteen days, the city will move to condemn the property."

"Who was the concerned citizen?" I said.

"I don't know, sir, and even if I did know, I couldn't tell you."

"This have anything to do with the resort Councilman Discenza is building up the beach?" I asked.

The man's intelligent face seemed to close up and contract. "I don't know about that," he said. "I'm just doing my job."

"Where we s'posed to go if you condemn the joint?" Candyman asked angrily. "There ain't no place else 'round here we can afford to live."

"I hear you, man," the inspector said. "I hope you don't lose your home. But there is nothing I can do about it, one way or the other."

He tore a pink sheet off the form on his clipboard and held it out to the two stooges. They looked at it like it was radioactive.

"You best give that to Miz Sharpnick," Candyman said. "She the owner."

"She'll get a copy, too," the inspector said. "This copy is for the tenants."

Candyman and Budge kept their hands at their sides, as if they could hold the reality of impending homelessness at bay by refusing the form.

The inspector raised his eyebrows at me and I walked over and took the sheet. It was crammed with check-marked boxes and scrawled comments. By the looks of it, the house would have to be rebuilt from the foundation up and then have a new foundation put under it in order to fix all the violations.

I walked out onto the front porch with him.

"Would a thousand dollars do anything to bring us up to code?" I asked, showing him one of the packets of hundreds I got from Fahim.

He looked at the money like a dry alcoholic at a glass of Chivas Regal, rubbing the polyester lapel of his suit with the hand that wasn't holding the clipboard. But then he shook his head.

"It wouldn't do any good, man. They are waiting for this report at city hall. If I said the place was up to code, they would just send somebody else out here to write it up. And this is one time they would be right. They've taken some houses north of here that really weren't in bad condition, but this place isn't fit for human habitation — no offense to you."

"None taken," I said. "The place is a dump. What do they want the property for? I thought the resort ended a few blocks north of here."

"There's a phase two," he said, "but you didn't hear it from me. I have to get going now."

I wasn't actually going to give him the money. I only offered it to him to get a sense of where the corruption lay. It wouldn't be beyond some city inspectors to take advantage of an atmosphere of redevelopment and the specter of eminent domain to extort money from frightened property owners.

Having the house condemned would actually be convenient for me and Reggie. If we took the necklace that night or the next morning, I planned to leave town afterward. But a sudden departure might attract attention. The threat of condemnation would give us a perfect excuse if anyone ever tracked us down and asked us why we took off.

"How'd Pete know this was gonna happen?" Budge asked Candyman as I walked back through the living room.

"He's probably the sumbitch that sicced that tricky inspector on us," Candyman said. "Mo'fucker made it sound like if we let him in he'd make Sharpnick fix the place up for us, but he's really planning to put us in the street."

Upstairs, I found Reggie standing in front of the wavy mirror in his bedroom, struggling to drag a plastic comb through his brassy curls, and not having much luck. Chavi was gone, leaving a neatly made bed and straightened-up room behind her.

"Word from the front, bro," Reggie said, looking at me in the mirror.

"What?"

"Guess who I saw sneaky Pete talkin' to yesterday afternoon?"

"Who?"

"Bubba Rubba."

"The guru?"

"If that's what you want to call him."

"Where and when?"

"Half a mile north of here, where they were having that meetin' on the beach. 'Round five."

"Anybody else with them?"

"A wop with a thousand-dollar suit who you wouldn't want to meet in a dark alley."

"What were they doing?"

"When I spotted 'em, they were a ways down the boardwalk, watching people walk away from the meetin', like they wanted to see who was there. Then they went into a bar. I couldn't hear what they were saying."

"Baba went into a bar in his dhoti?"

"Nah—he was wearing street clothes."

I was surprised that Baba would appear with Discenza in public. Maybe he thought no one would recognize him in an Armani. Or maybe he didn't care. With the deal poised to go through, he might be ready to abandon the guru dodge and become an ordinary corrupt businessman. Pete meeting with the two of them fit like a puzzle piece.

"What are they up to?" Reggie asked.

"The Italian is a crooked city councilman named Discenza. He's trying to develop a resort on the beach. That's what the protest was about. I think Pete's been helping him put pressure on property owners, coercing them to sell out. He probably met Discenza while him and the other stooges were doing demolition work up there."

"How's Baby Huey fit in?"

"He's Discenza's partner."

"What's it mean for us?"

"The financing for the deal is supposed to close on Tuesday, and Baba needs the necklace as collateral for his share of the equity. The way commercial real estate deals work, a bank puts up most of the money—tens of millions in this case—but the bankers want the developers to carry risk, too. Makes them feel more secure that the developers really believe in the project. If we take the diamonds and Baba can't come up with his share, it might torpedo the deal. Hard to say exactly how much shit that would stir up with Discenza and his crowd, but there would definitely be some wild-eyed Italians in the vicinity."

"You been busy, bro. How'd you find all this shit out?"

I told him about the documents in the guru's bedroom and my conversation with Evelyn.

He made saucer eyes. "You mean you took her out to dinner?"

"Yeah."

"How'd you manage that?"

"I was playing contractor when I met her at the ashram yesterday morning and she asked me to come over to her house to take a look at some work she needs done."

"That place by the canal?"

"Yeah."

"Slick! You got her liquored up and pumped her dry. Did you bang her?"

"No."

"Why not?"

"She was too drunk."

"Aw, man—that's what you want with a snooty piece like that. Lower her inhibitions and all that pent-up wildness comes out. She'd of let you do all kind of shit to her."

"Maybe next time."

Reggie made a sour face, annoyed by my failure to sodomize the rich lady.

"When we gonna grab the rocks?" he said.

"Evelyn's lawyer is bringing the necklace back from the desert tonight. He's supposed to take it to his office in Santa Monica. If he does, we'll B and E the place later on. I looked it over. It's a good setup."

"Prep work?"

"We need to buy some tools and find out where he lives."

"Why we need to know that?"

"If it's late when he gets back from Indian Wells you got to figure there's a chance he'll go straight home and keep the jewels there overnight. If we can find it, we'll case his house this afternoon and then stake out both places this evening to see where he takes the diamonds. You can watch his house while I watch the office."

"Speakin' of sparklers, when we gonna cash in those earrings?" Reggie had an above-average ability to sense fluctuations in the underworld ether. He usually knew when money he had an interest in had changed hands.

"They're cashed," I said, reaching into my pocket and handing him three of the bank-banded packets of hundreds.

Reggie's bearded face took on an angelic look as he riffled the currency under his nose, breathing in the bracing scent of Treasury Department ink. Then he caught himself and scowled. He was delighted by the newly printed bills, but felt compelled to quarrel a little bit.

"This all you got for them?"

"That's your cut."

"So six grand's all you got?"

"Shut up," I said. "You're lucky to get that after letting that goon sneak by you at the hotel."

"Don't start that shit again," he said.

"I'm not starting it, bro. I'm finishing it. I talked to Evermore, remember? She told me. Jimmy went in the front."

Reggie was silent for a moment, his face blank. Then he shrugged and grinned, officially retiring the lie.

CHAPTER THIRTY-THREE

We found Mr. Parker napping at the lot, leaning back against his shack in an old kitchen chair, soaking up the morning sunshine. I woke him gently but he didn't take it like a Christian.

"Lot of in-and-out for a weekday," he muttered as he handed me the keys.

I drove to the library to see if the home phone and address of Armand Hildebrand, Sr., was listed in the Greater Los Angeles phone directory. Reggie stayed in the car. The antagonistic years he had spent in the public school system before punching out his junior high school principal and walking out the front door of academia for good halfway through eighth grade had made him allergic to learning environments. He avoided bookish places the way most people avoid dentists' offices.

Hildebrand was listed, which was good. But I cringed when I saw his address. He lived on Laurel Way, just above Sunset behind the Beverly Hills Hotel. It was one of the most heavily patrolled neighborhoods in the basin.

We drove out Santa Monica Boulevard, past Century City Mall and the Los Angeles Country Club, and turned left on Beverly Drive. A few minutes later, we turned off Beverly onto Laurel Way. Hildebrand's place was an impressive brick-and-clapboard Colonial, probably five thousand square feet. The landscaping harmonized with the architectural style. There were mature sweet gum and sycamore trees along with an abundance of azalea and rosebushes, the kind of plants you'd see in Connecticut or Virginia. A Brink's Security sign by the driveway threatened an armed response.

I pulled over down the block and parked in the shade of a jacaranda tree to observe the house. This was where people with real money lived, the people who rich people called rich. The homes went for anywhere from two to twenty million, having doubled in value during the 1980s real estate boom and recovered from the early nineties crash in property values. If Hildebrand had hung his fedora here for a decade or more, he had made millions just waking up in the morning. Made we wonder what other valuables besides the necklace we might find in his house.

Before we'd been parked five minutes, a white Taurus with a Beverly Patrol decal drove past. The gray-haired security guard behind the wheel stared at us openly as he went by. While the exhaust from the Taurus still hung in the air, a Beverly Hills police cruiser rolled past in the opposite direction. Like the rent-a-cop, the real cop gave us a good looking-over as he went by. If we hadn't been in a new luxury car, he probably would have stopped and asked us pleasantly if he could be of any assistance, wanting to know if we were lost or visiting someone in the neighborhood. As it was, he likely noted my license number.

"This is no good," Reggie said. "Fuckin' cops are crawling out of the woodwork."

"You're right," I said. Between the armed Brink's guards poised over the horizon, the grim-faced Beverly Patrol, and the alert city cops, it was a dangerous location. "We'll focus on his office. If he doesn't show up there tonight, we'll rob him at the bank tomorrow morning."

"Where's it at?"

"On Wilshire, about a mile from here."

We drove to the Bank of America and looked it over. Pulling an armed robbery in the parking lot on a Tuesday morning would be risky, with lots of traffic on Wilshire and a steady stream of people entering and leaving the bank. Success would depend a little bit on luck and a lot on clean, fast execution. The best thing about the location was its proximity to the 405 free-way. An entrance ramp a quarter mile west made for a great getaway route.

We spent the rest of the morning and early afternoon buying burglary and safecracking tools at scattered locations to hide our intention. We bought a hand sledge, a set of Mayhew cold chisels, and some hardened punches at an Ace hardware in Van Nuys. In Reseda, we picked up pry bars and two extra-long eighteen-inch screwdrivers, one flathead, one Phillips. I paid three hundred and forty dollars for the best cordless recip-rocating saw at the Sears store in Northridge and another two hundred and seventy-five for the heaviest half-inch Craftsman drill. I still had the drill I had taken to the desert, but I wanted a backup.

We bought flashlights, rope, and two extra sets of titanium drill bits at another hardware store in the valley and stopped by a ski shop to pick up pullover masks and a couple of small backpacks to carry the tools in. All the stores were miles from Santa Monica. If we had to flee without the tools, the cops would never be able to canvass up a witness to identify us as the purchasers. We'd wipe them down before the robbery and only handle them with gloves after that. The power tools had serial numbers printed on heavy foil glued to their hard plastic housings. We peeled the foil off.

Later in the afternoon, I picked up a fresh set of fake ID, becoming Stephen Michaelson from Sacramento, and drove to LAX with my partner. Wearing the sunglasses and hat I bought at the Hyatt, I rented a nondescript white Chevrolet from Enterprise, giving the clerk a five-hundred-dollar cash deposit in lieu of a credit-card number.

If we had to do an armed robbery, I didn't want to be squealing away from the bank in my own car. Even with stolen plates, having the model and color identified so close to where I lived would have been dangerous. If someone got the license number of the rental, the cops would trace the vehicle to Enterprise. They might even dig up a videotape that showed me signing papers at the rental counter. But they wouldn't have my real name and they wouldn't be able to identify me behind the hat and glasses. Driv-ing a rental would make a burglary less risky, too.

Reggie drove my car back to Venice from the airport and parked in one of the big lots by the beach. I rendezvoused with him there, and we moved the tools from the trunk of the Seville to the trunk of the rental. Afterward, Reggie took the Caddie to Mr. Parker's lot while I stashed the rental on a side street near the flop.

Reggie was sitting in the broken-down armchair in my room, draining the last swallow from a quart of Budweiser when I got back. I spread a map of West Los Angeles out on the bed and showed him where the lawyer's office and the restaurant were.

Outbound traffic would be light on Monday evening, but it would still take Hildebrand two hours to drive to Indian Wells, at least half an hour to do his business and two hours to drive back. If he left at four, that would put him back in Santa Monica around 8:30 p.m. If he left at five and stopped to eat on the road, he wouldn't be back until ten or eleven. I decided to stake out the office from 7:30 on.

Norm's was ideal for our purposes, a big, busy restaurant with plenty of in-and-out traffic and yet one where denizens of the Los Angeles night hung out for hours on end. We could sit in a booth by the window for a long time over coffee and pie without attracting attention.

"Once Hildebrand comes and goes, we can leave too," I told Reggie. "We'll go back around midnight and wait for the cops to do their drive-by."

The Santa Monica police patrol a given street every four hours. Once they put in an appearance, we'd have time to do the burglary and be long gone before they returned.

"We're gonna stick out like a sore thumb if we sit in that coffee shop all evenin' and then come back and start hanging around after midnight," Reggie said. "They'll probably think we're getting ready to knock *them* off."

"Good point. We'll split the surveillance up. One of us can watch until Hildebrand shows with the diamonds and the other one watch for the cops later."

"I got dibs on the early shift," Reggie said.

"Suits me." There was something I wanted to do that evening.

"What's this chump look like, anyway?"

"I don't know."

"What's he drive?"

"Don't know that either."

Reggie made saucer eyes. "How am I supposed to spot the son of a bitch?"

"It shouldn't be a problem. The office and parking lot will be empty after six or seven o'clock. If guy in a suit shows up with a security guard between eight and eleven and goes inside for a little while and comes back out, that's him."

"How am I supposed to see all that in the dark?"

"There are lights in the parking lot."

CHAPTER THIRTY-FOUR

When we finished going over our plans, I gave Reggie the keys to the rental car and warned him not to get any phone numbers or rub jobs from the waitresses at Norm's.

"Don't worry about me," he said. "I'll be quiet as a church mouse."

We walked out the front door together and shook hands on the porch.

"Good luck," I said. "I'll be here from eight on. Call me as soon as he shows up."

"Where you going now?"

"Over to the ashram to see what Baba Raba's up to."

"Baba Raba or that tight little blonde?"

I shrugged and smiled. "What are you going to do?"

"Stop by Chavi's and see if she wants to get a burger and a couple of brews at Mulligan's."

"Make sure you are at Norm's by seven-thirty, and make sure you're sober."

"Yes, sir!" Reggie said, giving me the sneering salute of an insubordinate sergeant.

The ashram was quiet when I arrived. The front door was closed but unlocked and I walked in through the foyer to the main hall. Ganesha was sitting behind the cash register in the gift shop, reading what looked like the same copy of the Bhagavad Gita he had been reading the first time I saw him. I was starting to like him. He was caught in an impossible situation, trying to maintain a legitimate ashram in the face of creeping corruption. He was lovesick over Mary and facing a crisis with Baba Raba, but he was still on the job. He was reading the right book, too.

Seeing the orange-robed twentysomething poring over the most famous Hindu scripture, I remembered the first time that I had read the Gita, in Florida years before. It was a little book with a light-blue cloth cover, and I could feel it changing me as I turned the pages, as if I were a clay figure being resculpted into a more functional and durable form. The fact that I'd never managed to live up to the book's highest ideals didn't diminish its value as a source of existential guidance in the least, and I was always glad to see another human being latch on to it.

Ganesha looked up as I walked into the shop.

"Hey," he said.

"How's it going?"

He shook his head. "Not so great."

"What's the problem?"

Our eyes locked and I could see that he wanted to confide in someone. I had gained some stature by fixing the roof, and by being cool about his lapse in manners, but he had no reason to trust me or even think that I was truly interested.

"It's ashram business," he said. "I can't talk about it. I'm waiting for Swami Ramananda's assistant to call me back from New York. Swami Ramananda will know what to do." The last sentence was addressed more to himself than to me.

"Wasn't Ramananda a disciple of Paramahansa Yogananda?"

"Yes!" Ganesha's spiritual enthusiasm broke through his other concerns. "How do you know about him?"

"He's mentioned in a biography of Yogananda that I read one time. Is this center part of the Self Realization Fellowship?" That was the name of the stellar spiritual organization founded by Yogananda. The group had a beautiful ashram in Hollywood, a shrine in Malibu, and a domed temple on a cliff overlooking the sea in Cardiff, in north San Diego County. Swamis have even better taste in real estate than gay guys.

"No. Ramananda studied at the feet of Yogananda when he was very young but eventually recognized Sri Brahmananda as his guru. This ashram is owned by the Divine Light Society."

"What is the Murshid Center for Enlightened Beings?"

"That's an organization Baba Raba founded. He operates it from here, but he doesn't own the ashram."

"Sounds like a complicated setup."

"It has confused a lot of people," Ganesha said somewhat grimly. "Baba is an ordained monk in the Divine Light Society, and Ramananda made him head of this ashram when Swami Sankarananda left his physical body two years ago. But he has his own organization, too, in which he calls himself the Murshid, which is a term for teacher that comes from Sufism. I guess he studied with some Sufi masters at one time and adopted some of their teachings. He has studied with many different teachers, including Trungpa and the Maharishi and claims to be a synthesizer of traditions."

"It sounds like you have some doubts about him."

"I didn't at first. He has so much spiritual insight, and his *siddhis* are so strong. But now . . ." His voice trailed off and he shook his head again. "I really shouldn't be talking about ashram business. I'm sorry. What can I do for you? Meditation doesn't start for two hours—if we even have it tonight."

"I came to see Mary. Is she around?"

His glum face fell further. "She is here but she is not available."

"Why?"

"She is with Baba."

"Doing what?"

"He is initiating her."

My heart sped up and I felt the way a lion does before it roars.

"What does that mean?" I asked.

"I don't know exactly," Ganesha said, annoyed. I wasn't sure if he was irritated at me or at his own ignorance or at Baba's shenanigans.

"Forget 'exactly.' Get me in the ballpark."

"He is giving her a personal mantra and making her a high rank within the Murshid organization. It is supposed to be a big deal that he only does for people with great spiritual talent. Mary was all pumped up." He sounded angry and disgusted.

"Why her?"

"I don't know! I don't know what goes on inside that organization. It doesn't make any sense to me. She is a girl off the streets who has only been in the ashram a few months."

It made plenty of sense to me—and maybe to Ganesha, too.

"Where are they?" I said.

"They just went upstairs."

I turned and walked out of the shop toward the staircase.

"You can't go up there!" Ganesha said, following me into the hallway. "Only staff are allowed up there."

"What's the hubbub, Bub?" Namo drifted out into the hallway from the library, where he had apparently been lurking. He blocked the base of the stairs with his lumpy body.

"We already been through this once, haven't we, Bub?" Namo asked me.

"Get ready to go through it again," I said.

Namo grinned. He was missing his top canine tooth and the one behind it on both sides. "Sounds like my kind of game," he said, crouching flat-footed and bringing his clenched fists up in front of his chest.

"Stop it, both of you!" Ganesha yelled.

"You keep out of this, you fucking pansy," Namo said.

"Shut up," Ganesha said forcefully. "I'm in charge here, not you!"

"Yer the one better shut up," Namo snarled. "The big man ain't gonna be too happy when he hears how you been running your mouth to this prick."

"Doing a little eavesdropping?" I said.

"What if I was?"

"Sounds like something a snitch would do," I said to get his goat.

"Who the fuck you calling a snitch?" he yelled, shuffling toward me, swaying his overdeveloped upper body. A snitch is the lowest thing you can be in prison. Nobody wants to be called one because it can get you shanked.

"I'm sorry," I said. "I didn't mean a snitch. I meant a sissy." That's someone who has acquiesced to playing the female part in a prison relationship, either a homosexual who enjoys the role or someone who has been beaten into sexual submission.

With an inarticulate but seemingly hostile sound, Namo charged me.

I leaped back five feet, landing with my guard up and my left side toward the bodybuilder. Enraged, he had given up on the idea of a boxing match and was going for a tackle, coming in with his head down. I met his charge by pushing his greasy melon down and away from me with both hands at the same time as I skipped to the right, letting his momentum carry him past me, like a bull past a matador. As he went by to my left, I pivoted and kneed him solidly in the gut with my right knee, forcing a grunt out of his thick torso and sending him sprawling on the hall floor.

When he scrambled to his feet, he had a sheath knife with a four-inch blade in his hand. Before he could make a move, Ganesha ran between us.

"If you don't stop, I'm going to call the police!" he shouted at Namo, then turned to me: "I mean it, man. We have enough problems around here without this kind of shit. I will have you arrested if you keep it up."

Namo shared my disinclination toward the Venice Beach police. The knife disappeared and he didn't try to renew hostilities. Red-faced and panting, holding his side with one hand, he contented himself by giving me a threatening look as he stalked away, shoving past Ganesha and disappearing into the hallway beside the stairs that led back to the kitchen.

"I'm sorry, Ganesha," I said. "I don't want to make trouble."

"You have a funny way of showing it."

"He attacked me. You saw that. I was defending myself."

"You shouldn't have been trying to go upstairs."

"I know. I'm sorry."

He was right. It was stupid of me to try and charge upstairs and stop whatever was going on. What was I going to do? Mary was of age. If she let Baba take advantage of her, that was her karma, not mine.

As if my mental image had conjured her up, the blonde appeared at the top of the stairs, paused when she saw us, then came tripping down. She was wearing one of the flimsy white robes.

"Hi, Rob," she said casually, hurrying past me on her way to the meditation room.

"Hi," I said to her back as she went through the French doors.

When she reemerged a few moments later, she had two candles, some sticks of incense, and a bell clutched in her eager hands.

"What are you doing?" I asked her.

"Baba is initiating me as Murshida! He says we need this stuff."

"Mary—"

"I can't talk now." She sounded excited and happy and a little dazed, like a girl getting ready for the big dance with her girlfriends, caught up in preparations and anticipation. As she passed me on her way back upstairs I noticed that her pupils were big.

So the fat louse had outmaneuvered me. He was going to get in her pants by flattering her spiritual ambitions, making her some kind of assistant swami, and telling her how enlightened she was as he undressed her. And she was falling for it. I wondered if Baba would include any of the flower girls in the initiation ceremony or if he would save that for later, after he had fucked Mary silly and gotten her used to his perversions.

I wished I'd never looked at her. I wished I had fucked Evelyn the night before. At the same time, I still wanted to follow her upstairs and smash Baba's face and take her away from him.

Ganesha's gaze was directed toward the top of the empty staircase, same as mine, and he had the same expression of longing on his face that he'd had the night I met him, when he watched Mary moving lightly around the gift shop, snuffing out candles. But now the desire was tinged with bitterness. I didn't think he would be at the ashram much longer.

"Goodbye, Ganesha," I said, heading for the front door. "I hope everything works out."

"Goodbye," he said. "You are still welcome here."

"Thank you."

I didn't think I would be returning. We would grab the necklace and get out of town. I didn't know why I felt so bad about the girl. I'd only known her for three days. If she wanted to be with Baba instead of me, so be it. Southern California was well supplied with willing women. There were thousands of them everywhere, at the beach, in shopping malls, at dance clubs and restaurants and bars.

If only the vibe between us hadn't felt so special. There was no use lying to myself about that. It was hard for me to connect with people because of what I did for a living. Reggie was the only person in my life I could really talk to, and he was a mixed bag as far as emotional props go.

Yoga teaches that detachment is the supreme virtue. Because all physical objects, including living beings, inevitably decay, attachment to anything in the material world leads to pain and sorrow. The ideal attitude is

186 STEVEN M. THOMAS

illustrated by an expression the swamis teach: Pleasure or pain, loss or gain, fame or shame, all the same.

It's easy to say—it trips off the tongue—but much harder to maintain as an existential stance. I had let my feelings for Mary run away with me, more than I knew, perhaps, and now I was paying the price, an ache in the center of my chest as painful as a stab wound.

Walking down the dark street toward the ocean, I shook my head and shoulders to try and throw off the emotional oppression. Fuck her. Fuck him. Fuck everybody. I still had the robbery to look forward to.

The jewels.

The money.

The freedom.

CHAPTER THIRTY-FIVE

The lawyer must have stopped to dine in the desert, probably marking the meal up a couple of hundred percent and charging it to Evelyn's account. He showed up at 10:30 p.m. and went into the building with an ex-NFL type in a suit carrying a briefcase. When they left, fifteen minutes later, without the briefcase, Reggie called me from the pay phone at Norm's.

"Cat's in the cradle," he said.

"What?"

"Shyster showed up with ice."

After he dropped out of school, Reggie had watched a lot of old gangster movies on daytime TV.

He picked me up at the flophouse at eleven and we cruised north on Pacific Avenue to Le Merigot, a boutique luxury hotel a couple of blocks south of the pier.

"Turn in here," I said.

When Reggie pulled up at the brightly lit entrance, I waved off the valets and went in to rent a room.

"Whadaya want a hotel room for?" Reggie asked when I came out with the key card. "You got a date with Blondie later on?"

"No. It gives us someplace to go besides the house if there is any trouble."

We continued north past the pier, hung a right on Santa Monica, and drove inland to Norm's. Reggie planned to nap in the car while I went in and sat by the window to watch for the late-night patrol, but the cops showed up while we were still talking in the parking lot.

Ten minutes after the doughnut eaters circled behind Hildebrand's building and moved on to the next block, we pulled out of Norm's, rolled across Santa Monica Boulevard, and turned into the alley they had just checked. Reggie parked in one of the spaces behind the building and I got out and opened the trunk. There was a pair of lock snips I'd never seen before lying on top of the other tools.

"Where did these come from?" I asked Reggie.

"I boosted 'em from the bed of a pickup down by the boardwalk," he said. "Never know when you're gonna need a church key."

At least 10 percent of my affection for Reggie was based on his habit of referring to lock snips as church keys.

"They might come in handy," I agreed.

We carried the packs, clanking with metal tools, to the back wall of the building. Reggie boosted me up so that I could grab the retracted stairs and drag them down. While I lugged the packs up the metal-grid steps, Reggie drove out the other end of the dark alley and circled back to park the car in Norm's lot, which was still half full. By the time he returned, I had the tools on the top platform of the fire escape and had climbed up the ladder onto the roof.

The roof was an unobstructed rectangle, sixty feet wide by forty feet deep, sloped slightly toward the rear and dimly lit by ambient city light. The tar was covered with brown pea gravel. There was a low parapet along the sides and front of the building. As long as we stayed on our knees when we were near the edge of the roof, it hid us from the view of anyone below. At the front corners, the crowns of the two date palms gave additional cover. The two- and three-story buildings that backed up to the other side of the alley were all dark.

I pulled on a pair of brown cotton gloves and used a flat bar to pop the aluminum cover off a vent near the center of the building, exposing the top of a six-inch exhaust-fan pipe made of flimsy sheet metal and a jagged hole in the roof sheathing that was about ten inches square. While Reggie kept a lookout, I used the cordless reciprocating saw to enlarge the opening, cutting over to a joist, along it for twenty inches, over to the neighboring joist, back along that two-by-ten for twenty inches, then back over to the vent hole.

The saw made a racket, hacking through tar, sheet metal, and plywood, sending gravel flying, but the heavy demolition blade was sharp and the saw motor powerful and I was done in twenty seconds. It took another ten seconds to cut through the lath on the bottom of the joists and stomp the plaster out of the way, opening access to the interior of the building. When I was finished, dogs were barking on adjacent blocks but no lights had come on in any of the buildings around us.

"Goddamn, that was loud!" Reggie said, crawling over from the parapet.

"Anything on the street?" My ears were ringing. My gloves and the arms of my long-sleeve shirt were covered with sawdust and plaster.

"One car went by while you were cutting, but they had their windows up."

"We'll wait a few minutes to see if anyone comes. Keep watching the street."

Crouching, I made my way to the back corner of the building and lay down in the shadow of the parapet, where I could see the alley.

I wasn't too worried about the noise. People notice a strange noise at nighttime in a big city, it takes them a while to be sure they are really hearing it. They have to turn down the TV or wake all the way up and open the window, trying to tell where the sound is coming from. If the noise stops, they listen for it to start again to get a better fix on it. If it doesn't recur, ninety-nine people out of a hundred will shrug and go back to what they were doing, picking up the plotline of the nighttime soap opera or sinking gratefully back into the oblivion of sleep.

But I wanted to play it safe. If someone more acute or suspicious than the average city dweller had heard the noise and called the police, I was giving them time to arrive. As long as we were on the roof, the only crime they could charge us with was attempted burglary of an unoccupied building, not a serious rap. Once inside, we would have committed actual burglary, which carried more time. We also had a better chance of getting away while we were on the outside. If the cops rolled because someone heard a suspicious noise, it would only be one car and we would see them before they saw us. If all they did was circle the building and check the doors, we could still do the job. If they made a move toward the fire escape, we might be able to shinny down the palm trees in front and make it back to Norm's before they found the hole in the roof.

The dogs stopped barking after a few minutes. No one came into the alley. Several anonymous cars went by on Santa Monica, one on the cross street by Norm's. After ten minutes, I crawled away from the low wall and crouched back over to the hole. Shining a flashlight down into the opening, I saw a typical office bathroom with a vanity and toilet but no tub or shower. The smashed exhaust fan was half buried beneath lath and plaster.

"Let's go," I whispered loud enough for Reggie to hear.

He crawled over and looked down into the room.

"Yer gettin' good at this, bro," he said.

"Practice makes perfect."

Or, at least, hopefully, you get better.

CHAPTER THIRTY-SIX

I took a coil of rope out of one of the packs and tied it to the cast-iron soil stack that pierced the roof a couple of feet from the hole and lowered myself into the bathroom. Reggie handed the tools down to me, then slid down the rope, dropping heavily to the floor. It was a quarter past twelve.

"How we gonna get back out?" he whispered.

"You don't have to whisper," I said. "If we are in good shape, we can climb back up the rope. If we aren't in such good shape, we can move a piece of furniture in here, climb up on that like an old woman, and have someone pull our fat ass up onto the roof." I was still in a bad mood because of the thing with Mary.

"Excuse me for not being a fucking orangutan," Reggie said, taking a wholly justifiable tone. "Where's the safe?"

"Put these on," I said, handing him a pair of gloves, "and we'll go find it."

Besides the bathroom, the darkened suite consisted of a reception alcove; a large open office area with copying machines, file cabinets, and half a dozen cubicles for secretaries and paralegals; a small kitchen with a sink and refrigerator; and six locked private offices. The name ARMAND HILDEBRAND SR. was engraved on a brass plate on one of the doors.

The door gave way with a single stomp from Reggie's size-ten boots and we were in the large and finely furnished office of Evelyn Evermore's attorney. The blinds on the double-pane windows facing Santa Monica Boulevard were closed against the bright sunlight that would have poured into the room in late afternoon. Lawyers don't like bright light.

The wall safe was well concealed behind a hinged section of bookcase. It took us fifteen minutes to find it. The metal tag riveted to the front of the round steel door identified it as a Mosler, a classic brand that has been made in Hamilton, Ohio, since the nineteenth century. It had a class-A fire rating and an Underwriters Laboratories TRTL-30 security rating—a solid, well-made safe, but not impenetrable. For the first time that evening, I felt the happiness of the crime steal over me.

"Can we crack it?" Reggie asked.

"Yes."

There are dozens of ways to open safes, ranging from the stethoscope-and-sensitive-fingers method that predominates in the popular imagination to the use of high explosives. But the easiest way is to find the combination. People have a hard time remembering long sequences of numbers, and a surprising percentage of safe owners write the combination down someplace near the safe. We spent five minutes looking on the bottom of drawers and the backs of pictures and anyplace else that seemed likely. We kept our flashlights pointed straight down, careful not to shine them directly at the windows lest a glimmer of light leak through the blinds and alert the outside world that foul play was afoot in lawyerland.

We didn't find the combination.

That meant drilling.

I knew the Mosler had a hard-plate in the door to defeat attack from the front. The plate is made of special steel that takes a long time to drill through and may be embedded with chips of carbide that will shatter drill bits. The back of the safe would be ordinary high-tensile steel.

The small kitchen was adjacent to Hildebrand's office, with cupboards on the shared wall. One of the cupboards was a dummy, a matching door panel that didn't open. When the door was pried off, the back of the safe was exposed.

Before attacking the box, we took two file cabinets from the secretarial pen—one half-size, one full-size—and wrestled them into the bathroom, placing them side by side beneath the hole in the roof. Holding on to the dangling rope, Reggie had no problem climbing up onto the short cabinet, then onto the taller one and from there onto the roof.

"Stay up there and keep a lookout," I said.

"No way," he said, scrambling back down into the bathroom with an agility surprising in someone who had slammed into as many immovable objects on as many speeding motorcycles as he had. "I wanna see how you bust that Mosler."

Up to that night in late January 1996, Reggie's extensive criminal career had not included safecracking. I couldn't blame him for wanting to get some OJT, and we didn't have time to waste arguing. We had not been detected entering the building. The noise we would make drilling the safe would not be audible from the outside. The cops would only come now if we tripped an alarm inside the office that we didn't know about. If that happened, they would arrive in force and catch us whether we kept a lookout or not.

"All right," I said, giving the grizzled sergeant his due. "Let's steal some jewels."

The windowless kitchen was an ideal work area. I closed the door to contain the noise and turned on the light. We laid our new tools out on the counter and wiped them down again to make sure there were no fingerprints, using the cotton gloves that would not come off until we were back on the ground behind the building. I needed two holes in the back of the safe, one for the borescope, so I could see what I was doing inside the box, the other for the long screwdrivers we had picked up that afternoon.

Traditional safe locks operate via a set of notched wheels called the "wheel pack." The little click that guys with five o'clock shadows and Lone Ranger masks hear when they slowly turn the combination dial in B-movies is the sound of a lever, called "the fence," dropping into one of the notches. When all the notches are lined up, the lock bolt slides through a second set of notches and the safe pops open. Attacking from the rear, I would be able to see the wheel pack and move the wheels into proper alignment without using the combination dial.

We hooked up both drills and carved two holes simultaneously, standing shoulder to shoulder and using a series of bits. It's hard to drill a large hole in high-grade steel. It takes a long time and lot of muscular effort. It is much easier to drill a small pilot hole, then enlarge it with bits of increasing size. We started with bits three-sixteenths of an inch in diameter, followed by three-eighths, three-quarters, and one inch. The oily-factory smell of electric motors straining and the whine of steel cutting steel filled the small room. Hot metal shavings piled up at our feet.

Working silently with *tratakum*-like concentration, changing bits quickly and efficiently, leaning on the drills to make the whirling blades dig deep, it took us less than ten minutes to drill two one-inch holes in the "safe."

Inserting the lighted borescope in the top hole, I saw the metal plate that covered the back of the lock mechanism. It was secured to the inside of the safe door with four Phillips screws. Turning the scope, I saw the blue jewelry box on a side shelf.

I used the long Phillips screwdriver to undo the plate, working alternately from both holes. The safe was only sixteen inches deep, so the eighteen-inch screwdriver was plenty long enough. When the plate was out of the way, I studied the wheel pack through the borescope for a while, using the standard screwdriver to probe the action. After letting Reggie take a look, I began to painstakingly nudge the wheels into alignment. It was no picnic getting the entire set into position and I got stuck on the last one. I thought for a while that we were going to have to drill another hole to get a better angle to work from.

"Let me try," Reggie said, back to whispering.

Resolutely ignorant of history, politics, geography, and most other academic subjects, Reggie was a quick study in all things criminal, and a talented mechanic. After peering through the borescope for a minute or so, studying the mechanism, he took the screwdriver and with a flick of his thick wrist managed to pry the final wheel into place. The safe's spring-loaded bolt retracted with a loud click.

"Got it!" Reggie said.

We raced for the door. I squeezed out first, and ran around into Hildrebrand's office. Mysteriously unhampered by his limp, Reggie was right on my heels.

The heavy safe door swung open smoothly on concealed hinges, and I had the blue velvet box in my hand again. Taking it to Hildebrand's desk, I opened it and shined my flashlight on the rose-colored stones. A lot had happened in the eighty hours since I had last seen the necklace. The world had rolled on, becoming a new place each day as it always does. I had met

Mary, Baba Raba, and Evelyn. But the diamonds hadn't changed. More than almost anything else in the material world, they defied the yogic dictum and resisted decay, staying stable in the midst of the flux, like the still point around which the earth revolves. That genuine characteristic went a long way toward explaining why they were able to carry the artificial value that hucksters assigned to them so effectively. Diamonds were beautiful, certainly, refracting light into heavenly rainbows. But their deepest hold on the human heart was that they touched eternity.

Reggie lifted the necklace from the white satin interior of the box, letting it dangle from his stubby index finger. "Nice merchandise," he said.

Both of us were grinning. I could feel my cheeks begin to ache. Taking the necklace off his finger, I put it back in the box and snapped the lid shut.

"See if there is anything else worth taking," I said. "I'll pack up the tools."

I had just put the new drill back in its case when Reggie popped in the kitchen door, his eyes as wide open as they could get.

"You musta been good this year," he said. "Look what Sanny Claws left." He held out both hands. There was a canvas bag in his right hand, a thick five-by-twelve-inch manila envelope secured by a rubber band in his left.

The bag, delightfully heavy, was full of Krugerrands, bearded geezer on one side, antelope on the other. The lawyer was hoarding gold.

The envelope was stuffed with series EE U.S. Savings Bonds in denominations of $100, $200, and $500, inscribed to various little Hildebrands. Passing his ill-gotten gains on to the next generation—if they were lucky enough to ever actually get their hands on the cash. I could imagine a typical birthday party at the house on Laurel Way:

"Oh, look, Richard, your grandpa got you another hundred-dollar savings bond!"

"Can I have it, Mommy?"

"No, Grandpa will keep it in his safe for you along with all your other bonds."

CHAPTER THIRTY-SEVEN

We waited in the shadow of a palm tree at the front corner of Hildebrand's building until there was no traffic on Santa Monica, then started across the wide, well-lit boulevard, heavy packs bouncing on our shoulders.

"How much is the gold worth?" Reggie asked, hurrying beside me.

"Depends on the number of coins," I said, swiveling my head back and forth, looking in all directions. "Gold's somewhere between three and four hundred an ounce. Each Krugerrand is an ounce. If there are fifty coins that would be fifteen or twenty thousand dollars."

"That's good money," Reggie panted.

"Icing on the cake."

"Can we fence the bonds?"

"Yes."

"What'll they bring?"

"Depends on the maturity dates. We'll check it out when we get home."

There were ten or twelve cars but no people in Norm's parking lot as we headed to the rental. We put everything in the trunk except for the Tomcat, which stayed in my belt. I slid in behind the wheel while Reggie took shotgun.

"Good job, Robby," he said in his serious mentor voice.

"You, too, brother."

The pistol was digging into my side so I pulled it out of my belt and put it in the glove compartment. I had started the engine but not put the car in gear when a black-and-white swooped in out of nowhere and pulled up beside us, rubber barking as it jolted to a halt. It was such a shock that if I had been in the Seville I might have peeled out as a reflex. The Cadillac was faster than the cop car and I knew the terrain and we might have been able to get away. But I didn't trust the rental car's power and I wasn't used to driving it around corners on two wheels, so I turned off the engine and put my hands on the steering wheel.

They popped out of their cruiser like they were spring-loaded, the driver circling behind us to check our license plate and get an overview, the ride-along tapping on my window with his club-light. They didn't have their guns out, which meant they hadn't made us for the burglary, at least not yet.

"Let me do the talking," I murmured to Reggie, then rolled my window down six inches and looked at the cop. "Good evening, Officer. What's up?"

"Aw, not too much. What are you guys up to?" He was an old-school lurch, six-four, a good two-twenty, the kind of cop that predominated on big-city police forces before rookies started rolling with junior college degrees and mouths full of legal jargon. He looked like he was about sixty years old, poised to prove that he could still cut the mustard if some punk gave him half an excuse. The other cop—black, in his thirties—was of average height and build.

"Just getting something to eat," I said.

"Here?" He had a foxy look on his face.

"Yeah."

"What time was that?"

"Earlier this evening."

"Where you guys coming from just now?" He must have seen us walking into the parking lot.

"Just taking a stroll around the city, soaking up some Santa Monica scenery."

He looked at his watch. "At one-thirty in the morning?"

"Yeah, we're only in town a couple of days. Trying to make the most of it."

"Where you from?"

"Sacramento."

"What are you doing down here?"

Cops like to ask a lot of questions. It gives them a chance to read you, to see if you are nervous or evasive. They like to ask about times, locations, reasons, trying to pin you down, catch you in a contradiction.

"Vacation."

"Where you staying?"

"The Georgian, down by the beach." I could see the name of the hotel impact his thinking. Standard rooms at the Georgian were three hundred a night. The fact that we were staying there moved us up from transients to well-heeled travelers, whether he liked it or not.

"You got some ID?"

"Sure." I handed him my Stephen Michaelson driver's license. He looked at it for a few moments, then half-turned, keeping one eye on us, and handed it through the window of the squad car to the other cop, who was on the radio running our plate.

"How 'bout your friend?" He leaned down to look at Reggie. "Got some ID, sir?"

Reggie dug in his back pocket and came up with his fake license, which also had a Sacramento address. I handed it to the cop, who looked at it and passed it to his partner.

"What did you guys put in the trunk?"

This was what he had been leading up to.

"Our backpacks," I said.

"What do you have in them?"

"Water, a guidebook, a jacket, my camera — that kind of stuff."

"You sure that's all? They looked pretty heavy."

"Why all the questions, Officer?"

"I get curious when I see people putting bulky backpacks in the trunk of a car in the middle of the night. Makes me think they might be burglars."

"Not us," I said and laughed. "We're just tourists."

"Would you mind stepping out of the car?"

"Why, Officer? Are you detaining us?"

"Just get out of the car," he said, filling his voice with that cop threat they get so good at. "You, too." He leaned down to look over at Reggie again.

I rolled the window up and opened the door. As Reggie and I got out of the car, I pushed the button that snapped the locks down and then slammed my door.

"Why did you lock your car?" the cop said.

"Just habit. I don't want anyone to steal it."

"Can I see your car keys, please?"

"Why?"

"I need to do a routine check to make sure you don't have anything illegal in the vehicle. There's been a lot of burglaries around here lately, and your friend looks like a guy I arrested last year. You don't have anything to hide, do you?"

"No, Officer, I don't have anything to hide. But I don't consent to any searches." I paused, looking him in the eye. "Are we free to go now?"

Cops are so used to riding roughshod over people on the street that it confuses them if you assert your rights calmly and politely. After a moment's indecision, the lurch fell back to a default tactic honed during countless late-night encounters with scared petty crooks, drunk kids, and timid citizens. Stepping up nose to nose, looming over me with his extra two inches of height, he breathed salami fumes in my face.

"All right, smart guy," he said. "There are two ways we can go here. I think you got something in the trunk you shouldn't have and I'm gonna find out what it is one way or the other. If you cooperate, I'll make things easy for you. But if you give me a hard time I'll nail your hide to the wall. Do you understand that?"

He glared at me, waiting for an answer.

I didn't answer, just looked him in the eyes.

"We got a special cell down at the station for guys who don't play along with us," he said. "Guys walk into that room cocky but they crawl back out ready to kiss the ass of any cop who bends over. We make tough guys into sacred little schoolgirls in that room. Now, what's it going to be? You gonna be smart or stupid?"

Alert to conflict, the other cop had come up behind his partner. He held our licenses in one hand. His other hand was on the butt of his gun. I glanced at Reggie. He was leaning against the rental car, a couple of feet from the doughnut eaters, his face as impassive as a cigar-store Indian's.

"Why don't you let us take a look in the backpacks, sir?" the black cop said. "If there's nothing in them, you can be on your way. Save a lot of trouble."

"I don't want any trouble, Officer," I said, addressing the black cop. "I know you guys are just doing your job. But I believe it is my obligation as a good citizen to protect my constitutional rights and I do not consent to any searches of my vehicle or my person. My friend and I aren't doing anything wrong. If you think the fact that we put our backpacks in the trunk of our rental car gives you probable cause, then I guess you will search the car. But you don't have my permission."

The big cop was seething. He glanced around the parking lot to see if there were any witnesses. If he assaulted me and I fought back, he could arrest me for resisting, then search the car to his heart's content. Bad luck for him, an elderly gentleman wearing cowboy boots and a straw cowboy hat had just come out of Norm's and was walking across the parking lot toward us.

The black cop pulled the lurch back a couple of paces. Standing by the rear bumper of the squad car, they held a whispered conference.

"There are no warrants for either of them and the car is clean," I heard the black cop say, warning in his voice. "There haven't been any prowler calls or alarm trips within a mile of here tonight."

"I know they are up to something, goddamn it!"

"Then we'll get them next time."

The black cop walked back over.

"Are we free to go, Officer?" I said politely, keeping the pressure on them.

"Can you establish your local address so we know where to find you if we need to?"

"Why would you need to find us, Officer?"

"Don't push it," he said. "You have a key or receipt or something that shows you're staying at the Georgian?"

"Yes." I took out the key card I'd kept since our stay there six weeks before and handed it to him.

"If I call over there, are they going to tell me you're registered?"

"Absolutely. We have a suite on the top floor." Suites at the Georgian went for $500 and up. We were getting more respectable by the minute. The cop looked at the front and the back of the card, flexed it, then shrugged and handed it back along with our licenses.

"I wouldn't advise wandering around the city this time of night in the future," he said, trying to come out on top psychologically.

"I think you're right," I said. "It's probably a bad idea. Are we free to go?"

"Yeah, get out of here."

"If you're smart, you'll keep right on going until you get back to Sacramento," the lurch said in his menacing tone.

"Why's that?"

"Just let me see you around here again in the middle of the night and you'll find out why."

CHAPTER THIRTY-EIGHT

"Yep," Reggie said, nodding to himself, looking straight ahead out the windshield as we drove down Santa Monica toward the Pacific. "I picked the right partner."

"Why's that?"

" 'Why's that?' " He swiveled his head to look at me. "Listen to this shit. You outfoxed that flatfoot like a flimflam man on a Sunday school teacher. You were smooth as a sixteen-year-old girl's heinie, Robby, and you know it. 'Why's that?' Shit!"

"Seemed like the way to play it."

"How'd you know they wouldn't just search the car anyway and claim they saw something that gave 'em cause?"

"I didn't. I was gambling that they would play by the rules. If the cops are out-and-out corrupt, asserting your rights doesn't help. But if they are halfway honest, mentioning things like probable cause makes them stop and think. Even if they really want to stick it to you, even if they are really suspicious, they know they aren't allowed to search you or your car unless they have some evidence that a crime has been committed. A strong hunch isn't enough. If you know your rights, it makes them cautious. They wonder who they are dealing with and start thinking about getting bawled out by the district attorney, or being made a fool of on the witness stand by a good defense lawyer."

"What would you have done if they pushed it?"

"Fought them."

Reggie nodded. "I had that black cop measured."

"I know you did," I said. "That big prick had his legs too far apart for his own good. If the shit went down, he would have been singing soprano at the next smoker."

I pulled into the alley behind the flophouse a few minutes before two, popped the trunk, and got out, leaving the engine running. Reggie slid over behind the wheel while I retrieved the loot.

"Park wherever you can find a spot," I told him. "We'll take the car back first thing tomorrow. Be sure to check the street-sweeping signs so we don't get towed."

The back door that opened into the kitchen was bolted from the inside. Walking to the front, I saw a glimmer of light in the derelict house where Ozone Pacific slept. I was surprised he was awake this late.

Upstairs, I emptied out the bag of gold and the envelope of bonds. There were seventy-three Krugers. If gold was at $300, the coins were worth twenty-two grand. If it was at $400, they would be worth nearly thirty. The unexpected windfall put helium in my heart, made it light. The grin I had worn earlier, when we opened the safe, came back from wherever it had gone during the cop encounter.

The face value of the bonds was $18,300. The oldest issues had passed their maturity dates, which made them worth much more than face value. The newest issue was from the previous summer. It would be worth a little more than half of its nominal. All together, there was probably $40,000 worth of government paper. I could lay them off for 20 percent of that, another eight grand.

I took the diamonds out and held them up to the light, marveling at their beauty. Folding the necklace in my hand so that a single rose-colored crystal protruded between my thumb and the side of my index finger, I scratched a crude OM symbol in the mirror, then put the jewels back in the blue velvet case.

Fahid would be very happy.

But not as happy as me.

The money was the main thing, of course. But I also felt a glow of professional pride—pride in a tricky, high-stakes heist well-planned and executed, a feeling like I used to get in the construction business when a new room was latched solidly onto an old house, electrical and plumbing work up to code, interior paint job perfect, siding and roofing materials buttoned tight to protect the structure from the elements.

I was glad to be hurting Baba, too. I didn't like his yogic con game in the least. I didn't like what he was doing to Evelyn. I hated him because of Mary.

I hoped the real estate deal collapsed on him like an iron bridge.

When I hid the loot in the compartment I had constructed beneath the floorboards under my bed, I kept out one gold coin on an impulse. I wanted to show it to Ozone, to let him see the difference between plastic and real gold.

When I went back downstairs, I found Budge standing in the middle of the living room with his eyes closed. I couldn't tell if he had stopped to think about something or had passed out on his feet, sleeping like a horse in its stall.

"Budge." I tapped him on the shoulder, ready to catch him if he fell or duck if he took a swing at a dream-world enemy.

He opened his eyes and looked at me blankly for several seconds, then whipped his head back and forth rapidly, like a boxer shaking off a blow. When he recognized me, he smiled broadly.

"Rob!"

"Yeah!"

"Whatcha doin', man?"

"Just going to check on Ozone. I saw his light on."

"Little Oz! I love that kid, man."

"I know you do."

"Hey, Rob!"

"What?"

"You got that little blonde upstairs?" He spoke in the sly whisper he always used when talking about women or sex while he was drunk, nodding his head to try and provoke an affirmative answer.

"No."

"Don't let that get away, man. That's some sweet shit. Those pink shorts! I ever got my hands on her little behind I'd lick that brown eye clean as a whistle."

"It's a thought," I said.

"Got to lick the brown eye, Rob," he said with conviction. "Girls like it. Makes 'em squeal and squirm." He wiggled his big body to illustrate and lost his balance, stumbling a couple of steps sideways before getting his feet back under him. "That little girl had me around, she wouldn't need toilet paper."

"I'll let her know," I said. "You better get to bed."

"Yeah, um drunker na skunk."

Listing like a sailboat in the wind, my burly housemate staggered toward the hallway. I watched until he made it into his bedroom, then went out the front door and along the sidewalk to the abandoned house next door. There was a notice from the city taped to the front door, stating that the house was unfit for human habitation and had been condemned. Discenza wasn't wasting any time.

I left the door open for the light that filtered in from the street and picked my way through the debris on the living room floor to the hallway. Ozone Pacific's door was open, pale gold leaking into the hall.

I heard someone crying as I went toward the room. The boy was sitting on the floor wearing nothing but his old jeans. His cowboy boots and cowboy shirt were beside him on his sleeping bag. There was a book open in front of him and his shoulders shook as he dribbled his plastic coins onto the colorful pages.

"I'm rich," he sobbed.

CHAPTER THIRTY-NINE

Glimpsing Ozone's private world, I decided to give him not one but ten of the Krugerrands, or the value of them, to help him get off the street and do something with his life. Both of our houses were condemned, and I didn't want to leave him wandering homeless when I skipped town.

"Those coins are plastic," I said from the doorway.

Ozone looked around, frightened, and turned his back toward me as if shielding himself from a blow.

"Don't be afraid," I said, crossing the room to stand behind him. "It's me, your friend Rob."

"Hi, Rob," he sniffled, gathering up the coins.

In the light of the caged forty-watt bulb dangling above him I saw that the volume open on the floor was a children's picture book filled with farmyard scenes. It was old and worn with torn pages, as if it had been much handled. The lush illustrations showed a red rooster crowing in front of a yellow sun, and cows and horses grazing in green pastures.

"Don't you know those coins are worthless?" I said, trying to draw him back toward reality. "You're not rich. You can't spend plastic money."

"I am, too," he said, his pathetic tone tinged with anger. "My mom had a lot of money that she showed me. She told me we are rich."

"Did she finally show up?"

"No," he said miserably. "She never came back. I waited all day, but then I got scared and tried to find her. She told me not to cross Pacific so I walked down to the end of the beach, looking for her. I was afraid to go any farther. I was afraid she would come back and be mad when she couldn't find me. She told me to stay by the palm tree. Do you think she came back while I was gone, Rob, and left again when she couldn't find me?"

"I don't know, Oz. When did that happen?"

"I was eight," he said. "It was my birthday. It was summertime."

"You've been waiting for your mother to come back for you since you were eight years old?"

He turned his head to look up at me, keeping his body hunched protectively, his fistful of plastic coins clutched to his chest. Tears were leaking from his eyes. He nodded.

"Sometimes I walk back down to Ozone looking for her, but then I get afraid again and come back. I think she'll come soon, Rob, don't you? A man came and said I have to get out of here, and I don't have any place to go. I want to go with my mom but I don't know where she is."

Without wanting to, I imagined the long days he had lived through in the monotonous sunshine, days when loneliness gnawed at him until he couldn't sit still and he trudged north along the boardwalk, retracing his childhood route to that first stopping point. It had become a Pavlovian barrier, like a disconnected electric fence still restraining horses or cattle that don't know the shock is gone. Ozone Pacific. A nickname that took hold years before, when boardwalk denizens first noticed his odd geographical limitations.

"Look at this," I said, taking the Krugerrand out of my pocket and holding the heavy coin out to him. "This is real gold."

Keeping the plastic disks tight against his chest in his left hand, he reached out with his right to take the Kruger. As he grasped it, I saw that his arm was bleeding. Taking hold of his wrist, I turned his arm and saw several fresh cuts midway between his wrist and elbow. The cuts were surrounded by countless scars. The long-sleeve shirt in all weather.

"Oh, Oz, what are you doing?" The periodic misery that underlay his cheerful demeanor hit me like a knee in the gut. I guess I should have known. People who are always smiling are usually sad.

He pulled his hand free and hunched back over, holding gold in one hand, plastic in the other.

"I'm sorry, Rob. I know I'm not supposed to do it. Please don't tell anybody."

"But why are you doing it, Oz? Why would you want to cut yourself?"

I had heard of schoolgirls who supposedly sliced their delicate skin for some kind of perverse satisfaction, but I had never understood it. It seemed like something made up by daytime talk-show hosts to elicit maudlin tears from emotionally congested housewives, not something that actually happened in real life. I knew all about addictions to things that make you feel good, at least temporarily, like alcohol and heroin and sex, but I couldn't comprehend being addicted to pain.

"I do it when I feel sad," he said. "It makes me feel better. It hurts, and I think about that and forget about my mom and everything else."

"What else?"

He leaned his head back and moaned. "All my problems. Baba Raba won't give me my picture back, and I'm going to get kicked out of my room, and I'm never going to get out into the country. I'm all grown up and I've never even seen a cow. I am afraid I am going to be stuck down here forever and never see my mom or the country or anything."

I knelt down beside him and put my arm around his thin shoulders. He leaned his head against me and wept. He smelled sour. Tears dripped from his chin, jewels of blood from his elbow. I let him cry for a minute or so to get it out of his system, then squeezed his shoulder.

"I am going to make sure you get out into the country, Oz," I said. "Don't worry about that anymore."

It had occurred to me how much I owed the kid. He was the one who had put me on the trail of the necklace in the first place, and the necklace was going to make me rich. Not rich like Howard Hughes or Christina Onassis or any of the other sick superrich for whom money was a painful poison, but rich like a guy in the fairy tale who steals the ogre's treasure and exits the story whistling, bag slung over his shoulder, hat pushed back on his head, disappearing down a country lane.

More than that, in the hollowness of late nighttime, I felt a kinship with him in his sorrow, as if he were my son or brother. He had lost his mother, who I was quite sure would never return. I had lost my daughter, whom I probably would never see again. Oz and I were sandwiched together in the darkness between two devastations.

Reggie and I would be leaving Venice the next day. Or maybe the day after. I might try one more time. Before leaving, I would hook Ozone up with some kind of social-services agency and find him a place to stay, maybe some vocational training. Something better than sleeping in alleys.

"Come on, stop crying," I said. "Why don't you come over and sleep on our couch tonight? We need to put some antiseptic on those cuts so they don't get infected. What did you cut yourself with, anyway?"

He reached under the sleeping bag and pulled out a single-edged razor blade. I took it from him and slipped it in my shirt pocket, then helped him up.

"Bring your shirt and boots. We'll wash your clothes tomorrow after you take a bath and get cleaned up."

Following Oz out of the dim room, I tripped on some of his junk, kicking a pile of magazines so that they splayed across the floor. One of them caught my eye. It was the copy of *Riviera* with Evelyn's bejeweled picture that the boy had shown me on the boardwalk. I wondered if he had two copies or if he'd forgotten that Baba had returned it to him. I started to ask him as we walked back over to the flophouse, but thought better of it. I didn't want to challenge another of his delusions, if that's what it was. He was upset enough already.

Though he should have been dead to the world, Budge must have heard us go into the downstairs bathroom. I was putting Bactine on Ozone's arm when the former lineman's bulk loomed in the doorway.

"Don't let him see!" Ozone said, turning away.

But he had already seen.

"Oh, motherfucker!" Budge said, turning away from us and smashing his fist into the wall, punching through the plaster and lath, something I'd never seen anyone do before.

Any fool with a few drinks in him can put his fist through a piece of drywall without damaging his hand, unless he hits a stud. Most of my friends' homes when I was growing up had a hole or two in the kitchen or living room drywall, testament to some memorable domestic disturbance, as when a drunken father objected to his wife's shrill 2 a.m. accusations.

But plaster and lath is more like concrete than half-inch drywall. My man Budge had a big punch.

"Knock it off, Budge," I said. "Look what you did to your hand."

He held his fist up in front of his face and looked at the blood seeping through the white plaster dust.

"Who gives a shit?" he said.

"Sharpnick will when she sees that hole in the wall."

"Why should she? They're gonna tear it down anyway."

"Just behave yourself."

After Oz's cuts were disinfected and bandaged, I sent him to the living room to lie down on the couch.

"I'm sorry, Budge," he said softly as he went down the hall. But Budge wouldn't look at him.

"Let me see your hand," I said, pulling the big goof into the bathroom. He had gashed his knuckles badly, grinding old paint and plaster into them.

"I told that little son of a bitch if he ever did that again, I was gonna kick his ass," he said and hiccupped and began to cry.

"Oh, shit," I said. "Not you, too. Sit down on the toilet and let me see if I can do something with your hand so you don't get gangrene."

When Budge was patched up and back in bed, I checked the other downstairs rooms. Candyman was snoring in his berth with an anonymous companion of sizable proportions. Pete's room was empty, the hospital corners on his bunk undisturbed. I wondered what the ex-sailor was up to at two-thirty in the morning.

Upstairs, Reggie's room was empty, too. Probably gone to Chavi's to celebrate the score with a blow job after stashing the rental car.

I drifted off, thinking about the next day. The first thing I would do was take the necklace and coins to Fahid. Then we'd return the car and get the five-hundred-dollar deposit back. Then call someone about Oz. Then . . .

I slipped over the edge of consciousness, dropping down into a deep, cool sleep.

CHAPTER FORTY

"Wake up!"

I heard the voice from my vague location far down in the depths of unconsciousness. As I breast-stroked toward the surface, it repeated itself.

"Wake up!" It was cheerful.

When I opened my eyes, I saw Namo leaning over me, grinning, showing the black gaps beside his top incisors. He had a snubnose chrome six-shooter in his hand. He was pointing it at me. My gun was in the glove compartment of the rental car, parked beneath some ragged palm tree on a side street somewhere in south Venice Beach. Namo's little green eyes were sparkling with happiness. He was looking at me the way a sadistic kid looks at a cat he has just trapped, relishing what he will do to it.

Judging by the light pouring in the window, it was midmorning, around nine or nine-thirty. I had been asleep for about six hours. Baba was sitting in the armchair by the window, his ample ass more than filling the space between the splayed arms. He was wearing the blue suit I had seen in his closet, dressed for an appraisal.

"If you return the necklace now, without any difficulty, I give you my word that the police will not be involved and you will not be harmed," he said in his measured guru voice. Despite the sonorous tone, he looked scared. His face looked thinner than it had been, flesh worn away by worry in the hours since I had last seen him.

"Necklace? What are you talking—"

Namo jabbed the barrel of the gun in my face, striking my cheekbone with an explosive bolt of pain. Instinctively, I started to come up out of the bed but he cocked the hammer and I lay back down.

"Stop it!" Baba said. "There is no need for that. Not yet. I believe Mr. Rivers will be reasonable when he knows the facts."

"How did you know where to find me?" I said, rubbing my cheek.

"Our nautical friend put me wise."

"Pete?"

"Yes," Baba said. "He has been keeping me informed of your activities. When he told me last Saturday that you and your associate had been to the desert on some kind of criminal enterprise at the same time that a pair of thieves attempted to steal the necklace, I instructed him to keep what he might call 'a weather eye' on you."

"I'm in it with 'em, you asshole!" Pete said, bouncing into the room through the hall door. "You think you are pretty fucking smart, but there's a lot you don't know. I'm the one that found—"

"Be quiet," Baba said, cutting Pete off. "Loose lips sink ships."

Pete clapped his mouth shut and Baba turned back to me. "I congratulate you on your skill and perseverance. You very nearly got the necklace in the desert, despite my precautions. But you also very nearly came to grief. It was bold of you to quickly regroup and steal it last night from that idiot lawyer's office. Concentration of that order is a yogic virtue. But then I believe you have studied yoga, haven't you?"

"How do you know that?" I said, confused again by his insidious ability to pluck information from the atmosphere.

"Our lovely little Mary mentioned it to me. You are acquainted with her, I believe? A slender young woman with blond hair and a fairy's face? Street tough, but oh so tender underneath? Another prize you hoped to steal from me, perhaps?" Anger crawled up into his voice like a sewer worker emerging from a manhole.

I didn't say anything.

Baba nodded heavily, as if my silence confirmed his statement. "We will come to her shortly," he said. "At the moment, I am interested in the necklace. You must return it."

"I don't know what kind of shit Pete has been feeding you, but I don't have the slightest idea what you are talking about. What necklace?"

"Bullshit, motherfucker," Pete said, doing a perverse hornpipe of fury and glee. "I heard you and your prick of a partner planning a job before you went to the desert. When you came back you were tore up like a couple of sailors who tangled with a barroom full of Marines. When Baba told me someone fought Jimmy Z and tried to steal the diamonds, I knew it was you guys."

"How did you hear us?" I snapped.

"Through that floor vent," Pete said.

His room was below mine.

"How he heard is irrelevant," Baba said. "He did hear, and when I mentioned the attempted robbery to him last Saturday, we put two and two together and he started watching you. He has been helping me with . . . certain tasks since last summer. He is always most willing to be of assistance if his efforts are recognized in a monetary fashion." He smiled a mixed smile at Pete and then went on: "I was less confident than he that you were the culprits, but the possibility certainly existed."

That explained Baba's laser-like interest in me on the beach on Saturday evening. I tried to think when and where Reggie and I had discussed the burglary and when Pete had been around. They couldn't have known about the previous night's plan ahead of time or they would have moved the necklace and tipped off the police.

"So what are you saying? You think me and Reggie tried to steal a diamond necklace in Palm Springs last weekend and that we did steal it last night?"

"I know you did," Baba said. "And I have to have it back. I need it as collateral for equity in a real estate project I have in hand. My partners in that project are not the most spiritual of men. They have half a million dollars earnest money at stake, which they stand to lose if the deal falls through. The deadline is five o'clock tomorrow afternoon. If we aren't fully collateralized before then, our option will expire and the project will collapse. My partners have informed me several times this week that if I don't provide my share of the equity in time, there will be dire consequences."

His voice trembled a little. Despite his size and spiritual accomplishments, he was scared of the Italians.

"They will certainly kill you if they find out your actions were responsible for scuttling the deal," he went on. "That is an outcome I could, with regret, accept. But if they lose five hundred thousand dollars, they will also want to kill me, I think. As you might imagine, I am not so easily reconciled to that outcome. So I need the necklace back, and I need it back now. If you refuse to return it voluntarily, I will have to allow Namo and Pete to indulge their lower natures and use pain, and the fear of even greater pain, to compel you. Other people could be harmed as well."

"What makes you so sure that I stole the jewels?" I said. "Just because Pete suspects me hardly proves . . ."

"I see everything—here," Baba said, jabbing a blunt finger into his broad forehead. "And then of course there is this." He held up the Krugerrand I had left out of the stash. "Some of these gold coins were stolen along with the jewels. This one was on the table beside your bed when we arrived this morning. That is conclusive, I think."

I had taken the coin back from Oz for safekeeping, but was so tired when I came upstairs I hadn't bothered to put it away. It would give the cops enough for a search warrant and make it very hard to convince Baba that he was chanting up the wrong chimney.

"I've had that for years," I said and laughed. "Even if some Krugerrands were stolen last night, it doesn't prove I had anything to do with it. There are millions of Krugers scattered around Los Angeles."

"Have it your own way, asshole," Pete said, pulling a leather blackjack out of his back pocket and circling to my right so that he was on one side of the bed and Namo on the other. "I got a cut coming when this deal closes, and you ain't jewing me out of it."

"Wait!" Baba said. "The less trouble we have here, the better. If you don't value your own skin, perhaps you care more about the delicate epidermis of our mutual friend Mary. It would be a shame if her loveliness were to be marred."

"If you hurt that girl, I'll kill you," I said.

Baba nodded and smiled as satisfied a smile as he was capable of with Discenza and his men waiting in the wings, tapping their Italian loafers.

"It is as I suspected," he said.

"Where is she, you fat fucking hypocrite?"

"Watch yer mouth," Namo said.

"She is locked up, safe and sound," Baba said. "We had a disagreement yesterday evening when she declined to participate in the culmination of a ritual. Her refusal to submit led to an argument about the role of sexuality in spiritual development and human relationships. Your name came up in that argument in such a way as to make me believe that you two have formed a mutual attachment. Considering our suspicions of you, I thought that might make her a useful tool. In addition, I didn't want her running to the authorities with any wild tales. So I locked her up. Are you going to force us to knock you out and take you to watch her be abused in order to secure your cooperation? Would you enjoy seeing Namo have his way with her? Or will you play it smart, as they say, and turn over the necklace?"

When I didn't answer, Baba continued, putting a powerfully persuasive note in his voice: "If you give me the necklace, I will give you the girl, only slightly the worse for wear. I will also let you keep the golden coins and any other booty you may have taken from Hildebrand. You and the girl can go your way, richer than you were, and I will go my way. Neither of us want police involvement, and that will give us a comfortable level of what could be called mutually assured destruction. You don't have to worry about me turning you in for burglary and safecracking, and I don't have to worry about the two of you making any allegations about illegal activity at the ashram."

"All right," I said, resignedly. "I guess you've got me over a barrel. I'll give you the necklace, if you promise to let Mary go and let me keep the Krugerrands."

The loving smile, tinged with relief, widened beneath Baba's big nose. "This is wise, Robert. I knew from our first meeting that you were an intelligent man."

"Be careful!" Pete said. "He'll try and pull something."

"Not while we have the girl," Baba said. "And the gun. Where is the necklace?"

"I'll get it," I said, throwing back the covers.

Namo raised the snubnose as I put my feet on the floor.

"Tell this goon to step back so I can get out of bed."

"I am not sure that is a good idea," Baba said. "Why don't you just tell us where it is?"

"It's hidden under the house," I said, standing up. "I'll have to show you."

"Watch him, Namo," Pete said.

"I got him covered."

Baba shrugged. "Let him get dressed. There's no time to waste. The necklace has to be at the appraiser's by the close of business today in order for the bank to provide the funds by tomorrow evening."

The clothes I had worn the previous night were on the floor beside the bed. I stepped into my pants, put my shirt on and buttoned it up, then sat back down on the edge of the bed to put on my shoes.

Namo was hovering over me in a threatening way while Pete stood guard at the bedroom door with his sap in case I tried to make a run for it. He wasn't a big guy, but he was in good shape. It would be tough to get past him without taking a debilitating blow from the blackjack.

When I stood up again, I patted my pants pockets. "One of you guys got a cigarette?" I asked.

"No, we don't have a cigarette, asshole," Pete said.

"You shouldn't smoke, Robert," Baba said, disapprovingly. "It is bad for your health."

"I only do it when I am nervous," I said, fishing in my front shirt pocket.

"Let's go," Namo said, reaching out with his free hand to grasp my shoulder and turn me toward the door.

As he grabbed my shoulder, the gun swung wide. When it was pointing at thin air instead of my navel, I whipped Oz's razor blade out and slashed his left forearm and then his face with a quick back and forth motion of my hand. He screamed and dropped the pistol, using his gun hand to try and staunch the blood spurting from the arteries in his arm. I sprinted for the window.

"Stop him!" Pete yelled.

Baba bounded up from the chair to cut me off but jumped back when I slashed at his face.

I dove through the closed window. Its dry-rotted frame gave way like balsa wood and I landed among splinters and broken glass on the shed roof over the back porch, rolled down the roof, and dropped over the edge into the alley.

"After him!" I heard Baba roar, but no one came out the window. Baba was too fat, Namo too bloody, and Pete most likely too chicken.

I ran south half a block to Market, dodged over to the boardwalk and sprinted north, weaving around morning strollers. At Horizon, I circled back to Pacific, peeking around the corner of a brick building. There was no one in front of the flophouse. Namo's wounds had slowed them down.

I raced across Pacific and along Horizon to Mr. Parker's. He was situating a Corolla at the back of the lot. I grabbed my keys out of the shack and ran to the Seville, which was parked with its nose toward the gap in the chain.

"Hey, now," Mr. Parker said, hurrying toward me. He didn't allow people to get their own keys.

"Sorry," I yelled as I hopped in. "I'm in a big hurry."

CHAPTER FORTY-ONE

Things were bad. A slippery handful of lowlifes knew that Reggie and I had committed a series of felonies that could send us to prison for years, and they had at least one piece of potentially damning evidence. It was very possible that I had lost the necklace again, this time irretrievably. To have it and lose it and have it and lose it again was too much. I felt like I was flailing in quicksand. Baba might search the room and find it, along with the gold and bonds, leaving us nothing to show for our time and risk and effort and outlay on tools. Or the cops might move in, blocking a return to the flophouse, putting us on the run. And Mary. I didn't know what Baba had done to or with her. I couldn't think about it. To top it all off, there were homicidal gangsters moving in the shadows.

Things were bad. And they were about to get a lot worse.

I parked at Brooks and Seventh Street, one block over from Broadway, took a couple of deep breaths to slow my heart and calm my mind, then got out and took the tire tool from the trunk and jogged along Seventh to the ashram. There was a Magic Marker–scrawled sign on the locked front door that said the Murshid Center was closed for a staff retreat. No reopening date was mentioned.

There was no one on this residential street at ten o'clock on a Tuesday morning. The wooden panel door was old and shrunken in its frame. I stomped it open, leaving a splintered jamb.

I was headed for the stairs, intent on finding Mary, when something in the gift shop caught my eye. The French doors were closed and the lights were out, but when I glanced that way, scanning for enemies, I noticed something behind the counter.

Something orange.

Something still.

It was Ganesha, a young man who had had the highest of human ambitions. He was lying on his back, one arm pinned under his body, the other stretched above his head as if he was reaching for something. The front of his robe was soaked with blood. I would never know how or why or when, but at some point after he came, shocked and new, into the blinding light of a hospital delivery room, he had looked out at the sunshine and trees, or down into the pages of an ancient book, and felt the joy of God sting his soul. Turning away from common desires, or most of them, at least, he had devoted his life to seeking knowledge of the divine, trying for the ultimate goal of welding his being to the infinite.

He was in the infinite now, and I wished him Godspeed.

"May Christ protect you and have mercy on your soul," I said. "Sri Ramakrishna open the doors of heaven for this man. Yogananda and Muktananda receive his spirit. Saint Michael and all you angels of light surround him. Protect us now and at the hour of our death."

There are much better funeral prayers than the one I offered—in the Tibetan Book of the Dead and other traditions—but I didn't know them. I did the best I could for him. His body was still warm, so I knew his spirit was in the early hours of its journey. His eyes were open as the eyes of the dead always are before the living compulsively close them, symbolizing their expanded vision. With the eyes of his Akashic body, he was seeing sights more amazing than any ever seen on earth, and I repeated my prayer fiercely several times, willing my words to pierce the veil between the worlds and find him in the place where his soul was hurtling.

There was no smell of gunpowder in the air. It looked to me like he had been stabbed at the counter and then fallen and bled to death where he lay. There was blood on the stool where he usually sat and a few drops on the countertop and the phone book that lay on the counter. The phone book was open to the page that listed all the different numbers for the city of Venice, including the underlined number of the police department. He had been ready to blow the whistle, but someone had stopped him. Namo with his knife. I would settle that score if I got the chance. I was glad I had cut him with the razor blade.

Leaving the young monk's body where it lay, I pounded up the stairs, more frightened than before for Mary. I found her locked in one of the client rooms. She was gagged and hog-tied on the floor, half-dressed in what was left of the robe she had worn the night before. When she saw me burst through the door her eyes flashed heartrending relief that mirrored my own emotions.

"What are you doing here?" she asked with a sob in her voice when I loosed the gag.

"I'm here to rescue you, hot stuff," I said, working on the ropes. Her slender wrists had been rubbed raw as she struggled to escape.

"How did you know I was in trouble?"

"Baba paid me a visit."

When I helped her up, she put her arms around me and gave me a long, hard hug, then stepped back and looked me in the eye.

"Where is that fat motherfucker?" she said, all her maiden-in-distress emotion swallowed up in anger. "I am going to bash his melon head in."

"What did he do to you?" Rage seethed up inside me, turning my field of vision red around the edges.

"I'm okay, baby," she said, reining in her own outrage long enough to stroke my cheek and give me a quick kiss on the lips. "But he's not going to be when I get my hands on him. Is he here?"

The ferocity flashing in her flame-blue eyes reminded me that the worst fate a captured Native American warrior could face was being turned over to the women of his enemies for squaw torture.

"He's not here, but he's probably on his way with some armed men. We need to get out quick. Are you sure you're all right?"

"I turned my first trick at Disneyland when I was thirteen years old, Robert. No pimp. Just me and a fat Shriner on the Small World ride. I can handle what they dish out. What kills me is that I fell for his bullshit. I can't believe I let that bastard con me. You were so right about him. He's a total fake."

"We'll fix his wagon," I said. "Don't worry about that. Right now we have to move. Where are your clothes?"

"In his bedroom," she said. "He let me use his closet and his bathroom so that I could have some privacy from the other girls. He said it was because I had spiritual potential, but that was a lie. He was just trying to get in my pants."

"Gather up whatever you want to take with you while I toss his desk and file cabinet."

The oak file cabinet was sturdy but I got in, using a stone statue of Buddha to hammer the tip of the tire tool behind the lock, then prying until the tongue of the lock bent and the top drawer popped open.

There was nothing but old books and files in the cabinet. Most of the file folders were stuffed with precomputer typed research notes and manuscript drafts dealing with esoteric topics: "Splitting the Atom of Religion in the Modern Age"; "Situational Ethics vs. Absolute Morality"; "Triumph over Tradition: Renegade Teachers and Holy Fools." The books were dusty spiritual treatises in several languages, many of them annotated in a neat masculine hand. Baba had been an ambitious scholar earlier in his career, and all five drawers were filled with the remnants of his intellectual labors, nothing of use to me.

The locked desk drawers yielded more: a loaded .38 revolver with a checkered wooden grip (nice prop for a guru to lean on); several 35-mm film containers full of black-tar opium (to fertilize the flower girls, no doubt); a shoebox full of pharmaceutical drugs, including lots of Valium and injectable Demerol, complete with a set of glass works (more fun for the girls, and maybe for Baba); several years' worth of stock market trading records listing frequent margin calls (an explanation for Baba's growing financial hunger); and a set of files with names and dated photographs of important-looking men engaged in rude behavior with one or more of the temple prostitutes.

Some of the blackmail files had only one compromising photograph; some contained several. All included typewritten notes about the circumstances in which the photographs were taken—the names of the girls involved, their ages, the acts performed, and in some cases the places the men had told their wives they were while they were getting their jollies. Some also listed payment dates and amounts.

I recognized several faces. One was Councilman Discenza. Another was the mayor of Venice Beach. There were high-ranking police officers and prominent local businessmen.

The files explained a lot—how Baba was able to run a spiritual whorehouse with impunity and why the mayor had pushed the city council to promptly approve every phase of the Pacific City development despite voter outrage. They left other things unexplained. Had Baba converted his blackmail of Discenza into a business partnership or was he holding the photo of the churchgoing Italian engaged in anal sex with a teenager in reserve in case he needed leverage? Was Pacific City a project of Discenza's that Baba had wormed his thick torso into, or was it Baba's baby, which he was using Discenza's influence to accomplish? Judging by the fear Baba had shown earlier, it seemed more like the former—like he had gotten a piece of the project by making himself useful to Discenza and found out that he had a tiger by the tail.

"What did you find?" Mary said. She was dressed in a pair of blue jeans, a yellow blouse, and white sneakers with ankle socks. She had a small brown suitcase in her hand.

"Drugs, a gun, some stuff he's using to blackmail people."

She shook her head in disgust. "What a fucker. What's that in the back of the drawer?"

There was a leather-bound notebook stuck behind the hanging files in the bottom drawer. The leather was water-stained and scuffed, the cover latched with a rusty push-button lock.

"It looks like an old journal," I said. "Maybe Baba has been keeping a record of his badness."

I put the drugs, stock records, blackmail files, and the notebook in a pillowcase that I stripped from Baba's bed. I checked the cylinder on the gun to be sure it was loaded, then stuck it in my belt beneath my shirttail. It felt good to be armed again. Taking Mary's hand, I led her downstairs and back through the big white-and-yellow kitchen where we had made *prasad* together. Just inside the back door, I gave her my car keys and the key card from Le Merigot.

"Do you know where Le Merigot is?" I asked her.

"It's just south of the pier, isn't it?"

I nodded. "I'm parked on the next block. If we go straight across the backyard and cut through the hedge and the yard behind us, we should come out by the car. It's a dark-blue Cadillac Seville. If there is any trouble, drop your bag and run for the car. If I have to stop and fight, go without me. Drive to the hotel and wait for me there."

"Forget that, pal," Mary said, stepping close so that her body touched mine. "I love tough guys who aren't afraid of a fight. Especially really sweet tough guys. But if Baba shows up, I'm carving a piece of that blubber myself."

Reaching between the lower buttons of her blouse, she pulled out a pearl-handled switchblade and pushed the button, flashing four inches of razory steel.

"You are one surprising girl," I said. "And that is one impressive blade. But it ain't smart to bring a knife to a gunfight. If there's any trouble, please just get to the car."

"All right," she said after a moment, putting her knife away. "If it comes to that, I'll beat feet to your car and fire it up. But I'm not leaving without you."

We hustled out the back door and across the lawn and through the rose garden, passing the statue of the Virgin Mary. The hair was standing up on the back of my neck. I had a feeling that Baba was going to come bounding around the house at any moment, accompanied by wild-eyed Sicilians with machine guns. But we found a gap in the hedge and hurried across the adjoining yard and made it to the Caddie with no shots fired.

Mary popped the locks and tossed me the keys.

"Nice car," she said as we pulled away from the curb.

"I bought it to impress chicks."

"It's working."

CHAPTER FORTY-TWO

At Le Merigot, I gave the valet a five and told him to keep my car in front, then took Mary in through the lobby and up to the room I had rented the night before.

"*Very* nice," she said when she saw the marble whirlpool tub and the large luxurious room with a balcony and a view of the ocean. "Is this to impress chicks, too?"

"No," I said. "This is a hideout."

"I was right about you!"

"Yeah," I admitted.

"That's cool!" she said. "What are we going to do now? How are we going to get Baba?"

With no discussion, it was understood between us that we were a team now, in the situation together. Briefly, I filled her in on what was at stake besides revenge—the jewels and gold and my and Reggie's freedom.

"I heard someone tried to steal that necklace in the desert," she said. "That was you guys?"

"Yeah."

I finished telling her about what had happened in Indian Wells, at the lawyer's office the night before, and at the flophouse that morning. Most people would say it was foolish of me to take her into my confidence, but I was sure I could trust her. You don't stay free as a criminal as long as I had without accurate intuition.

"Do you think they found the necklace?" she asked.

"We'll know soon enough."

She knew Evelyn from the ashram and was riveted when I explained the rich lady's part in the story—the picture in Ozone Pacific's magazine, the missing daughter, Baba's extortion scheme.

"How does he know all that stuff about her daughter?"

"That's the sixty-four-dollar question. Maybe he read Evelyn's mind. Maybe he actually came across someone who knew the girl. Maybe a combination of things."

Mary asked a couple more questions, then nodded decisively.

"I like the safecracking," she said, treating me to a radiant smile. "I knew you weren't small-time. How can I help?"

"Stay here until I get back, then we'll see. As long as Baba hasn't found the diamonds, we won't have to worry about getting even with him. When the resort deal falls through and the Italians' half million goes up in smoke, they'll skin him alive."

"Sounds good," she said, looking around the suite with pleased anticipation. Its decor contrasted favorably with the ashram's faded ambiance. "Maybe I'll take a bubble bath while you're gone."

"Don't say things like that. It puts thoughts in my head."

"I know."

Checkout time was noon, so I stopped in the lobby and paid for another day, then jumped in the Caddie and drove south on Pacific. The flophouse was quiet as I rolled by, no cops or gangsters in sight.

I parked at a meter several blocks farther south and walked over to Chavi's booth on the boardwalk, searching for my partner.

He was standing near the fortune-teller, looking a tall thin black man up and down. There was an electronic bathroom scale on the asphalt in front of him and a sign tacked to the palm tree behind him that said "Guess Yer weight for five Dollers."

"Reggie," I said.

He held up a stubby forefinger to put me on hold, then punched the black guy lightly on the shoulder and tapped him on the chest with two fingers a couple of times.

"One fifty-seven," he said.

A furtive look of surprise flashed across the man's face before he veiled it with an expression of bored skepticism.

"You way off, man. I weigh one sixty-five."

"Step on the scale." Reggie pointed at the bathroom appliance.

"Why I wanna step on the scale?" the man extemporized. "You probably got it rigged."

"How else we gonna know if I'm right?" Reggie said. "You got a scale with you?"

"What you talkin' about, do I got a scale? Who carries a scale around with them?"

"Then cough up the five bucks, chump."

"Oh, so now you don't even want me to weigh in on your scale?"

"Be my guest," Reggie said.

The man stepped up on the scale and all three of us looked down at the digital readout, which flickered to 158 and froze.

"See? You off by a pound!"

"Said I'd guess within two pounds. Cough up the dough."

"Aw, shit, I don't care about no lousy five dollars." The man pulled a crumpled bill from his pocket and handed it to Reggie, then walked off with an air of disgust.

Stone-faced but with the hint of a smirk, Reggie straightened the bill out, snapped it once, then folded it and put it in his pocket.

"When did you come up with this brilliant idea?" I asked.

"This morning. Chavi's been telling me I ought to have a hustle, so I borrowed her scale and made me a sign. What's up?"

"Trouble. We need to move fast."

Saucer eyes. "What?"

"I'll tell you on the way."

Engrossed in the palm of a bare-chested young man with blond dreadlocks, Chavi didn't look up as we headed for the Caddie. Hurrying along the boardwalk and driving to the rental car, I told Reggie what had happened.

"That skinny kid in the orange nightgown?"

"Yeah."

"Who killed him?"

"Probably Namo, the guy I cut with the razor blade."

"How'd you happen to be packing a razor blade?"

"I got it from Ozone Pacific."

"That squirrelly kid who lives next door?"

"Yeah."

"Why'd he give you a razor blade?"

I shook my head. "I'll explain later." I wondered what had become of Oz in the hubbub at the house, if he was around when they ransacked the place.

At the rental, I retrieved the Tomcat from the glove box and wiped down the wheel, dashboard, and door handles. I had planned to return the car to get my five hundred back, but that now seemed too risky. The detectives investigating the burglary at Hildebrand's probably hadn't had time to look at the previous night's patrol reports and find out about the two Sacramento tourists who were questioned in Norm's parking lot across the street from the crime scene—but they might have. If they had, they would have traced the rental to Enterprise and planted a plainclothes lurker near the airport return counter.

By the time I finished erasing our fingerprints, Reggie had moved the tools from the trunk of the rental to the trunk of the Seville. We climbed in the Caddie and headed north. There was still nothing unusual as we cruised back past the flop. Circling, I drove into the alley behind the house, alert for blue uniforms and black fedoras. My heart was pounding when I pulled up by the kitchen door.

"Keep the engine running," I said, handing Reggie Baba's .38. "If you hear me yell or guns start going off, come in blazing."

Upstairs, my room and Reggie's had been torn to pieces. They had cut the mattresses, smashed the furniture, scattered clothes everywhere.

But they hadn't found the stash.

Besides the diamonds, gold, and bonds, the hiding place held several thousand dollars in cash, including two of the packets of hundreds from Fahim, two boxes of shells for the Tomcat, an extra clip (full), and my passport. I put everything in a shoulder bag and then looked around until I found a map of California in the debris on the floor. I opened it up and refolded it so that it showed the coast north of Santa Barbara, then circled the town of Pismo Beach with a pen, scrawled the following day's date beneath the circle, and tossed the map back on the floor. After taking a last look around the place where I had lived for six memorable weeks, I picked up the shoulder bag and ran back to the alley with springs in my heels.

"We're still in business, bro," I said when I got in the car. "Head for Le Merigot, that hotel we went to last night."

It was an overwhelming relief to have the diamonds back in my possession. If someone had dragged a bow across a violin, I might have wept for joy. I had spent four weeks and traveled hundreds of miles and been in three fights and committed at least a dozen felonies to get them and it would have been hard to remain detached if they had slipped through my fingers. I would have been bereft, as if I had lost a person dear to me, seeing the necklace in my mind's eye like the afterimage of a candle flame, for years to come.

Now I could turn them over to Fahid in exchange for a small fortune and we would leave town, riding high, for the time being at least, with a bundle of cash and a charming new companion. I hoped.

The only blight on the rose was our legal jeopardy. It wasn't clear exactly how much trouble we would be leaving behind us, but it didn't look good. The doughnut eaters would be snuffing for whoever cracked Hildebrand's safe. At some point my illustrious name would come up. Baba knew where I lived. Mrs. Sharpnick knew my identify. In the course of routine interviews, the cops would find out that I had had dinner with Evelyn and questioned her about the necklace. Two patrolmen had seen Reggie and me near the scene of the crime. With our mug shots, they would probably find people in the desert who could identify us, especially if the linebacker and her little man were still in town. Searching for me, the Santa Monica dicks would contact the Newport Beach police and get an earful from the family man. That would sharpen their interest. The two departments might pool resources to try and track me down. Warrants would be issued.

We were going to get away with the loot, but if there was electronic paper swirling in the slipstream, our lives would be forever less enjoyable and free. Crossing a state line doesn't do much good anymore. International boundaries put distance and probability on the criminal's side but don't block pursuit. Except in a few remote countries that don't have extradition treaties with the U.S., modern fugitives can never really relax. There is always the fear of a hand on the shoulder from behind.

Part of my mind started to catalogue which countries lacked treaties and how long a couple of hundred thousand dollars would last in a comfortable adobe. But I caught myself and shut down the mental travel agency to concentrate on the present moment. First things first: I had to make sure we did actually get away before worrying about the fugitive future.

Back at the hotel, we valeted the car to get it out of sight and went up to the room. It was perfumed with the bergamot scent of the hotel's expensive shampoo and lotion. Wrapped in a fluffy white robe, Mary was curled up in an easy chair by the French doors that opened onto the balcony, bent over a book that lay open in her lap. She looked faintly mermaid-like with her long damp blond hair hanging down and the blue sea splashing on the shore behind her.

"Rob!" she said when we came in.

"What?"

"I found out how Baba knew all those things about Evelyn's daughter."

"How?"

"This is her diary!" She hurried across the room, holding out the leather-bound volume we found in Baba's desk.

"Is her name in it?"

"No," Mary said, "but look, it mentions the things you said Baba talked about—restaurants in San Francisco, a ranch where she used to go horseback riding with her mom . . . what her father did to her."

She was standing close beside me, flipping through the pages to show me passages she had marked. The tops and bottoms of the pages were water stained and deteriorated but the middle sections were legible. The entries were in both ink and pencil. The handwriting was a loopy, girlish script that deteriorated in places to a scrawl.

"See there, where she mentions Kelly? Evelyn told you that was the name of her daughter's baby, right?"

"That's what she said."

Turning the yellowed pages, I saw that she was right. The notebook, which looked like it had lain someplace damp and dirty for a long time, was the diary of Evelyn's daughter and the source of Baba's mysterious information.

"Who is this 'he' Christina keeps mentioning?"

"I think that's the baby," Mary said. "She says how beautiful he is and how much she loves him and wants to protect him."

"But I thought Christina's baby was a girl."

"Kelly can be a boy's name, too. Did Evelyn tell you it was a girl?"

"I don't know. I don't remember her saying that, but she showed me a picture of a baby dressed in pink . . ."

"Who gives a shit what the baby was wearing?" Reggie interjected. "We can buy it a blue bonnet and a binkie on our way out of town. Right now we gotta figure out the next move."

"It's figured," I said. "Just hold on a second."

I turned to the last entry in the diary, dated July 4, 1984. Scanning the final few scrawled pages, I felt a seismic shift in my psyche. As the mental landscape re-formed, I saw a way out of our legal difficulties open up like a pass between two distant hills.

"What do you want to know?" I asked Reggie.

"How quick can we fence the loot?"

"I'll call Fahim right now and let him know I'm coming. I doubt if he has enough cash on hand, but he should be able to get it within a few hours. We'll drop the jewels and coins off there this afternoon."

"We going back to the flop to get our shit or splittin' from here?"

"Anything there you can't live without?"

"Nada."

"Then we leave from here. We'll have plenty of money to replace anything we leave behind."

"Where we going?"

"South of the border."

"The cops gonna be on our tail?"

I looked my partner in the eye. "Right now, I'd say they are after two guys from Sacramento who are supposed to be staying at the Georgian, but by the time they get done with their interviews in a day or two they may be looking for me and you."

Reggie gave me deadpan for a few seconds, then shrugged.

"We'll be long gone by then," he said and smiled a smile that reflected torchlight, tequila, and dark-eyed señoritas.

I turned to Mary. "I was hoping you'd come with us."

She sprang into my arms. "I was afraid you weren't going to ask."

We kissed long and lusciously. When I slipped my hand beneath her robe, Reggie made an annoyed sound.

"All right, you two," he said with a sour look. "That's enough of the lovey-dovey routine. Get it in gear."

CHAPTER FORTY-THREE

Mary went into the bathroom to put her pants and shirt back on while Reggie walked out onto the balcony and stood at the railing with his back to the room, looking toward the ocean. I called Fahim.

"It sounds like a most valuable item," he said. "The same stones as in the earrings?"

"Pink diamonds," I said, "but better."

"Ah! Come at two-thirty. I will be ready for you."

I glanced at my watch. It was a few minutes past one.

"See you then."

I called the valet desk and told them to bring the Seville around, then packed the stuff from Baba's desk in Mary's suitcase. I put the jewel case in my pocket and stuck the Tomcat back in my belt under my shirttail. A few minutes later, the three of us were strolling calmly through the richly appointed lobby and out into the portico, where the Caddie was idling.

Rather than cruise the cop-infested streets of Santa Monica, I took the 10 east to the 405 and drove north to Wilshire. We had lunch at a sub shop in Westwood, then rolled along Wilshire into Beverly Hills. It was 2:25 p.m. when I pulled up at a meter a couple of blocks from Fahim's shop and parked in the shade of a banyan tree. The banyan is sacred in the Hindu religion, its ever-expanding branches representing eternity. It is called *kalpavriksha*, "divine wish-fulfilling tree." It felt lucky to park beneath it.

"You guys wait here," I told Mary and Reggie. "Fahim doesn't like strangers."

Taking the canvas bag of coins from the suitcase, I walked away through the dappled sun and shade beneath the queen palms that lined the avenue. A well-to-do breeze stroked my forehead, cheeks, and bare forearms like an endless bolt of silk unrolling.

Fahim examined the necklace as he had the earrings, running his various tests. It took all of his savoir faire to keep from showing his excitement.

"Quality as always," he said. "May I ask how heated the item is?"

"How hot?"

"Yes."

"Very hot. I wouldn't even try to move the individual stones in Los Angeles."

"Thank you for your honesty, Robert."

He offered me $100,000, citing the difficulty of disposing of something so notorious. I scoffed and countered with $150,000, mentioning Evelyn's jeweler's $500,000 estimate of the necklace's value. Very shortly we settled on a price of $120,000. He paid full value for the Krugerrands, minus a 10-percent handling fee. At the day's quote, that came to another $22,600. He had all of the money on hand, in hundreds and fifties, and provided a sturdy leather briefcase with a combination lock to carry it in. It took all of my savoir faire to keep a calm demeanor in the presence of that much cash.

I wrote the combination on a piece of paper and put it in my wallet and shook hands with Fahim. We walked from the back room through the shop, past a lady in a mink jacket who was being shown an emerald ring by Fahim's daughter.

"When will I see you again?" he asked at the door.

"It may be a while."

"*Ma'a salaame*," he said. *Go in peace.*

"*Allay salmak,*" I said. *May God keep you safe.*

Back at the car, Mary and Reggie were swapping stories about where their alcoholic mothers hid the bottle.

"Whud we clear?" Reggie asked causally, playing it cool in front of the pretty girl.

"A hundred and forty grand after expenses."

"Holy cow!" Mary said, snuggling up to me and making a purring sound in my ear that sent shivers down my spine.

"That the gold, too?" Reggie asked.

"That's everything but the bonds."

"Not too shabby for a night's work," he said, as if six-figure jobs were run-of-the-mill for him.

Mary turned her head slightly so that Reggie couldn't see and rolled her eyes.

I laughed and hugged her, then reached back and gave Reggie a solid punch on the shoulder.

"It's the best fucking score either one of us has ever made by a long shot," I said. "You did great."

Reggie shrugged. "What now?"

"I have one stop to make, then we're in the wind," I said. "We'll leave the car here and take the Surfliner to San Diego. We can pick up some wheels there and cross the border at Tecate."

"Let's swing by Chavi's, too," Reggie said. "She'll worry if we just disappear."

"You got it, brother. Anything you need to do, Mary?"

"I'm ready to ride, sweetie."

A promising double entendre, if ever there was one.

I drove south to the canal district and pulled up in front of Evelyn's bungalow. She would have to get someone else to fix it up if she stayed.

"Who lives here?" Reggie asked, mystified.

"Evermore," I said. "You've been here before."

His eyebrows shot up to his hairline. "Whadaya want with her?"

"I'm going to give her Christina's diary," I said. "And there is something I have to tell her."

Evelyn answered the door the instant I knocked, same as she had on my earlier visit, as if she spent her time poised at the threshold of her empty house, waiting for someone to arrive and fill it with life and meaning. She looked like she had been crying.

"What are you doing here?" she asked.

"I have something for you. What's wrong?"

"Baba called me." Grabbing my arm, she pulled me inside, shutting the door behind us.

When we came back out a little while later, new hope was twisted tightly with old fear in her expression.

Reggie got out of the car as we came down the walk.

"Everything all right?" he asked, glancing around the neighborhood to see if a trap was about to be sprung. "What took so long?"

I opened the back curbside door of the Seville and Evelyn got in.

"What the hell is going on?" Reggie said after I closed the door. "Are we kidnapping her? What's she boo-hooing about?"

"Baba Raba took Ozone Pacific hostage."

"Why? What's he want with him?"

"He's trying to collect a ransom. He wants the necklace, or a hundred and fifty thousand bucks."

"Yer not going to give him the moolah, are you?" Reggie asked, horrified.

"No, but I am going to make sure he doesn't hurt that kid."

"Fuck that," Reggie said. "Play Dudley Do-Right on your own time. What's a homeless kid to us—or to her?"

"Oz is Evelyn's grandson."

"Her grandson?" His brown eyes went flat as he looked inward, thinking hard, then got bright as he glared at me. "So what? How's that our problem?"

"Baba told her we stole the necklace."

Reggie stiffened, hearing the clank of cell door in his skull. I nodded. "He has some evidence, too. But Evelyn will let us keep the necklace if we get the kid back and she'll do what she can to stop the police investigation. If she and her lawyer don't cooperate, the cops will be hamstrung."

Baba had seen Evelyn and me talking at the ashram on Sunday. Grasping at straws after I got away, he came up with the idea that she might have hired me to steal the necklace so that she wouldn't have to live up to her agreement with him. When he called, he told her that he had found her grandson but that if she didn't turn over the jewels or $150,000 in cash or securities by five that afternoon when he was scheduled to meet Discenza at the appraiser's, the boy would be lost to her forever.

Evelyn didn't believe him at first, but he used his powers of persuasion to convince her, claiming he had DNA evidence proving Ozone Pacific was her grandson. He also told her that he knew exactly where Christina was and would give her the girl's location as soon as the real estate deal closed. Evelyn told him she didn't know anything about the necklace being stolen but that she would get the money if he swore to reunite her with Kelly and tell her where her daughter was. She tried to call Hildebrand for advice and help in getting the funds together, but his office was in an uproar and she couldn't reach him.

When I showed up and admitted that I was, in fact, a burglar and not a contractor, Evelyn's confusion whirled faster, but then gradually subsided. I convinced her that I was on her side and wanted to help her. She was too desperate to bother about moral judgments. When I showed her Christina's diary, she saw that Baba had been lying to her all along.

I told her about Ganesha's murder and confirmed that Baba was telling the truth about Ozone. I also made it clear that he could not be trusted to return the boy. Even if she had been able to raise the money on such short notice, even if I was willing to use the money in the briefcase, I didn't think it would get him back. Baba was going off his rocker, resorting all at once to murder and kidnapping. There was no telling what he might do— kill Oz to keep him quiet about the snatch, or hang on to him so that he could extort more money from Evelyn, or use the threat of harming the boy to keep her from going to the cops.

With me coaching her, Evelyn called the guru and told him that she would be at the ashram with the cash by four-thirty. She swore that she hadn't told anyone else about the meeting and that she didn't care about the money, only her grandson and daughter.

"Don't hurt him, Baba," she said. "I know you need the money for your work, and it's worth it to me to get Kelly and Christina back."

I hoped the phone call would be enough to put him off guard.

"We're going to help her, aren't we?" Mary said when Reggie and I got back in the car. In her eyes I could see our future together hanging in the balance. If I had been undecided about what to do, her attitude would have tipped the scale.

"Of course we are."

It was 3:35 when I sparked the Northstar engine. My instinct was to charge. Go straight at the ashram, where I believed Oz was being held and take Baba by surprise while he waited complacently for Evelyn to deliver. We'd rescue the boy, find out if Baba really knew where Christina was, and then leave him incapacitated for Discenza to deal with.

"Stop by the flop," Reggie said grimly after I explained the plan. "I got a piece there."

"What's wrong with Baba's gun?"

Reggie shook his head. "Um used to mine."

"You live in this dump?" Mary said when we pulled up in the alley.

"Not anymore," I said. "Slide over here behind the wheel. I'm going in with Reggie. If any shit goes down, take Evelyn back to the hotel and wait for us there."

The back door was unlocked and we went in through the kitchen, slow and careful. I had the Tomcat in my hand. As we crossed the living room toward the stairs, Budge came rushing down the hallway from his room.

"Rob!" he said, then pulled up short when he saw the pistol. "Why you got a gun?"

"There's been some trouble. Have you seen Oz today?"

"Yeah," he said, looking scared. "I saw Pete and Baba Raba taking him away somewhere. It looked like he didn't want to go."

"Why didn't you stop them?"

"I would have, Rob," he said. "But I saw them from upstairs and they took off before I could get out there. Where do you think they're takin' him?"

"What happened to your hand?" Reggie said.

"I bust it while I was drunk last night," he said. "What's going on, Rob? Why you guys' rooms all tore up? Where they takin' Oz? He ain't gonna know how to act out there without someone to keep an eye him. He ain't been off the beach in years."

Tanned face puffy, hair tousled, eyes bloodshot, Budge looked hungover and badly constipated. Viewing him in his board shorts and ratty Los Angeles Rams T-shirt, most people would have seen nothing but an over-the-hill beach bum who had drunk too much beer and wasted too much precious time to be good for much of anything, except more of the same.

I saw backup.

"Is there anyone else in the house?" I asked him.

"No."

"Reggie, grab your pistol and a change of clothes for each of us as quick as you can."

"Why we need clothes? I thought we were leaving everything."

"We might get bloody."

He nodded and jogged up the stairs.

I turned back to Budge. "Pete and Baba Raba are holding Oz for ransom. I can't explain everything right now but they say they are going to hurt him if they don't get the money they want in the next hour. We're on our way to get him back. We aren't planning on giving them any money. You can come with us if you want to."

Budge's fat-padded body stiffened and expanded, like Superman's when he tears off his Clark Kent outfit. His face turned angry and hard. "Fuckin' A," he said. "Where are they?"

"We think they have him at Baba's ashram over on Broadway. You have a weapon?"

"I don't need no weapon for those two," he said. "I'll tear their fucking heads off if they hurt that kid."

"I don't doubt that," I said. "But they are armed and a weapon might come in handy. You got a knife or a blackjack or anything like that?"

"I got a fish club in my room."

"Grab it."

Reggie came down the stairs at the same time Budge returned from his room, holding a smooth, hard skull splitter. It was a cross between a police billy club and a principal's paddle, an inch thick and two inches wide, and flat, so that it wouldn't roll on a boat. It was ash, the same kind of wood they use for baseball bats, twenty-four inches long, with a round handle at one end and a rawhide strip that slipped around the user's wrist. Wielded edgewise by someone as powerful as Budge, it was potentially lethal.

CHAPTER FORTY-FOUR

We went back through the stinking kitchen to the Cadillac. Mary drove. I sat next to her, with Reggie riding shotgun. Budge climbed in the back with Evelyn, who I introduced as Oz's grandmother.

"I didn't know he had a grandma," Budge said, wonderingly. "Especially not one that looks like you."

We parked on Broadway, two houses down from the Murshid Center for Enlightened Beings. The girls wanted to come in, Mary to get a piece of Baba, Evelyn to make sure no harm came to her grandson, but I convinced them to stay in the car with the motor running.

"We'll be in and out," I said. "I'm not fucking around with these guys."

I sent Budge with his fish billy to the back door, warning him to stick close to the house so he couldn't be seen from the second floor and to duck below the first-floor windows. As Reggie and I crept across the front of the house, he pulled his pistol out of his back pocket. It was a little

.25-caliber automatic that most SoCal crooks would have been embarrassed to be seen with.

"When you going to get a real gun?" I asked him.

"Hah!"

That was all he needed to say. There were three notches in the plastic handle, one of them only six months old. He carved it after killing a psycho slave trader who had been about to kill me.

We went through the front door that I had broken earlier in the day. There was no one in the hall or in the rooms that opened off of it. Ganesha's body was gone from the gift shop.

I was heading for the stairs when I heard laughter in the kitchen.

It got louder as we went down the back hall and became recognizable as Pete's nasty cackle.

"What's so funny?" I said as I pushed through the swinging door into the sunny room with its tall wooden cabinets that hadn't been changed since the house was built.

Baba was sitting at the table in his Armani suit, eating cornflakes from a mixing bowl. Namo sat across from him, poking at his bandaged arm. Pete was leaning against the counter by the sink. All three froze when they saw the guns.

"I hope you're not counting your chickens before they're hatched," I said.

Pete opened his mouth as if to speak but then closed it without answering. He looked frightened. I saw him glance toward the back door.

"Don't try it," I said. "I'll drop you before you take two steps. Where's Oz?"

Pete, bug-eyed, stayed silent. I looked at Baba.

He swallowed a wad of cereal pulp and spoke. "Did Evelyn send you?"

"Yes."

"Did you bring the necklace?" The day had pared still more fullness from his face. It had a lean, haunted look, and his flesh hung more loosely on his frame. He couldn't keep his anxiety out of his voice.

"No," I said.

"The money?"

"Sure," I said. "We brought the money. Where's Oz?"

"He's at a safe location. Show me the money and I will tell you where to find him."

I walked over to Namo. He was giving me a dirty look. He didn't seem quite as worried as he should have been.

"Where's Ozone?" I asked.

"Fuck you," he said.

I lowered the muzzle of the Tomcat and shot him in his meaty calf. He exploded out of the chair with a shocked scream and landed on his back on the linoleum, clutching his leg and cursing.

Standing over him, my ears ringing, I pointed the .32 at his face. "Did you kill Ganesha?"

Face scrunched with pain, he shook his head back and forth so rapidly that his features blurred. I took the snubnose .38 from his belt and stuck it in my back pocket.

Reggie walked over to Pete.

"Where's the kid?" he said.

"Don't say anything, Pete," Baba warned. "It's a Mexican standoff! They have to pay for that information."

Reggie's left hand shot out suddenly and grabbed Pete by the throat. He bent the ex-sailor back over the counter, pushing the .25 against his cheek.

"Um gonna count to three," he said. "One . . ."

"He's in the closet under the stairs," Pete shrieked. "Don't shoot me. I'm a veteran!"

Jerking Pete upright, Reggie slung him toward the table. "Get over there with your punk friends."

"Keep an eye on them," I said, heading for the hallway.

"He's not in there!" Baba said. "You're wasting your time!"

The door, which had an angled top, wasn't locked. Crowded in among folding chairs and cardboard boxes, Oz lay gagged, blindfolded, and bound hand and foot. I pulled the blindfold off first, so he could see who I was, then half-dragged, half-lifted him out into the hall, where I could get at the ropes to untie him.

"Baba Raba and Pete tied me up and put me in there," he said in a trembling voice when I removed the gag. "I told them I wasn't supposed to cross Pacific, but they made me come here. Why did they do that, Rob?"

"They're bad men."

Ganesha's body was in the closet beneath the stairs, too, crammed in a cobwebbed corner. I had that curious urge to lay him out neatly on a bed or table, to cover his body with a blanket and make him comfortable. But he wasn't his body. He never had been. His spirit was far in flight now, God knew where. And I didn't want to leave my DNA on him in a stray hair or drop of salt water. The police would be going over his body carefully, seeking his killer.

So I left him in the closet and took Ozone back through the swinging door into the kitchen. When he saw Baba Raba, his body jerked and stiffened.

"Don't worry," I said. "You're safe now."

"You are a bad man!" Oz said angrily to Baba.

Baba's face flickered at the bitter words, registering an unwelcome stab of self-realization.

"Where's my picture at, you fat baby robber!"

"I know where it is, Oz," I said.

"Where?"

"I'll tell you in a minute," I said. "It's the one you gave Evelyn, isn't it, Baba?"

"Yes."

"Where did you get the diary?"

"I found it," Pete chimed in, eager to cooperate.

"Where?"

"In the crawl space under a house we tore down over on Navy. It was under what was left of the body."

"Christina's body?"

"I don't know who the cunt was," Pete said. "Her skull was smashed and there was nothing left but bones and clothes and that notebook I sold to—"

"You have a big mouth for such a little man," Baba said. "You just squandered our last bargaining chip."

"So you knew Evelyn's daughter was dead the whole time you were stringing her along?"

"Yes, my criminal compadre, I did," he said. "What's wrong with that? I gave her hope and hid the ugly fact that her own actions caused the foolish girl's demise, just as her earlier behavior contributed to the incest. If you read the diary, you know that Christina contacted Evelyn shortly before her death asking for a sum of money to settle a debt. When she was free of the people she had been involved with, she planned to go home to her mother. Evelyn sent the money and the girl was killed for it, leaving this pathetic child to fend for himself."

"How long we gonna stay here jawin'?" Reggie demanded.

"I just have a couple more questions," I said.

"I'll tell you anything you want to know," Pete said. "I'll sing like a canary if you let me walk. I wasn't in on any of the really bad shit. I just did what Baba Raba and Discenza told me to do."

"Like burning down buildings and smashing the windows of inhabited dwellings to drive the tenants away?" Baba said.

"Discenza told me to," Pete snarled. "You knew about it, fatso."

"Knowing about it and doing it are two different things," Baba said.

"Who killed Ganesha?" I asked.

"Namo did," Pete said.

"You fucking snitch," Namo said. He was sitting up against the wall by the table, holding a bandana over the bullet hole in his leg. "Yer gonna get shanked in the joint, you little faggot."

"Fuck you!" Pete said. "I'll keelhaul your blunky ass."

"Why did you do it?" I asked Namo.

Namo shrugged, indifferent, hanging tough. "He was gonna call the cops."

"About what?"

"The cunts."

"Ganesha was a good man," I said, raising the Tomcat so that it pointed at his head.

"Don't," he said, losing his nerve as he looked down the bore of the weapon. "Baba told me to do it."

"Who's the snitch now?" Pete said.

"I did not tell you to kill him!" Baba roared. "I told you to stop him!"

"What happened to you, Baba?" I asked the false teacher. "How did you go from studying with Muktananda to murdering monks in your own ashram?"

His shoulders lifted in a heavy shrug and then subsided back into the massive pyramid of his Buddha's body.

"Judge not, lest you be judged," he said sarcastically. "You don't know what I've been through or how hard I strived to lead a Sattvic life. You don't have any idea of the good I have done in the world, the spiritual heights I've scaled. I meditated eight hours a day for six months in the Himalayas. I saw into the center of reality and worked tirelessly for three spiritual organizations. And what did it get me? I was turned out of Naropa when Trungpa died with nothing but my robe and bowl. That was my reward for six years of service. They blamed me for the AIDS, but I was only doing the will of my guru!

"After Naropa, I came here and tried again. This place was a lukewarm backwater with no dynamism. I built it up. We have hundreds of students taking classes here. But half of them never pay, or pay late, and there's a mortgage on the building, and utility costs are sky-high. I found ways to make money and keep it afloat, but it all became too much of a hassle. You serve only yourself, so you have no way of knowing. It is exhausting trying to do good all the time. Having people come to you constantly to solve their stupid problems. I just want to enjoy life a little bit instead of slaving for a bunch of rich dilettantes who can't comprehend the first thing about meditation or enlightenment. They don't have any idea of the discipline and sacrifice it takes. I'm fifty-five years old and I have nothing to fall back on if this place closes. Monks don't have 401(k) accounts. I had to start putting something aside for retirement—or end up a crazy bastard on the street."

"Is that why you started playing the stock market?"

"Yes. There is nothing wrong with that, or with what I am doing now. Tantra is a true spiritual path, and the resort will be good for the community. Jobs and a place for people to relax and forget their cares. I have decided to take my spiritual knowledge into the business world. That's where the real energy is in this age. I will use the energy of money to better the planet. We will have hatha yoga classes and meditations at this resort, and others that I plan to build. It will be beautiful. I will be the first yogic billionaire. Wait and see. I'll be on the cover of *Time* magazine someday. Ganesha should have been obedient and not tried to interfere with my activities. You should not be interfering, either."

Baba's anthracitic eyes glinted as he concluded his self-justification, and two things suddenly occurred to me. He was talking very freely, almost like he was stalling, and he was referring to the resort in the future tense, as if he still expected it to happen. That made me wonder what tricks he had hidden up the finely tailored sleeves of his suit.

"Let's bonk these pricks on the head or lock 'em in a closet and get the hell out of here," Reggie said, picking up the same vibe.

"Get the rope from the hallway," I said. "We'll tie them up in here."

Reggie hurried into the hallway and returned with the half-inch hemp that had bound Ozone Pacific. There were two pieces, ten or twelve feet long, unraveling at the ends. I took the rope and put the Tomcat in my other back pocket so that I had two hands to work with. Reggie stood near the hall door, well clear of the bad guys.

"Don't give any warnings," I said. "Anyone tries anything, just shoot them."

I used a kitchen knife to cut one piece of rope in half. I planned to hog-tie Pete and Namo with those pieces, then use the uncut piece to cinch Baba's thick wrists and ankles.

"You first, Pete," I said. "Lie down on your stomach on the floor and put your hands behind your back."

I was wrapping the rope around Pete's wrists while he pleaded under his breath, offering to betray his companions if I would let him go, when a muscle-bound guy in a black leather jacket strode into the room from the hall, cradling a grocery bag in his left arm. As he barged in, the door hit Reggie's elbow, knocking his gun from his hand, then struck his body, sending him stumbling several steps across the linoleum.

Sizing the situation up while the door was still swinging shut behind him, the newcomer dropped the grocery bag, which burst, sending cans of beer rolling, and whipped out an ugly black automatic before I could reach for my gun. The nose on his long narrow face was covered with a bandage. Above the cotton strip, his eyes sparkled with malice.

"Jimmy Z," I said.

His voice, strained through a swollen larynx, was a gritty whisper: "The last one you think of. The first one to show."

CHAPTER FORTY-FIVE

"I was beginning to think you had abandoned us, Jimmy," Baba said.

"Yeah, what took you so long?" Pete said, throwing off the loose rope and jumping up. "I thought we were going to have to deep-six these jack-offs ourselves."

"You didn't tell me it was eight blocks to the liquor store," Jimmy growled. "I would've took the car if I knew it was that far."

Namo was struggling to his feet, clawing at the wall for support. Now that Jimmy had the drop on us, he wanted to get at me as soon as possible.

"Wend you get out of the hospital?" Reggie asked conversationally, edging toward his gun.

"You can ask 'em when they wheel you in," Jimmy said.

Namo was hobbling toward me, his face like a rabid animal's. As he passed Pete, he sucker-punched him on the side of his head, knocking him to his knees.

"Watch this bitch," he said to Jimmy as he came toward me. "He's got two guns on him."

Jimmy raised the fascist pistol, targeting my breastbone. He was no fonder of me than Namo.

"Go easy!" Baba said. "We have to get the money from him."

When the Muscle Beach moron was a step away, rearing back for a haymaker, and Jimmy's finger was whitening on the trigger, the hall door swung in again and Mary burst into the room, blond hair streaming behind her, pearl-handled switchblade held low in her right hand.

Jimmy was quick. Keeping the gun trained on me, he lashed back with his left hand, hitting Mary in the face at the same moment she plunged the knife into the back of his thigh. He howled, dropped his gun, and staggered toward the table with the blade buried in his muscular leg. I ducked Namo's awkward, time-delayed swing and sank my fist into his solar plexus, dropping him.

As Namo went down, Pete scrambled up, feet skittering on the lino like a cartoon character's as he darted to the back door. When he jerked it open, Budge was waiting on the steps, slapping the fish billy in his hand. Stepping into the kitchen, he hit Pete with a tremendous uppercut. There was payback for a good many existential eye pokes and light pay envelopes in that blow, and it made an airman of the ex-swabbie, sending him flying halfway across the room. Landing hard on his back, he convulsed just once, then lay unconscious.

In the confusion, Baba sprang from his chair and charged the open back door with surprising agility and speed. Years of hatha yoga had kept him limber despite his size. His three hundred pounds of human freight train should have been unstoppable. But Budge still blocked the doorway. He dropped down to a three-point stance and met Baba head-on with the strength and leverage that made him all-city in 1973. Living up to Coach's billing, he stopped the guru in his tracks and, after a brief sumo bout, shoved him back into the room, where he stood, slump-shouldered and panting, defeated.

Mary was sitting with her back against the wall, rubbing her cheek, watching Jimmy writhe on the floor. Namo was crawling toward the hall door. Ozone Pacific was crouched in a corner. Reggie had snatched up Jimmy's cannon and his peashooter and backed himself against the counter, keeping an eye on all the players. I had the Tomcat in my hand.

"Are you all right?" I asked Mary.

"Yeah," she said and then lit up the room with an amazed and amazing smile. "This is wild!"

While Reggie covered, I jerked the knife out of Jimmy's leg, evoking a piercing scream and releasing a spurt of blood. I tied a piece of rope above the wound as a tourniquet and dragged him over to the wall by the table. With Budge's help, I lugged Pete and Namo over and dumped them beside him.

Baba stood brooding, looking much sillier in his fine blue suit than he ever had in his ridiculous dhoti.

"You won't get away with this," he said. "I'll turn you in for the burglary and grand larceny. That necklace belongs to me. If the police don't get you, Discenza's men will."

"I'll take my chances," I said. "Turn around and face the wall."

Before he could execute the maneuver, Evelyn came into the kitchen from the hall. It was getting to be like Grand Central station in there.

"Where is my grandson?" she asked the disgraced guru.

"He's right here," Mary said. She stood up and took Oz's hand and led him to Evelyn.

"You're the lady in the picture!" the boy said.

"She's your grandmother," Mary said. "She's going to take care of you now."

"I'm going to take the best care in the world of you, Kelly," Evelyn said. "You are my precious jewel."

Oz looked from the elegant lady to me, and then back at her and back at me again, wonder emerging from the confusion on his face. Behind the wonder, something sly flitted in and out of sight, like the flash of a fish turning just below the surface.

"I'm rich," he said to me.

I nodded and smiled. "You were right, buddy."

"Help me, too, Evelyn," Baba pleaded. "Just give me a couple of the diamonds to get away with."

"Where's Christina? If you tell me, I will help you. I will help you get away."

"He doesn't know where she is, Evelyn," I said. "He was lying about that."

I didn't want her to find out about her daughter's death right then. The scene was fraught enough already. I could break the news to her later, in private, and let her explain it to her grandson.

Baba's eyes darted to mine when I spoke, not knowing why I was covering up but accepting the lie as wise. He didn't want Evelyn going banshee, either.

"Tell her to help me," he said, conspiratorially. "I promise no one will know of your involvement in any of this. It is in your interest to let me go."

"I don't think so, Baba."

Pete was stirring on the floor and Namo had pulled himself together. Only Jimmy Z was still incapacitated. He was in shock, his leg bleeding badly, despite the tourniquet.

"Get up," I said to Pete and Namo. They got to their feet slowly, wincing and cursing, and stood unsteadily beside the bulk of Baba Raba, looking like his abused children.

According to the Seth Thomas wall clock, it was 5:10. Baba was late for his meeting with Discenza and the appraiser. Budge was standing behind the three upright bad guys, looking at me, waiting for instructions. Pointing the Tomcat at them to keep them still, I raised my other hand and brought it down, a judge passing sentence. Budge grinned and nodded.

Like a man playing an oversize xylophone, he went down the row, cracking first Namo and then Pete on top of the head with the broad edge of the billy. As they collapsed in sequence onto the bloody floor, I was moving Mary, Evelyn, and Oz into the hall, Reggie bringing up the rear. He looked back from the doorway as Budge raised the billy above Baba's cannonball head.

"Hey, Baby Huey," he said, thrusting out his hip and slapping his broad ass, "meditate on this." Baba's eyes got wide with what looked like fury, then snapped shut as Budge rapped his thick skull. The house shook when his body hit the floor.

On the street, we piled into the Cadillac—me, Mary, and Reggie in front, Budge, Oz, and Evelyn in the back. We had only gone a block toward the ocean when a black Cadillac limo turned off Seventh and pulled up in front of the ashram. In the rearview mirror, I saw four men in suits getting out. One of them was Councilman Discenza. The malevolence on his beaked face etched the glass of the mirror.

"Where we going?" Reggie asked.

"The hotel."

We made it back to Le Merigot without incident. I didn't think anyone could trace us there. I was about to make a left into the hotel's semicircular drive when a blue Taurus cut in front of me and pulled up at the entrance ahead of us. When the valet opened the door, a giantess in a brown linen suit struggled out. Her big hash-slinger's face was mottled with anger as if someone had just skipped out without paying the check.

It was a face that had launched, at most, a single rowboat. The guy at the oars, who had proposed to it after a dozen longnecks and his first hand job, probably wished by now that he had drowned himself in the lake instead of plunging into matrimonial fire. It was a face I knew.

"We want our luggage brought right up," the snowbird said shrilly to the valet. "We left the last hotel because of poor service and we won't stay here if things aren't to our liking. My husband won't stand for any malarkey. We have been driving around this cockamamie town for two hours trying to find this place and we're starving. I hope you have good food in your restaurant and decent portions. They didn't give you enough food at the last place."

She was a lady who would always stuff herself and never be full, a spiritual cripple but a stellar consumer. Each expensive stop on her journey was an inevitable disappointment that took her nowhere but closer to the exit door of an oversize casket, lowered without emotion into a prepaid grave.

Reggie looked at me, making saucer eyes: "Ain't that the lady from . . ."

"Yes," I said. "It is. We'll have to go someplace else."

"What is it?" Mary said.

"Those people were at the hotel in Indian Wells. They saw us in Evelyn's room after the fight with Jimmy."

"I still can't believe that was you," Evelyn said, somewhat dreamily, stroking Oz's hair.

As I pulled past the Taurus, the valet opened the driver's door and the little husband popped out, making a mean face. I didn't blame him.

"My wife has to have the best of everything," he said angrily. "She is not easily satisfied."

Several blocks south, I took a right, cutting over to the expansive beachfront lot on Nelson Way. I parked at the far edge, near the creaming waves, and turned around to look at Budge.

"Do you know where Candyman is?" I asked him.

"I think he went to Shoshana's."

"Can you get in touch with him?"

"Sure, I got the number."

"Call him and warn him not to go back to the flop, and you stay clear of it, too. The Italians are going to be out for blood."

After Baba spilled his guts, Discenza's men would be fanning out to try and find the necklace. They would go to Evelyn's, the flophouse, maybe even Hildebrand's office.

"All right, Rob. I'll let him know."

"Thanks for your help, Budge," I said, stopping him before he could ask any of the questions that were crowding onto the tip of his tongue. "Take this for your trouble." I handed him a packet of ten hundreds.

"Wow! Thanks a lot, man." He shoved the money into his pants pocket and got out of the car. "I'll share this with Candy."

"If anyone asks you what happened at the ashram, you weren't there and you don't know anything about it."

"Gotcha."

"Take care, brother."

"You, too, Rob. Thanks again." Leaning down, he reached in the window to clasp hands with Reggie, biker-style.

"Fly low," Reggie said.

"You too, man. See ya, Oz."

" 'Bye, Budge."

He strode off across the lot with his head high and shoulders back, a valuable player returning to the locker room after a big game. Halfway across, he changed direction, slightly, angling toward the public restroom. I think it was a Teena Marie song that he was whistling.

"What now?" Mary said.

"We have to find someplace to regroup," I said. I didn't want to head for Mexico with Evelyn and Oz in tow.

"Why don't we check into another hotel?" Reggie said.

I shook my head. "We're too conspicuous. I don't know what kind of network the Italians have around here. Discenza may put out the word to cabbies and hotel clerks to watch for us. What about your place in Bel Air, Evelyn?"

She had her arm around Oz. His head lay on her shoulder.

"We can't go there," she said. "It's rented out."

"Any other thoughts?" I asked the group.

"I have a cabin in Big Bear," Evelyn said. "We could go there."

"Does Baba know about it?"

"No."

"Perfect."

I took the 10 to SR-60, following the same route we had four days ear-

lier when Evelyn had been ahead of me in a white Lincoln instead of behind me in the backseat of my Caddie. As we passed through Pomona
below the Chino Hills, Ozone cried out:

"Look! Cows!"

In a pasture that sloped up from the right side of the highway, Holsteins
were chewing their cuds in the evening light. I took the next crossroad and
circled back, winding along narrow lanes to a spot above the pasture where
the shoulder was wide enough to pull over and park.

"Can I pet them?" Oz said, excited.

"I don't know," I said. There was a five-strand barbed-wire fence between us and the cattle and I didn't want him to get torn up climbing over.

"Pop the trunk," Reggie said.

I pulled the lever and Reggie got out and walked to the back of the car.
The rest of us got out too, watching as he took his church key to the fence
and cut the top four stands of wire, pulling them back out of the way.

"Go on down," he said gruffly.

With a happy laugh, the boy stepped over the bottom wire and ran
downhill toward the cattle.

"Be careful," Evelyn said, following him.

Reggie leaned against the hood, lock snips hanging down in one hand,
watching them cross the pasture.

Mary and I were standing next to the car.

"You're pretty good," she said. "You got the necklace and torpedoed
Baba. You saved me and the kid and gave Evelyn back her grandson."

"Look who's talking," I said. "You were awesome with that knife. You
saved my ass."

There was a tumbledown barn on the other side of the tar road. Taking
my hand, Mary led me across the road and around the corner of the weathered building into a grassy area beneath an alder tree. Once we were hidden from view, her small hands with their heartbreaking nails went to the
button that fastened her pants. Unzipping, she wriggled her butt free,
pushing her jeans and panties down to her knees, then bent over, placing
her delicate palms against the rough gray boards of the barn.

"I like it hard," she said.

Curiously, I was not offended by this.

Afterward, as we walked down through the pasture to where Evelyn
was sitting beneath a pine tree, watching Oz stroke the coarse hair of a
drowsy dairy cow, Mary gave me a teasing look through her fairy eyelashes.

"That wasn't very tantric," she said.

"I felt close to you."

"I felt close to you, too." She squeezed my hand, making the chakras in my heart and throat swell. "But if it is tantra, the guy doesn't come. And I am pretty sure you did!"

"You got me there, baby. It may take a lot of practice before I get it right."

"You'd like that, wouldn't you?"

It was nearly dark by the time we pulled Oz away from his bovine friends and got back on the road. The world must have seemed magical that night to the homeless kid turned heir, his picture books and magazines coming to life around him. It was pretty sparkly for me, too, with the briefcase full of Benjamins and the tough blonde tight beside me, leaning hard against my shoulder and then away, as we switchbacked up Highway 330 into the San Bernardino Mountains. Above five thousand feet there were patches of snow, white among the black pines, and by the time we reached Running Springs the ground was blanketed with cold crystals. As we drove along the Rim of the World Highway toward Big Bear Lake, fresh snow began to fall, big flakes floating down through the headlight beams, carrying Christmas memories like candles and bringing smiles to all our faces.

We spent a week at Evelyn's lodge, a five-bedroom timber-frame over-looking the frozen lake. It snowed all through the first night and most of the next day, so there was fresh powder for sledding and skiing and snow-ball fights. Mary turned out to be a daring downhill racer, beating me to the bottom of the mountain two times out of three. Oz made a cow out of snow. It was hard to recognize if you didn't know what it was supposed to be, but it made him happy. He used a piece of rope for the tail. In the evenings we burned cedar logs in Evelyn's big stone fireplace.

We followed developments in Los Angeles on TV and in the newspaper. The ashram burned down the night we left town. It was a big, lurid story on the next day's evening news. Police found five bodies in the ruins, including those of Herbert Finklestein, who ran the ashram, and Pedro Sanchez, who was under investigation for arson in connection with several recent fires in the neighborhood. The Krispy Kremes were treating the ashram fire as arson and the deaths as homicides, in part because the victims had fresh knife and gunshot wounds. Oz had been prescient when he'd called Baba's place an ash farm.

With the guru and his amateur gangsters gone, the link between me and the Center for Enlightened Beings was broken. Nobody else except for Evelyn, who had seen me there, knew who I was. With Evelyn on our side, the link between Reggie and me and the safe job was broken, too. Hildebrand didn't know who had knocked off his office, so he was no threat. The cops who had questioned us the night of the robbery only knew us by our aliases, and we couldn't be traced through the rental car.

On Thursday, our second day in the mountains, a story in the local section of the *Los Angeles Times* reported that the controversial Pacific City resort plan had collapsed when the main parcel of land fell out of escrow on Wednesday. The article noted in passing that Herbert Finklestein, a.k.a. Baba Raba, who was killed in the Murshid Center fire, had been a partner in the resort deal.

Two days later, when I went down to the snow-covered *Times* paper machine in the village, there was a dramatic headline on the front page: CAR BOMB KILLS VENICE BEACH COUNCILMAN. Discenza's Cadillac had turned into a fireball when he started it in his garage on Friday morning. Police estimated that ten or twelve sticks of dynamite were used. Evidently, the other Italians had been irritable about the loss of their half million.

I was glad to hear that Discenza had gone to the Big City Council Meeting in the Sky. Even though I hadn't struck at him directly, those guys have vendetta in their DNA, and he might have made a career of trying to track me down for something other than a friendly warning. He might have bothered Evelyn, too, trying to take up where Baba left off, extorting money from a likely rich lady.

I broke the news about Christina's death that evening. Evelyn and I were sitting in the leather armchairs in front of the fireplace. She was drinking chardonnay from a brandy snifter. When I told her how her daughter had died and how Pete had found her remains and given the diary to Baba, she bowed her head and closed her eyes.

"At least I have Kelly," she said.

I was surprised that she wasn't taking it harder.

"I guess I knew she was dead." She bunched the fingers of her left hand together and touched the center of her chest. "I felt it here. But I didn't want to admit it to myself. At least now I know for sure."

She was leaning forward with her head down over her glass and after a little while the surface of the chardonnay began to pucker like a pond at the start of a rainstorm. Her shoulders shook and the hand that held the alcohol trembled.

Oz came in from the TV room then and asked her what was wrong. She took a deep breath, wiped her tears, and told him that nothing was wrong, everything was going to be okay.

That was her last drink. She called her old sponsor later that night and went to an AA meeting in Big Bear the next afternoon.

We split up when we left the mountains the following week. Reggie went to Las Vegas, where he won twelve grand playing craps and got gonorrhea from a redheaded lounge singer. Mary and I drove to San Diego and then flew to Cabo, where we checked into a resort like the one Baba and Discenza had hoped to build in Venice Beach. It had fancy restaurants and swimming pools and a spa and cabanas on the clean beach, but we didn't see much of it. Evelyn took Oz north to her in-laws' ranch. Her former husband's parents were both still living. Weathered and wise and nearing the end of their time on earth, they pushed aside past grievances and welcomed the boy, who was both their grandson and great-grandson. He lives there now in the rural Eden of his mother's memory, riding around with his grandfather in his pickup truck, supervising and working with the ranch hands, bucking hay and rounding up cattle. He has his own chickens and pigs to take care of in a barn near the main house and two horses. Evelyn says he has become a fine rider.

Evelyn sold her bungalow in Venice Beach and divides her time between the ranch and her sister's mansion in Bel Air. As soon as the lease is up on her house, she plans to move back in and make that her home. She has never wavered on the bargain we made. When the cops eventually questioned her about the robbery, seeking clues, she feigned ignorance and indifference. She had no idea who had stolen the diamonds and didn't really care. The necklace was insured and could be replaced. When they got around to her again, weeks later, going through a list of ashram students in the long, drawn-out investigation into what happened at the Murshid Center for Enlightened Beings, they pricked up their ears at the coincidence, but she froze them out. How should she know if the robbery and fire/homicides were connected? She couldn't talk to them at the moment. She had to get ready for a fund-raiser for her friend Senator Feinstein. They would have to talk to her lawyer if they had any more questions about the burglary or anything else.

When Mary and I returned from Cabo, she found us a fantastic apartment on the water in Redondo Beach with a huge two-story living room and big balcony where we sit and watch the boats entering and leaving the marina and occasionally do other things. Reggie moved in with Chavi. He guesses people's weight on the beach when we aren't on a job. He has a push-button electronic gadget that adjusts the scale to match his predication if it happens to be off by more than a pound. Most of the time, he doesn't have to use it. He is as good at sizing people up physically as his girlfriend is at sizing them up psychically.

Overall, things are great. Mary and I are a good fit in every way. She makes me happier than I deserve to be. She seems happy, too. She's back in school at City College and plans to transfer to Cal State next fall to get a B.A. in comparative religion. When she doesn't have homework, she helps out in the family business.

Sometimes I get to thinking about Baba's demise, both spiritual and physical, and about all the dead bodies we left behind in Venice Beach, and wonder what kind of karma we incurred there. We didn't actually kill anybody, but we left them to be killed. I wonder if I have gone off track like Baba and just don't realize it. Sometimes I even think about getting out of the life. Stealing has an honorable history and isn't necessarily a spiritual dead end. Among other things, it supports the dictum that people shouldn't get too attached to their stuff. But it is a high-stakes gamble, practically and morally. It is a form of living by the sword, and everyone knows what that is supposed to lead to.

I have a lot to lose now with the waterfront digs and the sublime babe and all the cash in my safety deposit box. But I can't imagine doing anything else. Not with the world the way it is today. Chavi told me a gypsy saying shortly after we met last December that sums it up in my mind. Reggie had told her what he and I do for a living and we were talking about our career choices—she an open-air fortune-teller, me a thief. I was trying to explain why I thought it was okay to be a criminal and she held up her hand to silence me with the gesture the swamies call "fear not," hand open, palm toward me.

"I understand, Robert," she said. "You can't walk straight when the road curves."

I think the gypsies are right about that.

ACKNOWLEDGMENTS

I want to thank my agent, Loretta Fidel, for her friendship, guidance, and support, and my editor, Mark Tavani, for his invaluable insights and suggestions at various stages of this book's composition. Thanks also to Dennis Ambrose and everyone at Random House who worked on the book and helped take it from concept to reality.

The thoughtful advice of Marty Smith, Diane Pinnick, Patricia McFall, Len Mlodinow, and other members of the Mavericks writing group is much appreciated.

To Charles Dickens, the godfather, patron saint, and archangel of literary orphans, I bow with profound gratitude and affection.

About the Author

STEVEN M. THOMAS is the author of *Criminal Paradise*. He is also the award-winning author of many short stories, essays, and poems that have been published in more than fifty literary and small-press magazines in the United States and England. A magazine editor and journalist, he lives in Orange County, California, with his wife and daughter.